The Marbella String Quartet

The Marbella String Quartet

Stuart Charles Neil

The Marbella String Quartet

The proceeds from all these books will be donated to
Stuart's two charities:-

Star Action (Reg. Charity No. 1111137)
www.staraction.org

The Quiet Mind Centre (Reg. Charity No. 1029636)
www.quiet-mind.org

For Jenny

So many years of love and laughter

ONE

It never ceased to amaze Erik, who always travelled with the minimum of possessions that, whichever female companion he was with on his travels, brought on to the aircraft an astonishing array of 'essential' items. This time Lindsay conformed to the airline regulations by only carrying one piece of hand baggage.

It was an enormous carrier bag.

Once she reached her allotted seat this was revealed to contain three smaller bags and a handbag, none of which could be put in the overhead locker as each contained items critical to the comfort of the journey; two and a half hours from London Gatwick to Gibraltar.

Erik looked on quizzically at his friend. She was clad in a thick woolly cardigan, knitted hat and two scarves, one short and one long with tassels. The plane was warm from its recent journey into Gatwick and the anticipated temperature in Gibraltar was expected to be 25 degrees. He thought she must be close to boiling. Lindsay produced a Nepalese blanket, that still smelt remotely of the Yak, and unwrapped the airline blanket to support it. She removed her heavy shoes and donned slip-ons from one of the bags. A thick novel, I-phone and make-up clutch bag were inserted into the net at the back of the seat in front. She began to blow vigorously into an inflatable padded neck pillow, a Zorro style eye mask hanging loosely around her neck.

Erik fastened his seat belt and closed his eyes. His small grip was in the overhead locker and today's Daily Telegraph folded in his lap. He was wearing shirt, shorts and sandals in readiness for the journey in the sunshine from Gibraltar to Marbella along the coast of Andalucia..

"I think I'll have to go to the loo before we take off" said Lindsay, setting off against the tide of boarding passengers and leaving her seat strewn with garments and belongings. She returned red-faced with exertion and began ferreting under the seat for one of her shoes which she had accidentally kicked into the row behind. Finally, ensconced in the seat, surrounded by belongings and suitably belted, she said to Erik

"I know what you are thinking. Don't say anything because I need to meditate"

Erik wasn't going to say anything. He was used to his companion calling on the Gods to preserve her on the forthcoming flight and wondered what the pilots would feel if they were aware of the limited confidence of their passengers.

He settled back to contemplate the next weeks at their new Tennis Academy beside the Mediterranean. Erik, real name Joel Eriksson, had been a successful competitor on the tennis tournament circuit for several years, ranked in the top ten men's single players and No 2 in the world in doubles with his partner Samuraja (Sammy). Having retired from all but exhibition matches and charity events he had been persuaded to invest money and time in Lindsay's dream business in Spain.

Knowing only the immediate surround of the Madrid open and its nearby hotels Erik was keen to learn more about his adopted country and familiarise himself with the language. The journey passed swiftly and they soon seemed to land on the short runway at Gibraltar. The tarmac strip stretched out into the sea at both ends and it appeared as though they were landing on water, whizzing past buildings and coming to a halt seemingly back on the water again. Negotiating the Spanish customs was quite rapid now that we were all 'brothers' in the European Union. The air-conditioned coach sped along the fast road towards Marbella.

Lindsay slept the deep sleep of a traveller who had survived the worst part of the ordeal whilst Erik recalled his Uncle's tales of life in Gibraltar in the early 1960s. This was before the nearby Spanish coast had been developed as the very first package holiday destination for Northern Europeans. There were always British Navy ships alongside or riding at anchor in Algeciras Bay and the Gibraltar pubs were full of matelots enjoying a day of shore leave. Negotiating Spanish Customs at La Linea was a nightmare. The officials took as long as they wished before allowing Gibraltarians to pass through. Spain strongly thought that Gib was theirs and that Britain should hand the Rock back to them, so they felt justified in being 'bolshie'.

Despite this animosity Sven would daily cross the border with his friends from the local Bank, at which he was a cashier, in order to eat in one of the restaurants that overlooked the nearest beach. A meal cost a quarter of the price of one inside Gibraltar. Wine was even cheaper, though it was rough enough to remove the stains from any surface. One evening he and a friend had stayed too long, drunk too much and missed the border closure at 1am. They had to spend the night trying to sleep on a hard pavement outside the Customs Post.

Spain was a very poor country in those days. The coastal road was full of deep potholes and there were shortages of many essentials. Lorry companies could not buy enough tyres to run their whole fleet and, as one arrived at the depot, the tyres were removed and quickly put on the next lorryload that was waiting to leave. Most had large cuts in them and lorries and buses often suffered catastrophic blow-outs.

Sven befriended a customer of his Bank and spent weekends staying at her pretty cottage that was one of six in a row along the beach at the tiny village of Los Boliches. It was peaceful and they ate freshly caught Salmonete fish and melons that had been left to cool, buried in the sand at the edge of the sea. In a later holiday he searched for the village, but realised it had been swallowed into the huge concrete complex of Benalmadena. Package holidays began the year after he left the 'Rock' and much of Germany, Netherlands, Britain and Scandinavia descended on Andalucia to boost the Spanish economy every Spring and Summer.

Fifty years later it was no longer a major adventure to travel to the Mediterranean and Erik hoped to persuade a number of wealthy parents to send their teenagers to complete their education at a private academy just outside Marbella. These were to be aspiring junior tennis players, who had enjoyed some success in the summer tournaments in Europe and dreamed of pursuing a professional career in the sport.

He and Lindsay had known each other for over twenty years. They had taken a year out from the tennis circuit to lick their wounds after an abortive string of results and gone to the Solomon Islands to emulate Sven and live on fish, melons and free love. However, access to their own little island required permission from the authorities in Honiara, and to acquire this they had to be married. After a ceremony of flowers and copious quantities of palm wine the newlyweds embarked on a life close to nature. Sadly they had been joined by a thousand little mosquitos. Their occupation lasted only a few weeks before they were driven reluctantly to leave their paradise island and return to a mosquito-free environment.

Lindsay went back to her native New Zealand and Erik resumed his relationship with the furry yellow ball. Still single Erik, and, 'separated from her new partner' Lindsay, with son Cameron, met again in England twenty-one years later. Two days after that they began the process of starting their Academy in Spain.

Carmen, their housekeeper, and Cameron, Lindsay's teenage son came to meet them from the coach. She had been feeding the boy whilst Erik and Lindsay had been in London. It had been only a two day visit to a Dickensian-looking solicitor in a modern glass building in the City. Erik's Uncle Thorbjorn had requested in his will that Erik should chair the Trust that invested his life savings and dispense the interest to deserving sports ventures. The solicitor was one of the other four Trustees and organised official acceptance of Erik's election as new Trustee and chair at the same time. Over the next years this Trust could become useful as a source of funding to the aspiring Tennis Academy in Marbella.

Carmen produced one of her legendary paellas to soothe the tiredness of their journey. An early night was in order because they were interviewing potential staff members all the next day. Cameron drifted off to look at his homework from the private Spanish tutor while Erik took his customary black coffee on to the verandah overlooking the distant Mediterranean and an almost-full moon setting into the sea.

How life had changed in the last year. Erik had found and lost the only true love of his forty years, although there had been no shortage of near misses. He had enjoyed several visits to his bolt-hole in East Devon in England, having grown accustomed to using his false name to shirk most of the inevitable publicity that followed a successful sportsman. He vowed he would keep his home there and return every summer at the very least. There were many friends from this community that had become close and he now regarded this part of the world as a second home.

The candidates for interview came from as wide a spectrum of humanity as it seemed possible to imagine could be found in Southern Spain. This was partly because they were planning to employ to fill a variety of posts in the new venture. Carmen provided frequently refreshed pots of coffee and irresistible thin doughnuts covered in a fine lemon icing.

The first three applicants came to satisfy Lindsay's curiosity about the local standard of professional tennis coaching. The initial scheme had written Lindsay and Erik as the only coaches needed to launch the Academy, but someone in reserve would be good to include to add cover when Erik disappeared to fulfil his commitment to Swedish Television as their principal summariser during tennis grand slam tournaments. Although Sweden was a country with a population of less than 10 million, success had come, particularly in men's tennis, with several top players during the last forty years. The inspiration of Bjorn Borg had been followed by Edberg, Wilander and Johansson and further by others in Erik's generation. The television audiences' interest in tennis inevitably had grown over the years. Although the two men and one woman being interviewed had all the accepted coaching certificates and varied experience, none of the three appealed as prospective members of their team.

Next came the teachers. Half of each day for the students would comprise academic studies to keep the aspiring tennis players up to speed with their peers in the mainstream schools and, hopefully, to finish with a clutch of examination passes that would ensure other gainful employment if tennis failed. It was expected that this would be a pre-requisite of every parent before entrusting their child to Erik and Lindsay. The teachers would need to be flexible and able to cover a wide range of subjects. Erik left most of the questions to Lindsay who was the qualified and experienced teacher. She had been head of PE and games at a large school in New Zealand.

Unemployment in Spain after the economic crises of recent years was high and several good applicants came to see them, including the humorous teacher of Spanish, whom Erik and Cameron had been using since they first arrived. He was the first to receive an offer of a permanent position. They then chose a scientist, who thought he could arrange to use the laboratory facilities at a local secondary school where he had been a supply teacher. Lindsay would teach maths herself.

They offered a place to a wonderfully flamboyant 50 year old lady who appeared in a rainbow of coloured flowing clothes and scarves and more or less interviewed them. She had taught all over the world and was competent in English and all the Humanities. Lavinia also was well versed in the examination variations available in Europe.

At lunch Cameron was interested to know who would be likely to teach him during the next months. It had been decided that those offered positions already would be enough for now, at least until they had some students in place to teach. Cameron was not in the list of likely tennis players and had thought he would have to attend a local Spanish Government School, but it made more sense to include him as a pupil. He was on a promise that the afternoons would be put aside for sensible private study whilst his fellows pursued their tennis potential.

After lunch the two business partners resumed their interviews with Carmen feeding in each applicant in turn. She, Carmen, was to be the Housekeeper. Now they needed a cook, who in turn would need an assistant in due course. They had decided to see three of the twelve applicants and chose one, who had been brought up on a specialist horticultural farm outside Seville and was prepared to learn about and serve nutritious meals. Groundsmen followed, with Jorge, who had already done some casual work, being offered a full-time post. The next best groundsman was a woman. Donna sat down and demonstrated an enthusiasm far in excess of the others. As she walked away they noticed that her apparent overweight was moving in perfect harmony with the rest of her frame and could easily be solid muscle. They may not need the mini-tractor and trailer after all.

Erik had circulated most of the coaches registered with their domestic federations in each of the European countries, blatantly using his own name in the hope it would be an attraction. The offer to students, who were to come with academic and tennis references, was of a term's trial at the Trocadero Tennis Academy in Marbella at a quoted fee, to include accommodation, food, tennis training and schooling to International Baccalaureate or UK Advanced Level. All ages would be considered from applicants who were prepared to live away from home for the duration of a full term at a time.

In addition Erik took out half page advertisements in the dedicated tennis magazines and in the official programmes that were to be sold at most of the major tournaments of the coming twelve months. He and Lindsay hoped to fill each of the two dormitories that builders had been preparing, one for each gender on each side of the main admin and residential house. There were eight beds for boys and eight for girls. This was an experiment to see how well the ages and nationalities got on with each other and how well the older children cared for the younger ones.

They were enjoying a cool drink, ten minutes after the departure of the last grounds candidate on his ancient scooter, when an expensive Mercedes Sports swept up to the main door and a an equally expensive-looking lady climbed out, changed from driving shoes into heels and strode in through the glass door. The accepted image of a well-to-do driver of an open top sports car in the Mediterranean was completed with a cream, sleeveless blouse and matching straight skirt and large dark glasses with hair held back under a white headscarf. A blast of something Dior preceded her arrival at the arm of Erik's chair.

"I 'ave come to give you my son" said a probably Italian voice.

Experience had taught Erik how to handle the forthright element of the upper classes who felt they owned a piece of every sportsman on the planet.

"You are too late" he replied "We engaged two new Groundsmen half an hour ago".

His reply was greeted by a speechless, partially open mouth. The visitor removed the sunglasses and scarf and shook out her long auburn hair.

"Ee is to be trained to be a star in tennis" she stated.

Erik stood and introduced Lindsay and himself.

"I know oo you are. Don't you remember me?"

Erik blankly returned the look.

"You stood beside me for photographs on the Nike stand at Roland Garros last year"

Erik, who had stood beside 100 sponsor's wives and publicity girls for photos each year since 1997, politely replied that it had slipped his memory. The visitor sat and accepted the offer of an iced drink.

"How old is your son?" asked Lindsay

"Ee ees not old. Ee ees a teenage protégé" came the reply.

"What has he won so far?" asked Erik

"The Uruguay Under 16 years Boys Federal Championship." replied his visitor.

Erik searched his memory to try to remember whether he had heard of

another Uruguayan competitor in recent years.

"How did you hear of us?" asked Lindsay.

"They are talking all about you in the Marbella Club. We spend some of the year here. Our yacht is moored in the Marina at Puerto Banus "

It sounded as though the Academy Fees were unlikely to pose a problem.

"We will need to meet him and see him play a little before deciding. Can you bring him along, say tomorrow at 11am?"

"Ignacio is in the car now!"

"Really. Then let's see him now". said Erik

A few minutes later Ignacio, a rather awkward and round shouldered 15 year old stood in the hallway looking as though he would rather be playing a video game somewhere else.

"I am Maria Carmelita Conchita Vasquez del Forlan and this is my only son, Ignacio"

Erik sort of waved and Lindsay said personably

"Come and sit down Ignacio. We are not too ferocious".

"Nacho is a tennis protégé" repeated Maria Carmelita.

Erik recognised this as a bad start. The expectations of the parents and probable expectations of most of a player's friends, neighbours and great aunts had proven in the past to overwhelm a player and many had retreated back into the undergrowth never again to brandish a racket in anger.

"Why do you want to join our Academy, Ignacio?" The inevitable question appeared early in their conversation.

"Ee wants to be a Grand Slam Champion" stated Mother.

Lindsay continued to look directly at the boy, who was slowly sliding lower into his chair.

"What about you. Why do you want to come?"

"I don't. I want to be with my girlfriend in Montevideo"

A visibly shocked Maria Carmelita spluttered:

"We 'ave decided that ee needs to come here. Thees girl is from a low family and ee is not doing school work any more."

"Come with me" said Erik. "Is your gear in the car?"

The boy nodded and a few minutes later was knocking a box of new balls across the net to Erik, one by one. Erik watched his service action, movement about the court and reaction to difficult shots like a high backhand and deep baseline ground strokes.

Quite impressed at the basic package Erik explained to him that he could come for a term if he wished. This would please his parents. He could Skype his girl back at home and impress her with any progress he made on a video, and maybe be happier with the school studies than he was at the moment. New place, new teachers and no parents on his case all the time.

Lindsay had explained the academy terms meanwhile to Maria Carmelita, who was delighted to hear her son agree to sign on for a term. It appeared that the boy was hindering the parents' jet set lifestyle, so it was agreed that he could move in in two weeks time. Cameron showed him around the newly re-furbished complex and pointed out where improvements still had to be made. He helped Nacho to set up a Skype link with Isabella back in Montevideo; something which his parents had tried to veto since they had come to Europe.

Lindsay and Erik sat on the verandah at the Sea Grill on Trocadero Beach and toasted the beginning of their enterprise. They had a complex of buildings, a skeleton staff and the first student. Lindsay relaxed in the knowledge that she had a stable companion to share the load and Erik felt he had the entrance foyer into a consuming interest beyond that of the competitive world of intensive sport.

TWO

What do you mean, you've lost the your boxer shorts?"
George looked down at the forlorn face of his eight-year-old son Luke.

"Someone has nicked them" said Robin, his brother, who was two years older

"He changed beside the pool and now they're gone. Somebody nicked them"

George took the little boy's hand and they headed for the changing room beside the hotel pool.

"I don't think any Frenchman would be so desperate as to need to steal your pongy pants. They are probably screwed up in the rest of your clothes or you have dropped them on the path."

Helen had been one of the besotted women who, last summer found themselves melting downwards or upwards every time they had anything to do with Erik. She was now with George, a good natured farmer who had been her almost-next door neighbour and was trying to raise two boys, a herd of Friesian cows and twelve acres of varied crops mainly on his own. She had finally cast her fate to the East Devon wind and volunteered herself as 'painter's model' and, in her mind, slave and mistress to Erik on one of his visits last year. Erik had let her down gently and the sensible part of Helen eventually realised that George was waiting to scoop her up in his big, rough farmer's hands and amalgamate their two families.

They were currently a good way down the West coast of France in George's four by four, having broken the journey at a small hotel near Bordeaux. They were heading for the Trocadero Tennis Academy in Marbella with the second student to be joined to the coaching scheme. This was Lucy, Helen's eleven year old daughter, who had been attending tennis lessons at the Sports Centre in Ottery St. Mary near her home. She had gone on to win the Under 12 tournament in Exeter earlier in the summer. Now, instead of advancing from Primary to Secondary School in the English education system, Helen had taken up Erik's offer of a reduced rate place at the new Academy.

Lucy sat between the two boys on the back seat of the car, her two racquet handles visible behind her, sticking out of the smaller of her two bags. She was very excited at the prospect of being one of the first at the Academy and seeing Erik again, who had given her his attention and guidance whenever he came down to Devon. She was also trying hard to be brave with the realisation that, in a few days time, she would not see her Mum again until just before Christmas.

In the time-honoured way four out of every five friends, with whom Lucy had discussed her adventure, predicted doom and gloom. They told her she would hate the food in Spain, that all Spanish boys hate girls, there were spiders the size of dinner plates and nobody would speak English. She may be kidnapped and kept prisoner or taken to Africa or she may never be allowed to come home because England's borders could be closed to outsiders. However, her friend Saskia said it would be amazing. Only half the day doing schoolwork would be brilliant and Spanish ice cream was better than English. She, Saskia, was going to start playing tennis and try to join Lucy next year. Mrs Kellogg at school told Lucy that she would be special – a truly international girl, and probably the only girl in Axmouth who could speak Spanish if she paid attention in class at the Academy. She emphasised that few girls or boys would ever have an opportunity like this one.

Lucy smiled to herself and this was seen by George in the rearview mirror. This heartened him because he realised that it had been a change for her to have to adapt to a life with two younger brothers to add to her own elder brother Callum. Callum was staying with a friend in Lyme Regis, whose sister he secretly fancied. It was likely to be a fruitless cause because statuesque Verity was two years older, three inches taller and only saw herself as prey for sixth formers with their own cars.

They crossed the border into Spain with George announcing that they had reached the halfway point and would celebrate at MacDonalds.

"Is there a MacDonalds in every country?" asked Lucy from the back.

"Probably" replied George.

"What about Antarctica?"

"It would be difficult to get the ingredients for a Big Mac down there" said Helen.

"What would they sell then?" joined in Robin.

"Dessert would be Ice Cream and Penguins" suggested George.

Everyone laughed because the families were at that early stage where they all wanted to please each other and grasped every opportunity to be personable.

Rather than take over the driving Helen announced that she had a secret that she wanted George's advice over and it would take a while to explain. She had been employed at a local Bank in recent months and had decided to try to cheer up the rather po-faced management by playing an April Fools prank on them. It had rather back-fired and now she was struggling to deal with an embarrassing spin-off.

On the 1st April she had announced to everyone at their coffee break that she wanted their help in supporting a deserving charity in South America. They listened attentively. She told them that one of the most dangerous occupations in Brazil and the surrounding countries was picking the Brazil nut crop. It was all still done by hand. The nuts grew inside a large kernel that was the size of a coconut and the workers had to climb the trees or ladders to pick these from the branches.In recent years the casualty departments of nearby hospitals had become filled with men and women with severe head injuries, sometimes proving fatal, from kernels that had fallen on their heads. Helen's Charity was raising funds to send motor cycle crash helmets to the poor workers to reduce the drastic reduction in the nut-picking population.

She opened a bank account at the Branch and managed to keep a straight face throughout, only bursting into uncontrollable giggles as she drove home. Not thinking much more about it until Friday she took a look at the computer ledger balance of the new account, fully expecting it to be unused. To her astonishment there was already a balance of £320 in it, comprising cash credits and, as yet uncleared, cheques.

Just before she left for a week off there was a pile of encouraging letters from staff members and a dozen customers of the Bank and over £600 in the account. Her dilemma went on for weeks. Helen thought she may buy a batch of postcards in Spain, write 'April Fool' on each one and post them to be received whilst she was away. However it seemed a little late to call someone an April Fool when it was now September. What could she do?

"I have been having sleepless nights over this" she said

"Well, that's a relief" said George. "I thought it was because of me".

George silently contemplated the dilemma. Lucy, who had heard every word and who, at age 11 years, missed nothing in the family emotional exchanges, said decisively:-

"Buy the crash helmets and send them to be given to poor people in Brazil with motor bikes".

"Actually, that is not a bad idea" said George. "Use the money to benefit the same workers in some way that will improve their lot. That would be acceptable to the donors and help people who are desperately poor by our standards. There will be charities working in the area who would distribute the money in the way you want."

Helen looked a little happier.

"I could get them to send some photos that I could show everyone at the Bank. OK, thanks. That could be the best way out of my crisis"

"I know I am going to be away for a few months, Mum, but you can always text me if you have any more problems that I can help with." said Lucy.

Helen caught George's eye and smiled to herself.

They motored on South across the wide Spanish plain.

"This is where all the rain falls" volunteered Lucy.

"The rain in Spain falls mainly on the train." said George

"It's 'plane', Daddy. It falls on the plane" contributed Robin

"If it falls on the plane the runway may be too slippery for it to take off"

"That's silly, George (Lucy preferred to call him George). It's a different kind of plain."

Robin looked puzzled and teacher Lucy launched into a long explanation of the difference.

The sun was setting as they came over the last hump of the Sierra. In the distance to the South West was Gibraltar with its fin shaped rock swimming in the Mediterranean. Above the Rock was hanging a halo of cloud. Just over the Rock, nowhere else.

"You can always tell when you are close to a British Colony. It is the only place it is raining" said George, tongue in cheek.

To the West was the best sunset Helen had seen all year. The golden globe sank gracefully into the distant Atlantic.

"When it goes into the sea like that I always expect there to be an enormous hissssss...." she offered. "This is paradise. I wish we could all stay down here with you Lucy Logic." Lucy's name extension had stuck for years because of her little girls honest, straight from the shoulder, remarks throughout her childhood.

The heat that had poured from the sun down on to the centre of The Iberian Penninsula now rose into the sky and cooler air from the sea rushed in to replace it at the lower level. This created a strong refreshing breeze to cool their perspiration from a long time in the car since lunch.

They walked a hundred metres to the top of a nearby rise to enjoy the last of the sun as it reflected pink from the underside of a dozen wispy cirrus clouds.

Fifty miles later George drove his, now dusty, X Patrol into the front gate of Trocadero Tennis Aca......... on the outskirts of Marbella. A weathered worker was fixing the last words of the main sign on to the front archway. He waved as they carefully drove past his ladder.

Erik walked in from the tennis court and held the car door open for Helen to climb out. She gave him a hug for a greeting as George came around the bonnet to shake his hand.

"You made good time. The last stage completed in daylight." said Erik. "Come and have a cool drink before I show you to your rooms"

Lindsay and Cameron joined them and began to hear descriptions of the journey across Europe. Cameron took the boys to enjoy the pool before the last of the light disappeared. They were to stay for two days before returning to the Channel Ferry crossing at Roscoff in Brittany. The new school term, the crop of rape seed and Helen's Bank all awaited their return with varying enthusiasms.

Helen thought Erik looked even better than when she had last seen him and thought how lucky Lindsay was to still be married to him. She had no idea what kind of relationship they were having now but vowed to find out so that she could relate the details to the gossip factory at Poppy Chocolatiere back in the village. Their rooms had balconies that faced South towards the sea. Soon, showered and changed, they were all sipping bottles of cold Saint Miguel at the bar in the sitting room. This was followed by a melon boat, delicious fish dish, Carmen's renowned crème caramel and a glass of the best Veterano Brandy.

Helen found herself sitting next to Lindsay whilst the men were in conversation.

"I'll bet you are happy to be back in a relationship with Erik" she asked.

"We are only business partners" came the reply. "No wild rampant sex on the beach any more" she laughed.

For some reason Helen felt better and less of a reject when she heard this admission.

Cameron appeared to change the subject.

"Mum. Do you remember our washing machine at home used to eat socks?" Without waiting for an answer, he continued "Spanish ones do the same. I now have three left socks and one right one"

"It is all arranged by the washing machine maintenance companies" interrupted George. "They fix the drum so that one sock falls down into a container at every wash, you know, in the way that one numbered ball at a time comes up in the lottery draw. Then, every time the machine is serviced, they collect the socks which are always clean by this time and sell them to organisations for ex-servicemen who have been unlucky enough to lose one leg. Next time you see one be sure to ask him where he buys his single socks"

"I can see the journey has not dulled your humour" said Lindsay, who was warming to this large, cheerful farmer. "Tell us about Lucy. Any comforts that we can provide to make her stay less lonely and more fun?"

They discussed all the relevant things that could arise around Lucy's term with the Academy and checked Skype addresses and emails, phone numbers and health insurance. Then they asked Lucy, who could only think of how she would get by when her secret supply of 'curly wurlies' had run out.

The next two days were filled with discussions around the academy programme and practical plans to expand the student attendance. There was a trip in two vehicles to the sherry bodegas around Jerez de la Frontera on the road to Seville. This included too much sherry sampling on empty stomachs and an exchange of very childish jokes and poems on the journey back to the coast. Over dinner they laughed at the memory of two of the employees at one small bodega, whose job was to put the cork in the top of the bottles at the end of a conveyor belt. As a bottle trundled past on the rickety belt, one placed a new cork in the neck of the bottle and his companion then hit it with a wooden mallet. Apparently each employee was allowed to drink the equivalent of one bottle of the fortified wine every day. This was late in the working day and these two were swaying in unison from side to side causing either the cork to be placed crookedly in the bottle or the mallet to miss altogether. A sympathetic girl was taking the incomplete bottles and placing them further back along the conveyor so that in due course there was a second attempt.

After Helen and George, the two boys and the 4 by 4 had headed north envying Lucy her term in 'paradise', Erik and Lindsay had been working with a local IT girl, who was creating the Academy website. They included photos of all the presentable aspects of the complex.

It was not long before the phone began ringing from a number of interested parents in a variety of countries in Europe. Enquiries came from Germany, Belgium, Poland, Ireland, three from Switzerland and, not surprisingly, another three from Sweden. A promising Girl from New Zealand, from a family who had emigrated there from South Korea, and who was known to Lindsay, had persuaded her parents to borrow the money to enable her to apply. Lindsay remembered how she had won every match with ease when Soo-Jin's school had played Lindsay's last school in a tennis match.

Each of the applicants was asked to submit a summary of tennis achievement and a recent school report. Most were then asked to visit the Academy with their parents for an assessment as soon as they were able.

Lindsay recommended that they accept Soo-Jin without the preliminary visit because her ability was known and it was a long way to come for an interview. Also, if her parents were borrowing the fees to confirm their commitment, they had every confidence in their daughter.

A busy three weeks followed entertaining parents, discreetly enquiring about financial status, touring the facilities and testing the tennis potential of the students. They accepted everyone except an over-indulged boy from Azerbaijan, whose parents were big in the new oil industry and whose son spent two days picking arguments with the other students, was rude and late for the tennis workouts and only ate cakes and drank Coke.

They now had 7 boys and 4 girls to begin the first term and the students began to arrive on planes, in trains and in expensive cars from all parts of the continent. Those who had already been deposited and whose parents had tearfully left were circling each other as new acquaintances do, each wondering what was in store for them and whether there would be any of the food available that their doting parents had lavished in their direction throughout their childhood.

Lindsay gathered together the five first arrivals before the first meal and explained that they were to have excellent, fresh food to help them grow strong and fit. As none of them had any allergies, and unless they were ill, she expected them to make a valiant effort to eat everything that appeared on their plates. This would befriend Carmen and the Cook, Juanita, and make everyone happy. There was a certain amount of muttering but the early meals went down well.

Lucy and Saskia kept in touch on Facebook and each told the other everything that was of interest. Saskia had now started at Kings School in Ottery St. Mary and caught the bus every morning from Seaton. She missed her friend but was determined to join her as soon as she could play tennis well. After school she signed on with Coralie, the tennis coach at the Sports Centre beside the school, and showed a determination to learn that was as good as any Coralie had encountered in recent years.

Lucy fuelled their exchanges with tales of her time spent with the older girls and boys in Marbella.

"How will your Dad pay for you to come here?" asked practical Lucy.

"I don't know, but Auntie Margaret has pots of money so I am going to be extra nice to her. I'll walk her dog and take her flowers on Saturdays. I heard her say that she needed manure for her garden and I know they sell Zoo Poo at Paignton Zoo, so I may order some for her because it is good for plants"

"Ugh!" came the reply. "What if it is from the Elephant House? The lumps will be enormous and crush her lettuces."

Ignacio and Thomas from Thun in Switzerland were swiftly on court loosening up and hitting balls from the baseline. Erik watched without making it obvious. He wanted to measure their enthusiasm for the game as well as give himself hints about individual techniques and habits that would later need changing. He began a notebook with a few pages devoted to each student.

By the following Monday only Kasimierz from Poland remained to arrive. The teachers came to a pre-term meeting and they and Lindsay prepared a provisional programme of lessons in all the subjects. It needed to be flexible until the standards, language skills and individual needs were discovered. They pored over the sample school report of each child to gain the best insight they could get before meeting the victims.

Kasimierz (Kaz) arrived with his Dad after a long road journey from Gdansk on the Baltic coast. With them was Agnieska, his older sister. Dad took Erik to one side and asked whether he still had any places for girls. His daughter was an accomplished horsewoman already but had recently developed a strong interest in tennis. She hadn't yet played in any open tournament but won the Ladies Singles at the prestigious Gdansk Club at her first attempt. Erik decided to call Lindsay over and hit a few balls to Agnieska. They were both stunned by the result. Agnieska had a most unorthodox style using both a double-handed backhand and forehand. This meant that she had to move closer to the ball on the forehand than others, needing extra speed and stamina. Although the fore hand was wild and needed a lot of work, her backhand was absolutely stunning. She was naturally putting almost as much topspin on it as Rafa Nadal and this alone would challenge any female opponent.

Establishing that Dad would not be economically embarrassed with two large accounts for academy fees, and that Agnieska (Aga) really saw herself as a tennis player rather than an event horse rider, both she and Kaz moved into the Trocadero. Dad had sensibly brought half Aga's clothes in a trunk in the car and would send the rest from Poland by carrier in a few days time.

The lessons started very well. Manuel (Lollo), the Spanish teacher, came to work dressed as a medieval Spanish nobleman to teach his subject and, halfway through the morning, Lindsay joined Lavinia's History class outside on a patio facing the sea. She heard her tell the four students how the Phoenicians had fooled the Romans when they had discovered the source of tin. They used to come past Marbella and head to the Pillars of Hercules (Gibraltar and Mons Abyla opposite on the coast of Morocco). They would wait until all the Roman galleys were out of sight, go out into the Atlantic and turn north towards Britain. For years the Romans believed the many tales of serpents and horrors that awaited any ship that passed through the Pillars of Hercules, and so would not believe that this was where the trading Phoenicians had gone. The secret was kept amongst only the Phoenician sailors and merchants and, when the Romans eventually began to follow the ships, some were deliberately scuttled on the coast of Portugal and France to preserve the secret destination. The brotherhood of merchants then reimbursed the shipowners for their losses. Tin remained an extremely valuable commodity for hundreds of years because of this and an excellent source of income for this North African community.

Lindsay was thrilled with this enterprise. She had always thought that as much teaching as possible should be carried out 'in the field' and not shut away in stuffy classrooms. It had been easy with her PE and games, and she felt that it should be equally easy teaching Geography, Biology and some History in the same way, thereby keeping the increased interest of the students. Lucy told Saskia that lessons were held outdoors in the sunshine. Lindsay complimented Lavinia on this and encouraged her to feel free to use the environment whenever she felt it would enhance the children's learning situation. She laughed with Lollo and his outfit that was causing rivulets of perspiration to flow down both cheeks and a huge grin on his lugubrious face. Cameron was enjoying every moment of his Spanish class and completing homework with an enthusiasm she rarely saw in New Zealand.

They were thinking how well this whole venture was going as they shared a bottle of Rioja at 10pm in their sitting room when little Gabriella came in barefoot and in floods of tears.

THREE

Gabriella eventually stopped sobbing for long enough to tell her story. Sitting on Lindsay's knee in her nightie she told them that she didn't want to see the enormous dog that was the size of a donkey, or the ghost with the rotten teeth or the smugglers who lived on the beach. It seemed that she was the victim of beastly nighttime tales dreamed up by the boys with the sole purpose of scaring little girls. Now all Gabriella wanted was her Mum.

She eventually calmed down and slept on the spare bed in Lindsay's room that night. It seemed that Nicholas, the 13 year old Belgian, was the creator of the ghost stories. Before the adults had a chance to reprimand him for scaring the little Gabriella, she had exacted her own revenge. Beside a small pond two feet deep and full of weed were two of those whicker chairs that hung on a spring from a metal frame to enable the sitter to swing gently whilst peacefully sitting. Nicholas approached these for the first time saying

"I like swinging on these".

Gabriella called that the springs were old and you have to jump on to the chair to make them work. Nicholas took a run at it and jumped on to the whicker chair with its thick cushion. He discovered that in fact it was the opposite. The springs were especially taut and lively. His body landed on the cushion, the chair sank on the spring and fired him gracefully into the pond. He walked into breakfast soaking wet and covered in green pondweed to the giggles of the naughty Italian and most of the others in the room.

"Already it is just like being back in my teaching job" laughed Lindsay "Teachers are rather like the police. You never know what is coming around the corner." She pulled the leaves of a decimated water lily from Nicholas' hair and sent him to the boys' block for a shower and change of clothes.

"This is what happens to people who make up ghost stories" rang in his ears as he departed.

Erik was anxious to establish the tennis element of the Academy in the local area and not to have the students regarded as weird and privileged outcasts. He phoned the largest of the local schools and offered to entertain their tennis teams to matches back in the complex. He remembered when he was a boy back in Sweden the most enjoyable school matches were those which had the best tea after the games, and he vowed to have Juanita produce the best possible spread for the teenage visitors. He was also aware that his students would be expected to win easily and planned to make up his teams with a mixture of talents rather than the best team available. In his mind was the embryo of a scheme to devote at least an evening a week to coach a handful of locals who showed promise but would never be able to pay the fees to join the Academy.

The immediate response came from Sister Magdalena from the Marbella Convent, who was well known as an outdoor enthusiast. She phoned and arranged to bring a team of six girls to play doubles matches. Erik asked her to bring a reserve player as well. A week later seven faces peered out of the Convent minibus, eager to check out the rumours they had heard in school about the new arrivals. Erik had not mentioned that he only had five girls at the moment and immediately asked whether the Convent reserve would like to play for the Academy team.

Sister Magdalena had instilled some steel into her team and they set out with determination. Each pair played each of the pairs in the opposing team in turn, with the second match being against their opposite numbers. The reserve, who was 15, played in the second pairing and the Convent won two of their three matches. Lucy and little Gabriella, the two youngest by at least two years, ran until they were exhausted and won against all but the top Convent pairing. There was no stopping the Academy No 1 team of Petra and Agnieska who swept aside all opposition with ease with Sister Magdalena clapping Aga's amazing backhand each time it fizzed across court or down the line out of reach of the net player. Trocadero Academy won by 6 matches to 3.

"Thank you Joel" said the Sister. "This has been a good lesson for us. The girls have won every match for two years up to now. We shall go home, discuss and learn."

Lollo took his two bosses to a little bar a few kilometres along the coast towards Gibraltar. He warned them that it was unusual but that they would enjoy the ambiance. The building was white with blue window shutters and half pots of terracotta attached to the walls, each having a trailing plant or flower leading from it. Steps led from the street to a verandah with four tables and inside to more tables and a bar against the far wall. The barman was about the most extrovert gay man that Lindsay had ever met. He was wearing leather shorts and a floral shirt with red braces and had a personality to match. Clarence threw his arms around Lollo in greeting and limply shook his two guests by the hand.

"Welcome. First drink is on the house" said Clarence "Tapas are along the bar, but get in first before 'guts' here eats the lot" glancing at Lollo as he spoke.

As they sat down at one of the inside tables Lindsay said "I didn't think you were gay, Lollo"

"He isn't, dear" called Clarence from the bar. "Despite my best efforts over many years Lollo still lusts after pretty women or, actually, any women he can get his hands on."

"I come here for the entertainment"added Lollo. "After eight hours of telling teenage brats to blow their noses it is a pleasant relief to enjoy a beer and listen to the banter between Clarence and anyone who takes his life in his hands and comes into the Bar Lulu."

"Bar Lulu?" asked Erik.

"Named after Clarence and his career as a Drag Queen."

"Clarence was a legend in Amsterdam only a few years ago"

"I had to retire, dear, after a bad month, and invest my meagre savings in

this superb establishment."

"What happened?" asked Lindsay

"The curse of all drag artists" replied Clarence "a run-in with a group of homophobes coupled with a chronic case of crushed nuts."

Erik asked for a more detailed explanation.

"You try jamming your nether regions into a tight pair of lady's nylon knickers twice nightly and matinees on Saturdays without excruciating pain."

Erik and Lollo winced audibly.

"I do it all the time without any problem" said Lindsay.

This continued throughout the evening with Clarence always the centre of attention. The Bar had a loyal local clientele and groups of holidaymakers joined them from the hotels nearer Marbella town and seafront. Clarence obviously enjoyed his notoriety and he was rapidly becoming one of the area's 'must see' attractions.

"That description makes me sound like a new promenade that has just been laid" said Clarence

"You should be so lucky!" added one of his regulars as he came to the bar for another round of drinks.

"If you are going to question my desirability I'll call Rex and set him on you. He hasn't had his dinner yet"

"Rex presumably is the Doberman guard dog" suggested Erik.

Lollo laughed. "No, Rex is his latest partner. Until last Christmas he was a crane driver on the container docks at Valencia."

Later Lollo ate a handful of peanuts from one of the small dishes that Clarence brought from the bar. He sneezed at the same time as he swallowed and caught the sneeze in his handkerchief. Apologising, he stared into the white handkerchief.He announced that he had blown a peanut down his nose to the great amusement of all the others. From the bar Clarence was unable to resist a quip

"If your nose wasn't so big you couldn't have done that"

Poor Lollo looked embarrassed in the presence of his new bosses. Clarence continued "Actually I did the same thing when I was about eighteen with a baked bean. Everybody was horrid to me afterwards. It became grossly exaggerated in the next years. My family members referred to it on every possible occasion, usually when I was eating something. I was accused of producing an increasingly large object from my quite shapely nose. It grew into a blueberry, then a strawberry. My brother told the story about the walnut that Clarence had sneezed out and put everyone off their food. Then the staff at The Night Club got to hear about it and it became a Brussels sprout. After three months it had become a tomato. Only last Christmas I listened to my young nephew, in the next room, relating the tale of the potato that Uncle Clarence blew down his nose. Perhaps that will make you feel better Lollo."

The next day Maria Carmelita arrived with a wardrobe of new sports clothes for Ignacio that she had purchased on line in Madrid. They had been delivered to her yacht in the smart Marina at Puerto Banus. At the same time she invited Erik and Lindsay to drinks on board that evening.

They negotiated the tight security at the Marina entrance and were welcomed by Maria and her husband, Victor, and encouraged to mingle with the dozen or so guests who were sipping cocktails on the main deck of the sleek white motor yacht, that was designed as much for ostentatious entertaining as for crossing the seas.

A slim, dark, good-looking man of approximately 45 to 50 years immediately approached them from the port guard rail.

"I am Joseph, brother to Victor", he announced. "Everyone calls me Pepe. It is the accepted nickname of Joseph in this part of the world."

"I thought your family were from Uruguay" said Lindsay.

"We are. But I have business interests in Spain and live most of the year on this coast"

They exchanged details for a few minutes and Erik noticed that Pepe was directing all his attention towards Lindsay. Not wishing to cramp her style, as she appeared quite flattered with Pepe's constant gaze, he moved off to speak to some of the other expensively dressed and beautiful people on the deck. Maria Carmelita took his arm and introduced him to several others, emphasising his name and reputation as if it was her own.

Lindsay had already finished two cuba libres when Pepe came back with a third. This one seemed to have a lot more cuba than the others and she was beginning to feel the rum seeping into her head and freeing her feelings. Maybe this was the 'libre'. She had not consumed much alcohol in recent years and the effect was nicely relaxing as well as this being her favourite tasting drink. Always having been athletic and good at sport she had steered clear of the late parties and pub crawls in her younger days, and thought that drink was a curse to be avoided most of the time. Recently, there had been precious few invitations to break out of her routine of caring for a lively son; her engineer husband having left whilst Cameron was still at play school. Several men had dated her in New Zealand in the last ten years, but none had appealed to her in the way that husband Jerry had, nor had been as considerate a lover as Erik on their South Seas Island. Hidden deep inside her was still a glimmer of the wild Lindsay from her tennis tournament days when her interest in male company eventually played havoc with her tennis career. Too many late nights out with coaches, other competitors and desirable men from the media circus had created limitations on court. Now, in the presence of a good looking South American, who had not reduced the intensity of his attention, and the re-discovered relaxation, the more extrovert Lindsay was beginning to emerge.

In a corner of the deck area a group of four, very hairy musicians had begun playing quietly. The bass guitarist now produced a mandolin and increased the tempo.

Pepe was very adept at the Latin System.

'Give the woman your total attention and she will be flattered almost to the point of submission'.

No Northern European man will do this so it was probably her first experience of this approach.

'Whilst she is facing you only look into her eyes'

Other men would be gazing around the room and frequently down the front of her dress.

'Always wait and only assess her physical advantages from a distance, not when she can see you are looking'.

'Speak only to HER, and only things that need to be said'.

These are tactics that have held up well for generations of Italian men, Spaniards, Greeks and itinerant South

Americans and they have managed to concertina 'chatting up' into an art form. However, Lindsay once had a mixed doubles partner called Casanova Firmani, whose ambition was to emulate his namesake and whose interest in her athletic capabilities continued beyond the tennis courts. She had therefore already experienced the Latin System and it had worked remarkably quickly on a New Zealand girl, even with Mummy's cautionary words still ringing in her ears.

"Shall we start the dancing?" asked Lindsay, to divert Pepe from gently stroking her arm.

The group were playing tunes with a strong beat that encouraged everyone to take the floor. There were only two couples to begin with and Erik watched Lindsay over the heads of two ladies who were trying to interest him in their somewhat limited knowledge of the tennis circuit. Living in a country of mainly shorter people was sometimes an advantage to Erik who was well over six feet tall. The downside, however, was that he bumped his head on the doorways in their houses. He was glad to have a head of quite thick curly hair as a protection. He watched his 'wife' with interest and realised that this was the first chance she had been given to have fun since they met in East Devon and hatched the idea of a Tennis Academy.

It takes a lot of energy to match a wild Lindsay, especially when fuelled with a latent dancing bug and a quantity of Bacardi Rum. Pepe was torn between playing the discreet brother of the host and keeping pace with his partner. South Americans are seldom embarrassed in public, so he opted for the middle of the road approach. After four numbers his ready smile became lopsided and perspiration was dripping from his jet black hair down the neck of his shirt and off one of his ear lobes. Another guest stepped in, during the short pause between songs and a relieved Pepe retired to the drinks table.

Erik was still watching the entertainment whilst being

given a ball by ball account of the one day his latest companion had used her complimentary ticket to watch a tennis
tournament. He thought that he must initiate a formal
divorce from Lindsay in some painless way to free her for
any future permanent suitor, and berated himself for not
having considered this years earlier.

"Don't you agree Erik?" Erik's attention was brought to
book with a bump.

"Sorry, I didn't hear that above the Music"

"My friends all think Rafa Nadal is the best looking
player at the moment, don't you agree?"

"I can't say I have thought much about it. I tend to put
tennis skill at the forefront, and Rafa certainly has been one
of the most skilful. I have also heard that he has a lovely
nature and that success hasn't changed him from the nice
lad he always was at home in Majorca."

Erik smiled and then excused himself. He asked one of
the waitresses for a café solo, waited, and then took it to the
bow of the ship. Looking out across the sea he began to contemplate the prospect of a lonely love life if he couldn't erase
the memory of the perfect harmony he had found many
years before. There was a hole in his heart that he feared
may never heal. Ever since his agonies as a gawky, skinny
ten year old Erik had grown his hair, which was blond and
curly, dressed largely in denim, spoke very little and had
become the boy every girl in his school desired as company. This continued through College and on to the tennis
court. He had never been rejected by anyone he had asked
for a date and found himself the one who always finished
relationships. He had been the darling of sponsors and his
picture was displayed advertising products and tournaments
in many countries. Ironically it was his one ideal love who
became the first to push him away – Sally, who had chosen
the second of the two men who loved her intensely. Erik
carried his painting of her in the top of his tennis bag.

He was wondering whether Sally's rejection of him was the reason why he yearned after her.

He was jolted back to the present when he saw a movement in the darkness. The Motor Yacht Rosario was too large to be moored on any of the pontoons so she had been secured to the promenade at Puerto Banus. This made it easy for the party guests to embark from the roadside immediately on to the lower ledge of her stern. The bow was fixed to a buoy in the harbour by a stout double rope. The bright lights of the promenade and on board left the water beyond the bow in darkness. Erik sat quietly on a capstan and watched. Behind him was a metal cabinet that prevented his silhouette from being visible to anyone on the water. A small skiff had been tied to the Rosario's buoy and he could see the outline of a young boy or girl sitting in the skiff. The child began to climb the double rope with a half full plastic bag in one hand. He or she was barefoot. Peering into the darkness Erik's eyes became more able to detect details. This was a boy of around eight years. He reached the edge of the deck and grabbed the rail, swinging to one side and then disappeared. Erik waited for a full minute before standing up and looking over the side. There was a hole in the side of the yacht where the main anchor would exit when it was in use, behind which would be a chain locker and many metres of heavy chain. The lad had climbed into this locker and vanished.

Maria Carmelita was preceded by her voice as she finally found Erik in his secluded place.

"There you are. I expect you needed a cigarette. I 'ave been seeking you. Come and meet the Mayor."

Erik thought this would be a good connection and so followed her back through the dancers. He took one look at his business partner and her energetic palpitations and decided it was for the best if he met the Mayor alone.

Senor Alvarez was an ebullient character dressed

impeccably in grey suit and blue tie with a large polka dot blue and white handkerchief in his top pocket. The warm evening and the alcoholic haze had not moved a hair on his head out of place. He greeted Erik courteously and with the respect that showed he had researched his name and reputation.

"I know you have been here for many weeks but welcome to Marbella. We are hosts to many celebrities, and even royalty, but your intentions are extra welcome because you plan to stay and also to provide some jobs at this bad time for employment. I was sad when the old school closed and was empty for a long time, but I hear you are advanced in re-furnishing many of the buildings".

"You must visit us and let me show you around. We plan to start slowly and wisely. If we become popular and train these young people well the Academy will be a credit to the town." said Erik.

He decided to grasp the chance to float an idea that had been in his mind from the first, partially because they now had an audience.

"Perhaps, Senor Mayor, during your period of Office, you may consider sponsoring one of the promising local boys or girls with a scholarship to the Academy. You will have many wealthy contacts who may be pleased to contribute to the, shall we call it, the Alvarez Bursary. It would give a talented poor child a chance to succeed and carry the Marbella colours around the tennis tournament circuit. It would also ensure the continuing celebration of the name of Alvarez."

The Mayor did not respond immediately. However he noticed several nodding heads amongst the listening contingent and gave a hint of approval by stroking his moustache with one finger.

"We can discuss this when I come to see you" he replied.

Pepe was back on the dance floor with Lindsay, this time pressed together shuffling to a slow tune. Erik positioned himself close to the dancers and beckoned Lindsay to him when she looked in his direction.

"I am close to leaving" he said. "How about you?"

Pepe, who had walked over with her, answered

"I will drive you back to your house if you stay".

Erik just raised his eyebrows and waited for her reply.

"OK. I'll stay another half an hour. I can return with Pepe."

Erik smiled and went to thank the hosts, leaving with an invitation to join them at the prestigious Marbella Club at any time he wished.

The next morning at breakfast Lindsay was first there and full of life.

"Best time I have had for ages" she called from the mini-buffet table they used for a rolling breakfast with Cameron and the students.

"What about Mr Smooth?" asked Erik quietly. "He was the perfect gentleman. Drove me here. Peck on the cheek. Didn't run out of petrol or drive to the woods and jump on me." Lindsay said, a little pointedly.

"Are you keen on the intense Latin types?" he added

"If they treat me nicely and are at least the same height. But I am not looking for any permanent connection. We have enough to think about getting this operation running successfully. To say nothing of the travelling to and from tournaments."

FOUR

The Academy settled into a boarding school style routine. Classroom in the mornings and tennis coaching or fitness exercises in the afternoons. The evenings were free and weekends devoted to trips out, often with an educational bias. It was time for the next meeting of Uncle Thorbjorn's Trust in London and Erik planned to extend the visit to include some time at his second home in East Devon.

The Trust made a number of small grants to sports venues and one large one to the Trocadero Academy to finance the building of two new outside tennis courts and better equip the small gymnasium that was already operating. The limited facilities were putting a strain on a programme for twelve students and the juggling of times for training had become a challenge.

The four trustees enjoyed lunch at Pauls in the French quarter near South Kensington tube station before Erik left to collect his old Porsche Carrera from a friend who owned a garage at Turnham Green and kept the car until each of Erik's visits to England.

"Off to the country again, I suppose" commented Georgiou

"Got a woman in every country now you've retired have you? Dozens of kids all over the place as well? Bet it costs you a bloody fortune."

"Yes"agreed Erik to Georgiou and his grinning chief mechanic. "I've been sowing the Eriksson seed in every continent to help improve the local strains. Soon, every other face will look like mine."

"God forbid" replied Georgiou. ."It used to be bad enough in Wimbledon week with posters of your mug all over the buses."

It was one of those clear, sunny October days for which the South West was famous. All the holidaymakers had gone home and the sun had decided to appear after a gloomy cool August and September. The locals had come out too, having spent a self-imposed curfew indoors since June. Many were winding up the summer season clearing their businesses from the beaches, closing cafes for six months or bringing boats in from moorings in the rivers and harbours of this established English holiday playground. Nobody had made a profit – or that's what they told each other in the pub, in case there was a taxman lurking nearby. The 'Indian Summer', as they called it, was lasting well and Mums and Dads were picnicking with their children at weekends. They had been too busy working all hours to do this in the school holidays. Erik put down the hood of the white sports car and began to feel relaxed as he entered the area of high hedges that was East Devon.

The first road makers in this part of England had levelled the road surface by piling the mud, stones and grass in a heap on each side. This heap continued along the roads with only gaps to access the fields beyond. During the next 150 to 200 years substantial hedgerows had grown creating a perfect haven for mammals and small birds, but an annoying barrier for the later car driver to enjoy the views. Only the drivers of tall lorries and touring coach passengers could enjoy the scenery as they drove from town to village.

Erik stopped in a layby on the top of Askers Hill in Dorset on the way, to drink in the Dorset/Devon coastline and the sparkling sea to the West. Opening a bottle of water he wondered how long he could stay in England with Lindsay stretched to cover all the tennis work. He also was not quite sure where he would be staying tonight. Erik still owned Kirkhaven House on the coast side road after Lyme Regis from Rousdon village to Axmouth and, almost beside it, 'The Umpire's Chair', an old water tower that he had converted into a bed sit with spectacular views across Lyme Bay. The house had been let to a young couple with three children and 'The Chair' was a successful holiday let that had been occupied from week to week throughout the summer. His only other option was to camp on his boat 'Viti Levu', which may still be moored in Seaton Harbour.

Probably the best place to begin was with Phil Mercer, who looked after the boat and also ran a little sideline letting 'The Chair' on Erik's behalf. Phil and his Dad ran the boatyard beside the harbour and there was not much that happened in Seaton or nearby Axmouth that his family did not know about.

"Hallo Boy" he greeted Erik in his gentle Devon accent. "Didn't reckon to see you down here again this year. How long you staying?"

"Just a couple of days. Have to get back to the new project in Spain. I see you've taken the boat out of the water already, so I can't stay there tonight."

Viti Levu was sitting on blocks in the storage park looking as though she needed a good clean and anti fouling after a summer in the water.

"You can use the Tower for three days. It's empty this week. Someone comes in on Saturday. It's clean. The girls always do it straight after people leave on Saturday morning. Hey, that Maggie is up at the Stables this month. You could shack up with her."

Phil was grinning, knowing something of the history between the two.

"Too dangerous!" Erik quipped "though I'll try to catch up with her whilst she is here."

He decided to go up to 'The Umpire's Chair' and took the key from Phil before driving up the hill. The parking space was underneath the tower. It was painted green to blend in with the surrounding trees and hedges. Erik climbed the wide metal steps that led, in two stages, towards the large single room. He stood beside the bathroom, which had been suspended below and to one side. Releasing the folding ladder from above with the key, he brought it down to the top platform and climbed up with his grip containing a few clothes.

He was pleased to see how clean everything was with the bedding perfectly folded. The SouthWest facing picture window revealed the sun setting into thin cloud above the fishing village of Beer and a wide view below of the Axe Valley and its haven for wading birds. Erik sat on the sofa that was placed in front if the window and drank in the greys and browns and greens of sea, village and the countryside he had grown to love.

Inevitably he also reflected the deep emotions he had experienced in this very place during his, all too short, life-changing relationship with the only real love of his life. Some of this emotion and creativity he had released into painting the woman, draining any desire to set a canvas again for some years afterwards.

He put his feelings away and decided to eat at the pub in Axmouth, where he enjoyed two pints of Otter Ale and a catch up with the locals, some of whom had had such a 'bad' summer that they were planning to spend November and December at resorts close to Erik along the Spanish coast.

"Us'll call in to check you are teaching they kids proper" said Harry Kerslake, who, rumour had it, had won a prize in the National Lottery the previous month. He wasn't saying how much, though, but he had been buying drinks for three weeks. This was a give-away because, whenever he had previously entered the pub with his mates, he made a point of holding the door open for them so that he would be last to reach the bar in order to avoid having to buy a round.

Erik ordered the steak and kidney pie to go with his second pint, putting aside the Scandinavian dislike of eating offal of any kind i.e. kidney, liver etc. He found this the most tasty English dish available and had consumed a good many when in Devon and away from the strict dietary routine of tournament training. Whilst there he called Helen, who was now living with George at the farm, along the road from 'The Chair'.

They couldn't join him that evening, being without a baby sitter, but Helen agreed to meet him at her favourite haunt in the village the following morning, whilst George was clearing the field that had harvested the rape and the boys were at school. Helen had recently given up her job in the Bank to become a farmer's wife. At her farewell in the Office the Manager had worn a Hells Angels crash helmet in memory of the Brazil Nuts joke, and told her he was relieved that she wouldn't be with them when April 1st came around again.

Erik then called Maggie, who was thrilled that he was in the area and jumped in her car to join him. Maggie was married to Sammy, his long time doubles partner, and lived on their estate in Bangalore in India. Erik reminded himself that he must remember to call it Bengaluru now, as it had reverted to the correct name in the Kannadam language rather than the one used by the British Colonials, who couldn't or wouldn't pronounce it properly.

The pub froze in mid-sentence as Maggie entered and, without even closing the door, shot across the room and pinned Erik in his seat as she smacked a full-on kiss on his mouthful of pie and potato.

"I haven't seen you since, well since, since forever" she said and all the men sitting at the bar went "Aaahh" in chorus.

Erik, who had managed to swallow the pie by, now corrected her

"It was only two months ago at the U.S. Open"

"Oh, oh" said the chorus.

"But it seems like forever" added Maggie.

"Aaahh" said the choir again.

"Shut up, you lot, or I'll come over there and sort you out" said Maggie.

"Right on, girl. I'm first" said Harry

"Harry Kerslake. I remember when Emma Hardy and I were cleaning at the Rugby Club and we caught you in the showers, and you couldn't get your towel without walking past us. You had the whitest bottom we had ever seen"

The choir dissolved in laughter and Harry went rather quiet.

Maggie owned the stables at the top of the village and, in recent years had leased them to Oliver and Malcolm, who were horse lovers and needed a change from the seafront café that Oliver had run in Seaton. Oliver had suffered in a riding accident and was confined to a wheelchair so Malcolm did the hard work whilst his partner kept the books and the kitchen in order.

"I decided to stay for a week this time to make sure the boys are really coping. They have had a busy season and need a holiday. Malcolm is not getting any younger. They have agreed to let a couple who were advertising in 'Horse and Hound' take over for a month so they can get a break. The two young ones have been there for the last three days learning all the oddities about the place and the walks we use."

"How is Sammy?" asked Erik

"I don't know. The bugger hasn't contacted me for days. We have a new, very pretty childminder at home. I hope he isn't bonking her insane while I am over here."

"I shouldn't think so. Sammy is a pretty constant sort of

guy and I am sure you are a hot enough number to keep him loyal." offered Erik.

"Anyway, in that culture, the girls parents will be looking over the fence every five minutes to preserve her purity."

"Yeah. I suppose so. He is not like me. 'See it, fancy it, go for it!'"

"I doubt you are any different from most horsewomen."

"It's not true – that rumour – we are just used to telling big four legged beasts what to do, so when a big two legged beast appears on our doorstep the inclination is to do the same."

Erik looked sideways at her.

"It doesn't always finish up in the hay, either" said Maggie "Look at us. I never managed to get inside your shorts when you were here."

"I would never have kept up the pace"

"You managed to keep pace with Sally.

"That was different. We had a special rapport. Like we had brought the love here with us from another life. I think we had been waiting for each other."

Maggie thought of her friend, whom she had known since college days.

"She gets maximum points for loyalty. I don't know that I would have stayed with Chris in those circumstances."

" I can see that now. It is what makes her even more special. She loved us both equally, but he needed her most. A decision that took a lot of courage."

Erik bought Maggie a drink and they shared a chocolate ice cream dessert with three scoops.

"I have already eaten a massive dinner. One of Oliver's game casseroles. So I shouldn't be sharing this with you. I'll never get into my thong at the pool when I get home."

"I imagine the workers on your Estate have an emotional disturbance every time they see you sunbathing in next to nothing."

"No they don't. I can't. I mean it is a cover-up society. In the countryside, where we are, everything is traditional. Women don't have legs. The older ones are always in a saree and the young ones in the chuttidah – thin, pretty trousers. Actually I can only sunbathe on the roof of the house and then very discreetly."

"What about swimming in the pool?" asked Erik

"I choose my time carefully. Usually when the staff are out shopping or away on the other side of the Estate with the horses. We had a pool party once and all the women, who wanted to swim, went in the pool wearing long nightdresses. It did look funny and one of them got into difficulties trying to swim."

They discussed the developments at the Tennis Academy and, inevitably, Erik's relationship with Lindsay before Maggie had to leave.

"When will I see you next?" she asked.

"I am going to be tied up in Spain until the Australian Open in January, when I have to honour my commitment to Swedish TV. See you both there."

"How about Christmas in India? Bring Lindsay if you are still talking to each other by then"

"Thanks" said Erik "I'd like that. Let me call you nearer the time."

They embraced warmly and the bar chorus added "OOoooo Nice" and a round of applause. They received a wide smile from Maggie.

Erik bought the lads a round and left shortly afterwards to spend the night high up in his unique 'Umpires Chair', as Sally had named it during their short love affair.

He was shaving in the lower room early next morning when he heard footsteps pounding up the metal staircase. He peered out to be greeted by Callum, Helen's son.

"Mum said you were here. How long for? I would have left Viti in the water longer if I had known you were coming down again."

"Hi Callum. I'm only here for a couple of days. No time for sailing on this visit. Have you been out on her much this year?"

"Quite a lot. Most days in August when the weather was not too bad. She was labouring a bit in September. Too much weed and barnacles on her."

"Yes. I saw yesterday. On the Hard by Phil's workshop. You can get all that off before it dries too hard and give it a good couple of coats of antifouling." said Erik.

"I've got to get the bus to school in a minute. I'll call in again later and chance you are here."

Callum and Erik were equal partners in Viti Levu, which they had bought and done up together two years before. Erik had taught him to sail at a time he was coming to terms with his Dad having left Helen. Now he was a competent sailor and the envy of many in his Sixth Form at school in Lyme Regis.

Erik called after him

"How is Verity?"

"Waste of time" came the reply. "Only interested in boys with cars. Took her out on Viti once and she was sick all the time. Bye."

With a wave he was gone. Down the road to catch the school bus to Lyme.

Coralie Matthews is a sports coach who works for the Sports Council and is based at the Sports Centre in the small town of Ottery St. Mary in East Devon. She has always preferred and specialised in coaching tennis and uses the indoor court at the Centre. There is no shortage of aspiring young players, partially due to the limited indoor facilities in this part of the country. More accurately, there is no shortage of mothers with aspirations for their children. They arrive for the first lesson with all the kit, often bought by parents who have not consulted an expert. They have saved themselves trouble visiting a sports shop by buying online. Therefore, many have the wrong sizes of racket for their child's weight and strength and sometimes the wrong type of shoes.

This morning, a weekday and a school day, Coralie was introducing a dozen eleven year olds to tennis. They came from the Secondary School next door and this was one of their games lessons. Her enthusiasm kept their attention and, although Erik could see that it was unlikely that any of them would be playing as an adult, they were going to learn enough about the game to be interested spectators.

Coralie had been Lucy Walker's coach in the evenings until Erik had stolen Lucy away to join his new Academy. She had shown him that she had the natural teaching skills that probably fewer than 20% of practising teachers possess. Her bubbly enthusiasm captured the pupils and kept them inside the subject. She had always liked Erik and had kept his secret when he had arrived incognito in Devon as she had immediately recognised one of her tennis heroes. Seeing him today waiting in the gallery, she dismissed her class as soon as the clock moved to 9.50am.

"Hallo. How lovely to see you. I had not expected you to pass this way again now Lucy is with you in Spain"

Erik was impressed with how Coralie looked for her first lesson of the day. She had taken care to wear a full set of clean tennis gear. Her trainers were not new, but had been cleaned and she wore a minimal make-up designed for those to whom she was speaking rather than her own comfort whilst playing. Many coaches and P.E. Teachers that Erik had seen over the years just threw on yesterday's T shirt and shorts and their shoes had not seen a cleaner since they had been purchased.

"I have come to see you. Will your boyfriend let me take you out to dinner this evening?"

"Er. Wow. Yes, no. I'm sort of between men at the

moment. You know – finished one and not looking too hard for another. Help. I don't know if I have anything good enough to wear to go out with someone like you. What have I done to deserve this?"

"I have one or two things I would like to ask you."

"Well, I hope at least one of them is a proposal of marriage". Coralie giggled. Her confidence was rapidly surfacing.

"Here comes the next batch of monsters."she said.

They exchanged phone numbers and Coralie's address for the 7pm collection.

"Don't dress up too much. It will only be a small place, but the food will be good." said Erik as he set off to walk back to the car.

He drove back to Axmouth and parked outside a pretty little shop/café called Poppy's Chocolatiere. Inside he met up with Helen again. Behind the counter was Rachel and from the kitchen at the rear, came Poppy, the Rev.Penelope Duguid, the owner and creator of chocolate dreams. They knew each other well and enjoyed a warm greeting. Erik had been their favourite customer since he first appeared in his tournament days unrecognised and having assumed the name 'Erik' rather than his real one.

He sat with Helen drinking his black coffee and indulging in a chocolate covered fruit flapjack. They discussed Lucy's progress and how well she had settled in with all the older students at the Academy, about her friendship with Gabriella and Nicholas' visit to the pond. The cafe was quiet this October morning and Rachel and Poppy came over to join them. They told Erik that this season had been the best so far and they were now mentioned in ramblers' magazines and had a long article written about the Chocolatiere in Devon Life last Spring. All these had helped to increase the visiting trade. Rachel told him that Poppy couldn't now move to another parish and would have to die in the pulpit at Axmouth or tasting the products in the kitchen behind them. However she may die the richest and tubbiest vicar in the Westcountry.

Erik took Coralie to Moores in the village of Newton Poppleford near Sidmouth. There were only three tables in this cosy and exclusive restaurant set back from the busy road. Erik told Coralie that she looked stunning. He didn't know that she had driven into Exeter immediately after school and spent far too much on a royal blue flaired minidress and low heeled peep toe shoes. Her almost black hair was tied in a chignon and complemented by earrings of tiny lanterns she had been given by a friend last Christmas.

Having spent some time watching Coralie's coaching techniques and her teaching skills, as well as checking Lucy's progress in previous visits, Erik had not taken in fully how attractive she could be 'off court'.

They enjoyed the main meal, every item of which had been made on the premises and, before dessert was served, Erik came to the point.

"I wanted to take you out to thank you for the great job you have done with Lucy. She now has the makings of a good player and the attitude to enjoy competition and widen her view of the world, almost all down to your infectious enthusiasm."

Coralie was flattered. She had been praised before and her skills recognised by the Sports Council, but not by one of the top ten tennis stars of the nineties.

"How tied are you into a contract with the Council?"

"I am hoping the funds will be there for them to renew from January 1st." she replied

"So, no serious boyfriend and a contract until the end of the year. Any other major commitments?"

Coralie thought.

"About two years still to pay on the car and I take Grandma for a drive most Sundays".

Erik continued

"How would you fancy half term week with us in Marbella?"

Coralie's eyes brightened. "Would I...............!!?"

"We'll pick up the airfare, but you will have to work. Not just a holiday?"

She caught the eye of a man on the next table, who had been listening and was nodding his head perceptibly. She grinned back at him.

"OK. What do I have to do? I can cook a bit and am a whizz at washing dishes."

"Nothing like that. Just a little more coaching of Lucy and her friend Gabriella."

The party next to them rose to leave and the same man came over to Erik and shook his hand. Thanks for the entertainment – all those matches at Wimbledon."

Then he looked at Coralie.

"You do realise you are dining with a legend?"

FIVE

Lindsay had been struggling to cope with the programme for tennis in the afternoons without Erik's support.

"We must get teaching cover on court" she told him.

"I may have the answer."

Erik was waiting in the departure lounge at Gatwick Airport.

"Coralie who trained our Lucy may be interested. She doesn't know it yet. However I have invited her out for a week during the UK school half term to help us with the tennis and for you to see what you think of her. If no good she has had a week's holiday. If she is OK and keen to come to us, she will be free by the New Year."

"Sounds good. I was even thinking of texting my old school assistant back in Otago and persuading her to come. We may be exhausted by New Year."

They agreed to talk more that evening over a glass of wine on the balcony.

Pepe had been trying to take Lindsay out for a meal ever since Erik had left, but she had used 'tiredness' as a reason to decline. This evening the excuse was that she was meeting Erik from Malaga Airport and needed to discuss the Academy with him quite urgently.

She was thrilled to hear that he had secured the funding for the two new courts and they decided to call the specialist builders from Granada first thing in the morning and to press them to begin as soon as possible.

The next day was wet so tennis practice was substituted by a video of one of the close quarter-finals of the previous summer's Wimbledon. The students were told to make notes of any improvements each player could have made to improve their grip on the tie, and a discussion of these lasted half an hour afterwards in their own sitting room. It was beginning to show who analysed a game well and who had not spent much time before studying this aspect if the sport.

That evening Pepe succeeded in taking Lindsay away from the Trocadero. The chef on board the Rosario produced a delicious meal for the two of them on the top deck. He grilled beef over a special barbecue of hot coals in front of them (asado) and served it with an avocado and tomato salad that had been given a light dressing of grappamiel, a Uruguayan drink of alcohol and honey. Lindsay managed two portions of the salad. Pepe explained that Victor and Maria Carmelita lived in their apartment overlooking the Marina when in Marbella, whilst he and the crew stayed on board the Rosario.

Tomorrow Pepe would be taking the yacht away on business, as he often needed to.

"No point in having such a versatile and expensive craft sitting idly in harbour all winter." he volunteered.

"How long do you go for each time?" Lindsay asked.

"Usually three days"

"Always to the same place?"

"No. Round and about in the Western Mediterranean."

"What do you do on these trips?"

"It is not very interesting. Mainly political meetings in other ports"

Lindsay ventured

"Can I come with you, one day? I love the sea and spent all my childhood on and off the water in New Zealand?"

Pepe's expression changed.

"I don't think this type of yacht would be for you. No sails or rigging to keep you involved."

She decided not to pursue the topic for the time being.

They relaxed after the meal sipping brandy under the stars, that had become more visible now the Marina lights had been dimmed. Pepe asked her more about herself and she told him tales of her younger days, friends and holidays. He knew little about her home country and how isolated many felt, driving them to scrimp and save to come to Europe and America to see if it was the same as they saw on television.

"Are you married?" Lindsay bluntly asked him, aware that, although he wore no ring, it would be likely that a straight man of his age and good looks either was or had been.

"I was. My wife died trying to deliver our first child. A rare thing these days, but the good maternity hospital in Montevideo could not save either of them"

"How terrible" exclaimed Lindsay. "It must have taken a long time to get over such a shock."

"I am not yet over it fully. It was eight years ago next month. For two years I just roamed around Argentina and Chile on my motorbike. Sometimes staying in one place for a few weeks, sometimes just sleeping rough; drinking too much, getting into political arguments, generally being bad company to whoever I met. Then Victor and Maria Carmelita discovered where I was, near the border with Paraguay, and sent a truck to get me. They knew I would object so they sent two heavies who found me with a hangover and bundled me in the back of the truck with the bike, locked the door and drove until I stopped shouting. By this time we were halfway home.

The two guys stopped in a small town, bought jeans, boots and T shirt and took me down to the river. They threw me in the water and sat on the bank while I thrashed about, made me take off all my clothes and then threw me in again ignoring the increasing size of the audience or my privacy. After another five minutes I persuaded them to give me a towel and managed to dress in the new clothes without giving the onlookers too much to talk about. Still no words were exchanged. They sat me between them in the front if the truck and stopped at a roadside café, slung all my old clothes in the garbage and bought a meal."

"For you too?"

"Yes. Me too. They were both about 230 pounds in weight and nearly two metres tall, so I didn't even ask for the menu. Just ate what they had ordered. We drove overnight and reached Victor's house at 6am back in Uruguay. He set me up again and now I do my own thing, sometimes borrowing his beloved yacht."

"He doesn't mind you taking it?"

"No. To him it is only a convenient way to get from one luxurious place to another, and a party venue for his friends and contacts. He likes to be the centre of attention and this suits him well wherever he chooses to go."

"Now, pretty Miss New Zealand, I must take you home. I have to leave early in the morning when it is dark."

"Where is it you are going?"

"If you must know. We sail to Rabat in Morocco and I need to be there by evening."

"Isn't it easier to fly from Malaga or Gibraltar?"

"More fun on the yacht and the food is good." Pepe replied.

"If it is like the meal this evening I can see why you stay on board."

Lindsay collected her wrap and they headed across the Marina to his car.

There were no pressures from this guy and he was well connected and good company. In a way she felt she was partially securing the patronage of his brother and son Ignacio at the Academy and contributing to the sources of students that Erik seemed to have found in abundance.

Another chaste kiss on the cheek as they parted made her wonder whether Pepe was either playing a clever waiting game or she was no longer as attractive as she had hoped. However this was no time for deep emotional relationships to hinder the establishment of their new venture into training young sportspeople.

Erik met Coralie from a Saturday morning flight at Malaga. She had left home during Friday night for Bristol Airport, a little confused over the actual time because the clocks in Europe were due to go back one hour that weekend. She discovered that it was not to happen until 3am the next morning and that she had less time to wait for the flight that she had thought. Her last lesson at Ottery had finished at 3.30pm the previous day and she was packed by 7, in bed by 7.30, but too excited to sleep more than a couple of hours before leaving home in her little Peugeot at 4am.

It was much warmer than in Bristol when she walked out of the airport with Erik towards the short stay car park. Coralie had not been to Spain since a wild student fortnight in Benidorm to launch her gap year. She loved Spain and could have loved one of its residents if the holiday had been a little longer. They drove through the developed coastal strip and its hotels and resorts to Marbella, further West than the larger Malaga. Erik had asked Carmen to treat her as a special guest because he hoped she may agree to come out permanently. Carmen had put flowers in her room and scented the sheets on her bed. The guest room had a matching set of dark wooden furniture and traditional shutters at the windows.

Lindsay and Coralie became instant friends. They seemed to have that rapport that one imagines is the exclusive right of sisters. After the meal Erik resorted to the Spanish papers as there was no chance he could add to the constant chatter between them. Dan came to see him on behalf of Agnieska.

"She won't say but she is missing her horses. We have some money. Is there somewhere near that she could ride at the weekend?"

"Leave it with me" said Erik. "We will find a riding stable for her. I am glad you told me. Are any of the others missing anything badly or homesick?"

"Soo Jin is very quiet. She doesn't say but I think she is lonely here."

"What about the boys?"

"All good so far. They will be better when they have had the first visit home at Christmas."

Erik watched Dan and thought he was mature beyond his years and could make a good leader in time - one to give extra responsibility when the opportunity came.

He broke into the intense conversation and asked Coralie if she wanted a day to get acclimatised or dive straight into the tennis tomorrow.

"I know it is Sunday but I don't want to waste any of the short time we have you with us."

"OK. I'll start in the morning. Who with and what do you want me to do?"

They decided to leave Lindsay to set her up with one if the girls to begin with. Erik suggested Soo-Jin as she probably will be at a loose end at the weekend.

Lindsay looked at him

"What makes you think that?"

"Something Dan just said. He thinks she could be lonely."

"Mmm. I hadn't noticed. OK then, start with her. We can talk over breakfast about the next thing she needs to improve" she said to Coralie.

By Wednesday afternoon Erik joined Lindsay on a bench at a discreet distance from Coralie, on court working with Nicholas and Lucy.

"She is just what we need" said Lindsay before Erik could speak.

"I have been looking at the finances and reckon we can afford her now that it seems that all twelve will stay. I'll be surprised if we lose anyone after Christmas. Everyone is paying too, some have covered the whole term already."

Erik nodded "I hope she agrees to make the change. The kids love her"

That evening they took Coralie to Bar Lulu and enjoyed some of Clarence's cuisine.

"Pretty good food for a pub" offered Coralie

"Pub?" Shouted Clarence from the bar. "You just be careful, young lady, or I will ban you from this excellent bar restaurant with its features, the like of which has rarely been seen along this whole Andalucian coast."

Coralie was sipping Campari and Soda and looking fit and happy.

Lindsay brought up the main topic of the evening.

"Coralie, we would like to offer you a job. This is really why we have dragged you away from a restful half term break. We have unashamedly been watching you from behind the curtains and would love to have you as a full time tennis coach at the Academy."

Coralie looked from one to the other and said

"I thought I was just helping out at a busy time, and it has made a great break for me from sitting at home in my poky flat. The highlight of the week was to be Guy Fawkes Day on Saturday."

"Keep calling this a pub and you can still be home for that" muttered Clarence from the bar.

"Shut up, Clarence, or we will stop using your establishment as an office." said Lindsay.

"Before we talk money and accommodation how do you feel about leaving the Sports Council and working for a new, barely started, teaching academy?" asked Erik.

"If I had considered it before I should have realised I was ready for a change. Lindsay knows that I had hopes that my last boyfriend may have been 'the one', but that fell apart in the summer. Yes, this will be a great opportunity to spread my wings a little. I am twenty-eight now and it's time I got out of Devon and experienced some real life. I decided last year that coaching was my forte and that I was in the right kind of job. This would be an ideal next step – to work with 'improvers'."

"We can only offer you a contract for a year. This is because we still are new and unsure that the students will keep coming. After a year we may have some achievements to put on a prospectus and continue to attract good players with winning potential." Lindsay continued.

"You'll be fine" chipped in Clarence again. "I feel it in my water."

They paused and ordered another drink. Coralie insisted on paying for this round.

"I have all these Euros burning a hole in my bag" she said.

"Before you sign your year away we need to talk about salary" said Erik.

"What are your earning now?"

Coralie told them and Lindsay said

"To begin with we can pay you the same but include accommodation and food. How does that sound?"

"Amazing. I will work really hard for that" Coralie replied.

They all shook hands on the deal.

"Barman, bartender, a bottle of champers please to celebrate this auspicious occasion" said Erik.

"Now you are trying to show me up" said Clarence. It is a

weekday and I haven't anything cold enough. Can you wait a few minutes whilst I freeze the best Krug?"

"Just the best Spanish will do" added Erik. "Put it in a bucket of ice and we will open it after eating one of your tempting desserts."

"Yes, sir. Right away, sir" said a mildly embarrassed Clarence.

Erik drove the two, slightly inebriated, ladies back to Marbella. They were giggling in the back of the car. He had no idea what at, but was delighted that the deal was done and they got along so well.

The next morning Erik set off to look at two riding stables. One was a standard stable designed for a few regulars but principally for holidaymakers to hire and hack. The other was more in Agnieska's range, with four racehorses in training and three others that had been retired and still enjoyed a gallop. He arranged for Aga to spend an afternoon on Saturday riding out a mare of sixteen hands. The owners were pleased to be able to help once Erik had explained the problem and emphasised Aga's competence in the saddle.

Lindsay took Aga out to the lower slopes of the Sierra to the stable whilst Erik drove Coralie to catch the plane back to Bristol.

"If what you told me about Lucy's friend Saskia continues can you fix her up with your successor or someone good to take her forward. I think it will help Lucy to have a long-term friend out here and we could trial her during the Summer Holidays next year. Let me know when you can be free and can return."

They gave each other a hug and Coralie disappeared into the Departure Lounge.

The first half term completed they decided to hire a mini-bus and spend a camping weekend on the beach at Tarifa between Gibraltar and Cadiz. This is a famous surfing beach and VW camper vans can always be seen parked on the sand along its length. All the students were up for this weekend and all tried surfing. Soo-Jin and Ignacio were already good and showed the others how it should be done. Two metre rollers coming in from the Atlantic were quite challenging. Lindsay was also useful on a board. Like Soo-Jin she had grown up beside the Pacific waves of New Zealand. Nacho had been able to visit a number of good surfing venues on his parent's motor yacht since he was small. The weather was good for early November and the water still reasonably warm. A change from the routine at the Trocadero lifted the spirits of everyone.

The two owners were now beginning to draft a programme of tournament entries for the first half of the next year. Some were ready to try their hands against Europe's best juniors. Others needed to work on newly acquired skills before trying them out in a competitive arena.

The junior scene in Europe had changed since Erik's early career and there were many junior tournaments sponsored by the equipment manufacturers and even a ranking list for 'under 16' and 'under 14' players, both in girls and boys categories. If the junior had the resources there was a tournament every month from February to November and one each week in the summer. In addition, to support this, a number of other tennis academies had appeared across the continent, including some in Spain where the expensive indoor facility was not so important due to the ambient climate.

Each of Trocadero's students had a package of sponsorship, even at their young ages, from one or other of the major sports companies to support their tennis equipment and expenses entering tournaments over the next year. This would be renewed from time to time and became a essential for those from the poorer families.

Lindsay had now engaged Maria Elena, newly qualified in accountancy, to look after the financial commitments of the students and issue invoices to the respective families. For the first year she herself planned to use her maths abilities to keep abreast of the Academy's own accounts. Having had a long relationship, and mixed doubles partnership, with a Spanish player in her competition days Lindsay was managing to revive her Spanish sufficiently to cope with office duties.

The Christmas break came around very quickly. The students were all anxious to spend time at home and Lindsay took Soo Jin with her on the long flight from Madrid to Auckland. She spent some time with her own parents and visited Soo Jin's home to see if there was something that she could return with to make her less of a loner. The visit spawned an idea that may solve the problem. She did not stay for Christmas and was back at the Trocadero Academy to supervise the final stages of the two new clay courts.

Erik also returned early, having spent a few days with relatives in Sweden. He brought a box of Christmas goodies from Gothenburg in his luggage.

Coralie said farewell to work colleagues and friends and drove her Peugeot 206 (Ethel) across France and down through Spain to her new job. She offered to bring Lucy back early but, in the end, realised that there was no room in the car. Lucy wanted to spend longer at home and to elaborate on her daily Skype messages to Saskia about her recent experiences. She, Lucy, was quite happy to fly down later as an unaccompanied minor from Bristol Airport.

Carmen came back to cook for their New Year celebrations. She was glad to return away from catering at home for all her extended family who, according to her mutterings, had not even chopped an onion to help over Christmas. She took over Juanita's kitchen and seemed in her element cooking for the three of them, with a 'frequently visiting' Lollo, who lived nearby and usually happened to need a book from his classroom at mealtimes.

Occasionally they ate at Bar Lulu to give Carmen a break.

"Did you have a happy Christmas?" asked Coralie to Clarence.

"I don't do Christmas dear" he replied.

"Whyever not? It's the best time of the year for most people."

"There is nothing sadder than waking up on Christmas morning and not being a child." replied Clarence.

"OK. But you can always find a child to make happy somewhere nearby."

"It's not so easy for us to befriend other people's children, you know. Their parents usually think we have ulterior motives. Anyway Rex doesn't do Christmas either. He even thought mistletoe was a mutant form of athlete's foot."

"You are a funny man, Clarence." Coralie said

"Funny ha ha or funny peculiar?" He asked.

"Both" said Erik "Now stop loafing and bring us our drinks."

Erik was impressed with Coralie, who kept up a high fitness level with a sensible diet, jogging at 7am every day and sessions in their small gym. He thought that he too had better run off the extra weight that he had gained eating the Christmas feast, and vowed to begin tomorrow.

SIX

Lindsay finally persuaded Pepe to take her on his next expedition on Rosario. They had become good friends, though not yet lovers, and held deep discussions on international politics and especially how to improve the lot of the poor and displaced peoples of the world.

The motor yacht Rosario moved across the Marina from her berth beside the Puerto Banus quayside at 5 am on January 2nd. Lindsay brought an overnight bag and was shown into a comfortable single cabin and told that breakfast would be served in the dining area at whatever time suited her. She had not been sure whether Pepe would be planning to sleep with her for the first time on this voyage, but the single cabin put that idea out of her mind.

Out at sea Lindsay was joined at breakfast by Pepe who seemed preoccupied with his mobile phone, more than usual.

"Any problems?" she asked

"Not really. I am waiting to hear about a rendezvous. We are going again to Rabat today. The weather is windy and will make for a choppy sea, but you will be fine as you are used to the water."

"What are you doing in Rabat this time?"

"Officially, we are delivering a cargo of ladies shoes, made in Alicante.

But, we may come back along a different route tonight and it will take until mid-morning tomorrow before we arrive in Marbella."

They docked in Rabat amongst the fishing boats and, whilst the crew were discharging boxes and wooden crates, Pepe took Lindsay to the Souk where they bargained for a pretty scarf and the inevitable round leather pouffe that everyone used to bring back from Morocco. In the late afternoon, after a lazy hour in a street corner café sitting outside at a metal table, they made their way back to Rosario.

"Don't you have a meeting to attend?" Lindsay asked.

"Not this time"

"Just the delivery of shoes then"

"And a return cargo to make the journey pay." He replied.

The Rosario pulled away at just after 4pm and Lindsay leant on the port rail later to see the sun setting into the Atlantic Ocean. Having become friends with the Pacific throughout her childhood this was her first feel of the Atlantic, about which she had heard so much in Geography at school. She estimated the yacht travelling at around twelve knots and was enjoying the constant warm breeze, although it was mid winter in these latitudes. Pepe was back on his mobile and she wondered what was so important for him to miss the beautiful colours that followed the sunset.

Lucas served dinner early at 6.30pm and told Lindsay that Mr Joseph was busy in the hold of the yacht so would not join her this time. After watching the lights of the Morocco coast diminish to just a few here and there Lindsay read for a while and decided to retire to her solitary cabin. At 10pm she turned off the light and went to sleep, only to be woken almost immediately by a click from outside her door. She wondered whether the romantic side of Pepe was bringing him into her cabin for a passionate night, albeit in her single bed. There was no more noise so she just dreamed of being held in his arms and quietly ravished beneath the expensive sheets.

A thump against the hull woke Lindsay up. She looked at the luminous hands on her watch. It was 11.15pm. The ship seemed to have stopped moving. There was a porthole high above her, so she stood on the bed and tried to see what was going on. The only thing was to get dressed and go out on the deck. She threw on some clothes, intrigued as to where they were and what was happening. Slipping on her flat shoes she turned the door handle. It didn't open. She tried again, turning it the other way. Still no joy. She realised it had been locked. Now this was scary!

Climbing on to the cabin hard chair Lindsay could see more of an angle through the porthole, and more clearly once she had turned out the cabin light. She slowly got her night eyes. There seemed to be a long rope leading from the Rosario out into the darkness and, at its far end, what looked like two torchlights. Although they appeared to be stationary the engines were throbbing gently; maybe to keep the ship steady on station. The rope was now moving, winding in towards the ship.

She watched and, at the same time, realised that something underhand was happening. The locked door and the low key lighting. She couldn't see any reflection on the water of lights from the Rosario. Then, out of the darkness, a big shape came towards the side of the ship and disappeared beneath the porthole and further towards the bow of the ship. There was a lot of scrabbling and scratching for several minutes. The shape reappeared and then dissolved into the far darkness again. Then the rope was there again, faintly visible slanting downwards from the deck also into the darkness. More torchlight, but quite distant. She could see the rope hauling in towards Rosario a second time, then the huge black shape and more scratching. What on earth were they doing?

Lindsay sat on the bed and tried to imagine what was happening. Was she part of a drug-running trip? Whatever it was must be illegal or there would be more lights. Maybe they were smuggling something. It must be from the Moroccan coast because the shape was coming from the Starboard side. It could be from another ship, but she thought there was the outline of hills in the black distance. She decided that, whatever was going on, she was better off inside her cabin. Provided they let her out eventually. Outside now there was a lot of splashing followed by a metallic squeaking.

She lay on the bed with a whirl of thoughts passing through her mind.

'I hope they will let me escape. We have only just got the business started.

How will Cameron cope on his own? Perhaps Erik will adopt him. Oh God, this is North Africa. I once saw a film about the Lord of the Rif and all his harem. Maybe I am going to be sold for the pleasure of some Arab Sheik who is looking for a white woman to indulge his fantasies!'

Almost asleep and her imagination developing an erotic dance of the seven veils that she would be expected to perform in front of her captor, Lindsay was aware of a dramatic increase in engine power and a surge forward of the ship. Her watch now said 'almost midnight'. Whatever had gone on had lasted less than an hour. She dozed in the darkness and woke with a start sometime later. It was 2.10am. The ship had stopped again.

'Help, this could be the Sheik's palace and her turn to be delivered as cargo'

There was a fire extinguisher in the corner of the cabin. She sat on the chair and held it between her knees pointing the hose towards the door. There was less noise this time.

She realised that things must be happening on the port side on this occasion. Looking out of her porthole again she could only see the distant lights of a passing freighter and a glow in the sky above what must be a town in Morocco. She sat back down and waited for her door to open. She loved dancing, but not naked. Maybe he would let her keep one veil on.

After half an hour there was the squeaking again, like a winch. Two minutes later the engines increased in pitch and off they went once more. There was nothing else to do but to go back to sleep and try to eliminate any more scary dreams.

Lindsay awoke at 8 o'clock! How can it be 8 o'clock when I was so scared. She was still dressed, jumped off the bed and out through the door into the passageway. Halfway along she realised that her door had been unlocked. Now angry, she arrived in the dining room to be greeted by Lucas carrying a silver plate of croissants.

"Do be seated Madame. These are hot and perfect to eat immediately,"

"Lucas. Please find Mr Joseph and ask him to come here, whatever he is doing."

Pepe appeared as if by magic through the other door.

"Pepe. What the hell is going on?" shouted Lindsay.

"We are making good progress and should be in Marbella by 1100 hours"

"I mean last night. What was happening and why was my cabin door locked?"

"You must be mistaken. No-one would lock you in. Sometimes the doors stick when the yacht moves from side to side. We had to stop a couple of times on the way to deal with engine problems, but they were soon resolved. Let's have some breakfast together"

Lindsay thought for a moment. She may have been

mistaken about the door, but engine trouble. They wouldn't need a long rope and what was the big black shape?

She sat opposite Pepe and buttered one of the large croissants, looking him straight in the eye. He was looking somewhat shifty.

"Pepe. There is something not right here. I could see a lot from my porthole window in the cabin". She didn't say how much.

"Yes, I saw your light on briefly and realised you were awake."

They completed their breakfast without saying much more.

The last few kilometres along the Spanish coast was pictur- esque with the sun shining on the cliffs and beaches, tiny boats scudding along and bottle nosed dolphins swimming in beside, under and in front of the ship. Lindsay enjoyed the view from the rail and decided she could relish a life with a beautiful yacht like this under her control. Pepe took her back to the Academy but excused himself from the offered coffee pleading pressure of work back at the Marina.

At lunch, in reply to Erik's enquiry, she told him that she had enjoyed the trip and loved Rabat. However there was a mystery stop on the way back, two in fact, that made her suspicious of the true purpose of the journey.

"What was it that made you suspicious?" He asked.

"Well, firstly this was a visit to deliver cases of shoes to a merchant in Rabat and to bring something back that I never saw. It was probably loaded whilst I was buying things in the Souk. Pepe spent a huge amount of time on his mobile. Unless he was talking about something quite unconnected I couldn't see what there was to talk about."

"Doesn't sound too mysterious to me" volunteered Erik.

"Wait, there's more. On the way back we stopped. It was around 11 pm. I tried to go on deck to see why but my door had been locked from the outside. So I peered into the dark out of the porthole. I could see no lights except a couple of faint torchlights in the distance, either on shore or on another ship. But there was a thick rope running from our ship towards the torches. Then the rope was pulled in to the ship and connected to a big black thing. It was let out and then pulled in again. Then some scratching and splashing and squeaking before we set off at full speed."

"Mmmm. Go on" Erik was thinking as he listened.

"Three hours later we stopped again and something went on on the other side of the ship following by the same squeaking, like a winch, and off we went again, arriving here mid morning. Pepe said we had had engine trouble causing us to stop twice and then he said he had seen my light on. It would only have been visible through the porthole which means he must have been over where the torches were."

"It doesn't sound too bad and his reasons could be correct. I can't imagine they are smuggling guns or drugs on the Rosario. I don't think you were in any danger." said Erik.

"I thought they had locked me in and were going to sell me to some Bedouin Potentate for a vast sum of money."

"Ha ha ha. No chance of that. They probably wouldn't give more than a couple of camels for you."

"Oh. Thanks very much indeed, my hero." replied Lindsay as she left the dining room.

In the evening Erik remembered the young boy that he had seen climbing on board the Rosario during the party and disappearing into the anchor locker.

That same evening there was a huge commotion in the students' sitting room. Coralie looked in to see Petra rushing across the room with a casserole dish full of water and Lucy trying to reach something in the goldfish bowl on the sideboard with a soup ladle. It seems they were trying to catch the goldfish, though quite why was not clear. Agnieska was watching so Coralie asked her what they were doing.

"That one there (pointing to Nicholas) put Alka Seltzer into the goldfish bowl and Petra thinks that Jaws is dying."

Nicholas was sitting on the arm of the sofa.

"Nicholas. Why?" asked Coralie.

"He was bored. I thought he might like a jacuzzi for a change."

Trying not to smile she added "He could die in all that fizz"

"Well, it's only a fish. I had a different one for lunch today and he was already pretty dead."

She left them to sort it out amongst themselves and walked out shaking her head.

Lollo took Lavinia to the cinema that evening and the school teachers' room was buzzing with this piece of gossip, and speculating on which film they went to see. Suggestions were 'Don Juan', 'The History Boys', Emmanuelle in the Classroom', 'One flew over the Cuckoo's Nest', 'Driving Miss Daisy' and 'Indecent Proposal'. Lindsay told them not to be so beastly and let them have their fun. There was good harmony in the staff room and the teachers were particularly enjoying teaching much smaller classes than they had previously, even though they were made up of mixed abilities.

Science was sometimes conducted in the laboratories of a large secondary school in Marbella town, the small groups fitting in with the school's own timetable and hardly being noticed as they came and went. The Academy had promised a suitable gift to the school for allowing use of the facility.

Lavinia was arranging to enter the older children for exams with 16 and 18 year old examination boards relating to the country system that each set of parents preferred. This involved a lot of research, paperwork and timetabling around tournament schedules. Some of them would have to sit controlled exams between Easter and the end of the Summer Term this year.

Everybody had arrived back on time after the Christmas break. There had been some ferrying from the airport at Malaga. As Dan had said some weeks before, all the students were happier now they had made one visit back home. They began to discuss each other's chances in the forthcoming season. Their coaches were not so interested in results this year as establishing shot making techniques and a mental game plan for each match that was put into practice. Lindsay and Coralie coached more than Erik, who did a lot of sitting and watching. He told the students not to be perturbed by his constant presence at the court side as he was there to notice small things that may not be seen so clearly by the ladies as they stood on court and hit balls to each of them.

Inevitably Erik watched more of Coralie's sessions because Lindsay had Maths lessons to prepare and mark and the accounts of the Academy to keep up to date. He found himself watching Coralie as much as the student she was coaching and once or twice deliberately tore himself away to one of the other two courts to watch 'students only' practising. He found it impossible not to enjoy looking at her. Today was a sunny Tuesday and, still being winter, it was cool enough to play comfortably in the early afternoon.

Coralie had invested in several new tennis dresses. Today she wore a pale blue one with matching peaked hat. Her dark hair was tied in a ponytail and channelled through the small Velcro band at the back of the hat. In the sun of southern Spain she had already tanned enough to enable her to be mistaken for a local. Women's magazines often extol the virtues of stick thin legs with no shape, but men always prefer a nicely shaped leg on their girlfriends with a calf muscle that looks as though she has, at least, run a few times to the bus stop. From a man's point of view Coralie had great legs and, unsurprisingly to Erik, was setting an example to her young students with freshly cleaned tennis shoes.

Erik went indoors to the coffee machine and poured a black coffee into a polystyrene cup to take outside and try to focus his eyes more on Kas and his half volleying practise. He was much older than Coralie and berated himself for his stirring feelings. He had not brought her all this way to take advantage of his position as her boss or his tennis reputation. He also felt disloyal to Sally, his 'special' love of fifteen or more years previously, after whom he had decided to stop dating women for the foreseeable future. Erik pushed his thoughts away and went back to the idiosyncrasies of the half volley.

The new clay courts were of the red variety that was used on the continent of Europe at most tennis clubs and was the court base for the principal tournaments including the Grand Slam in Paris played in May every year at Roland Garros. They had deliberately added these surfaces to the green painted hard court that they had inherited at Trocadero to get the children used to the speed of court, on which many of their early matches would be played. The red surface created a dust that coated their shoes and required cleaning every day. Erik saw this as a good exercise. He had always regarded his appearance on court to be an example to others as well as a compliment to sponsors and to his country, and wished to impart this to all who may represent the Academy around the world.

The Mayor of Marbella, Senor Alvarez, arrived the next day to honour his invitation to the new complex. He was suitably impressed and emphasised that he saw the Academy as an additional feature of his town to enhance its position in Spain. Erik had discovered that he had a background in Marketing, so was not surprised to hear that he had followed up the suggestion of an Alvarez Bursary to sponsor a teenager to attend the Academy full time. The Mayor had used his influence with a half dozen of the wealthier members of the Marbella Club to raise the funding.

Lindsay was able to provide the details of the actual amount needed to cover a year's tuition. She emphasised that the student would need to become a boarder in order to integrate better with the others. They shook hands on the arrangement and Erik felt this was an important step to the Academy becoming accepted and established, at least in the locality.

Felipe completed the complement of boys at the Academy, all eight beds now being occupied. He was another 15 year old and the son of a stallholder at the Marbella vegetable market. They had been unable to afford the annual subscription to the Club de Tenis and Felipe did odd jobs to be able to pay for hourly use of a municipal tennis court. His problem was that he could easily beat his friends and all his friends' elder brothers and many of their fathers. The groundsman, who cared for the courts and took the money from players, knew Senora Alvarez, Mother of the Mayor, and recommended Felipe for consideration for the first bursary. Lindsay quickly saw his potential and heard all about his determination from the Groundsman, who came with him for the assessment. He told of watching him practising serving on his own and spending hours hitting balls against the wall of his storage shed beside the courts.

"I let him pay me for an hour on the court, but he stays on if there is nobody waiting, sometimes all evening. Felipe says that, when he is a champion, he will buy me a small villa to retire in."

"You will be pleased to know that he has a place here and can start as soon as we have met his parents and they have arranged with his school for him to leave and come to us" said Lindsay.

Felipe's Mother and Father came the next evening and almost had to be dragged in to meet Lindsay and Erik. Lindsay had written down, with Maria Elena's help, all the relevant things they would need to know regarding his place at the Academy. She explained that Erik would use his connections with the Sports Equipment manufacturers to obtain sponsorship for his clothes, rackets and equipment. They looked very relieved at this news and asked what they had to do.

"Just come and see him whenever you like. We will keep you up to date with his progress and in which tournaments we plan to enter him."

Felipe arrived during the next weekend with his bag and was greeted by Dan, who had naturally become a kind of student 'minder'. Erik left him to show Felipe around and to meet the others. Head, who had become a leading supporter of juniors in Europe, took Erik's recommendation and Felipe signed a cursory agreement to solely use their equipment for the next twelve months. The Iberian representative met him with a car boot full of clothes in his size and three rackets at Erik's suggested weight with different string tensions. They saw the first of Felipe's cheeky smiles that afternoon.

The target had been to fill half the places in the first year and manage with one court. In practice, after five months, they had two additional courts thanks to Uncle Thorbjorn. There were now thirteen students, all being paid for and only three spaces left, all for girls.

SEVEN

Lucas, the cook from the Rosario, had heard from Lindsay what she did in Marbella as a job and began coming out to the Trocadero in his free time. He was Brazilian. The owners had lured him away from his kitchen in the prestigious Miramar Hotel in Recife with promises of an increase in salary and a chance to see more of the world. It transpired that he had played a little tennis at his local club to keep fit whilst he was in Recife. He liked to watch it whenever it came on television. To come out and sit watching the young players was a complete relaxation from the galley kitchen on board the yacht. Sometimes Erik would bring his folding camp chair and sit beside him and point out what the coach was doing with the player currently on court.

On this occasion Lindsay had joined Lucas and they began chatting about the Rosario and her owners, and about Pepe and what they were all like to work for. Lucas was loyal but not too secretive.

"Lucas" she said "What caused the ship to stop in the night when we were part way back from Rabat?"

Lucas supposed that Pepe had told her everything because she was his girlfriend and would not have invited her aboard without doing so.

"I expect you were asleep. We have to stop. You cannot pick up and drop off when the ship is moving forward."

Lindsay played along with this line of conversation.

"Yes, of course. I was so comfortable in my bed that I didn't get time to go up and see for myself this time." she said. "Did everything go smoothly."

"This time it was good. Not like last week when we had to pull away leaving Joachim in the cove."

"That was a problem. Did he manage all right?"

"He arrived on the bus later in the morning, and did his shopping on the way in Estepona."

"This time all the packages got through?"

"I don't know. We only deliver them on to the beach and then get out of there fast"

She did not want to kill this source of information by asking too many pointed questions, so changed the subject. Perhaps Lucas would reveal more when he next came over.

"I asked Lucas about the other night out at sea." Lindsay told Erik at dinner

"He thought I was already in the know. I was careful what I said but found that it was not an engine problem, but a clandestine delivery".

"What on earth is a prandestine delivery?" asked Erik

"Clandestine, Clandestine! You know, sort of secret, under cover"

"Never heard that word before"

"You had better start coming to classes in the mornings instead of reading the paper and chatting up Coralie" Lindsay added.

"I don't chat her up. We are planning the afternoon sessions."

"I've seen you watching her every move. Just because she has the body of a glamour model and you have discovered her tucked away in the back woods, doesn't mean she is prey for randy Eriksson."

"I am speechless. You can't read all that into my mind."

"I remember you, Joel Eriksson, and how you lured an innocent virgin out to a South Seas Island and did even more things to her than she imagined possible."

"Virgin indeed?"

"Yes, in a way. A virgin is someone who has not had certain experiences, and I certainly had no idea about some of the things you did to me, even underwater."

"That was different and you were panting for more than just fishing and watching the sunset. Just because you were irresistible doesn't mean I go around bonking every eligible female."

"OK. We shall see if I am right"

At this moment the subject of the discussion joined them late for dinner.

"Sorry I am late. I was checking that Felipe was happy with the food." apologised Coralie.

Erik frowned at Lindsay but said no more until they took the rest of the bottle of wine out on to the balcony.

"So what was the delivery then?" He asked

"I still don't know. I mentioned packages and he accepted that and said they just left them on the beach and sailed away. Oh. He did say that they had to leave quickly last time and one of the crew was left behind. He appeared later having caught the bus via Estepona.

"That means they dropped him on the Spanish side and further West along the coast." Erik deduced. "Was that all?"

"Yes. I didn't want to push my luck. I just hope he keeps coming back here to watch the coaching."

"There's something I should tell you." said Erik. "When we were on the Rosario I went up to the bow for a breath of air and saw a young kid climb up the mooring rope and go into the anchor locker. It seemed strange on a smart motor yacht owned by a millionaire. Though I can't see any connection with your shifty packages."

"No, I can't see any link either." replied Lindsay.

"I think you need to be careful. If they are running anything illegal, and it all sounds dodgy, you could get sucked into it and be in danger. Even from them if they think you may blow the whistle. How much do you like this Pepe character? Is he the love of your life?"

"I like him quite a lot. He is a gentleman. After years as a student and then on the circuit being hounded by men looking for a one nighter, it has been pleasant not to be fumbled in the lift, so to speak."

"Well. Keep away from his activities and just meet him socially. You are a precious commodity around here and indispensable."

"Worth more than two camels?"

"Two healthy ones at least." Erik grinned.

Pepe phoned the next day to ask to take Lindsay for a drive into the hills the next weekend. Lindsay accepted. They stayed at a small resort with a central reception building and restaurant and small villas dotted in an olive grove. He explained that there were two bedrooms in the house but he would like it if they decided only to use one of them. Lindsay thought this was the gentlest introduction she had ever had to a seductive evening and appreciated the opportunity to refuse, rarely made so openly by a partner.

Probably this was the reason she decided to give in to the advances of this attractive South American playboy as they made their way between the olive trees in the late evening moonlight. The next morning breakfast was brought to them on a tray from the restaurant, and they sat buttering hard bread rolls and spreading them with delicious peach jam. The coffee tasted smooth and earthy, needing a little more sugar than usual.

"We need to talk" said Pepe as they sat listening to the

birds welcoming a new morning. "I have an apology to make. Lucas told me that he had told you a different story about our nighttime stops on the yacht. He had thought that you were in on our scheme"

"Does this mean I am a danger to your plans?" Asked Lindsay.

"No, I doubt it. What we are doing is close to the topics we had been discussing together."

"Drugs or guns?" Lindsay asked"

Pepe laughed. "Would you say that I am a dreamer?"

"I think you were dreaming last night. I could see you lying on your side with a smile on your face."

"I was probably dreaming of passionately ravishing you again before dawn. We talked about the inequality in the world and how you wanted to make a difference for people on the breadline with no prospects. Lindsay, I am going to confide in you something you may not approve."

"Go on. I can keep a secret." She said.

They were interrupted by a shy waitress who had come to collect the breakfast dishes.

"Leave the coffee" Pepe said. Their conversation paused for a few minutes whilst she cleared and wiped the verandah table.

"If I tell you all that we were doing it will put you in danger if we are discovered and you are on board so, either I tell you and you never come with us again or I don't tell you and you promise to stay in your cabin when the ship is moving at night."

"Why can't you tell me and let me continue to go with you?" Lindsay asked.

"If we are caught by the authorities and you are with us you can plead ignorance. You were just an innocent passenger."

"I want to continue coming on the yacht, breathing the sea air and visiting exotic places, so don't tell me. I will continue to guess. Promise me though that, whatever cargo you have, it will not harm anyone innocent."

"No problem. You have my word on that."

They drove back via a more scenic route and Pepe bought a large bunch of narcissi for her from a roadside stall. He kissed her farewell telling her that the next voyage of the Rosario would be on Thursday to a different destination.

On Tuesday evening Pepe called Lindsay's mobile

"We have an emergency and I must take the Rosario out in about one hour. Can you get away to come? It is a quicker trip this time and we should be back by midday tomorrow"

"If I can get away I will meet you on the quayside before the hour is up." came her reply.

She changed one of her maths groups to Spanish for the following morning, and threw a few clothes into a bag. A thicker jumper and skirt than last time, then asked Erik to take her to the Port.

"I shouldn't let you do this. I am not happy about you zooming around the Med with a bunch of crooks, even if you are sleeping with them now." he told her as they made their way through the evening traffic in Marbella.

"I don't think they are bad crooks, and I have only slept with one of them."

"Be careful. Have you got your mobile? Call me if you need me."

"Yes sir." She ran across the promenade to the Rosario, which was still attached to the quayside.

Pepe greeted her and she noticed he and the crew members were all wearing dark clothes and woolly hats. Maybe they had before when they left Rabat, but she had not noticed. This time she was determined to find out what they were doing, despite the danger of too much knowledge.

Five minutes after she had climbed on board the big

yacht motored out of the Marina and quickly picked up speed, heading in a southerly direction straight out into the Mediterranean. The Rosario seemed to be travelling faster than last time. Lucas served dinner and Pepe, phone in hand, joined her for the main course.

"Where are we going?" Lindsay asked.

"Out into the middle of the sea, short stop and back to the Spanish coast."

His phone rang a bright little tune and he picked it up and walked towards the stern of the yacht. She couldn't hear the conversation, which was in Spanish.

They must be meeting another ship. Lindsay convinced herself that this would be safer than going close to North Africa with its dodgy police forces.

Pepe returned.

"We should reach our destination by midnight. Can you think of a good way to pass the time until then?"

Lindsay was not expecting him to spend very long with her on this voyage.

"We could play cards with some if the crew, if you like, or you could come down to my cabin and help me with some decoration"

"Decoration. I like doing up other people's property." she replied.

They made their way across the ship and down stairs at the stern end of the dining area. Pepe showed her into his cabin, which was lined with oak veneer and had a double bed on the side of the hull. He closed the door, pulled her close to him and kissed her long and hard.

"What about the decoration?" she asked

"Oh. Yes. Very important. You see this ceiling is black. I think it makes the room seem smaller and more cramped. Come over here and tell me what colour I should paint it to brighten up the cabin."

He led her over to the bed and helped her to lie on her back, taking off both her shoes as he did it.

"You study the ceiling whilst I help you feel cooler by taking off these hot clothes. When you have decided on the colour we could spend the next four hours exploring our differences."

Lindsay giggled. "You are a bad man Joseph…..Joseph….. What is your other name? You haven't told me.

Removing more of her clothes he said

"del Forlan. Joseph Ricardo del Forlan. Are you feeling cooler?"

"Cooler, I am practically naked"

"Yes, so you are. Now what is hiding under here? Ah! I remember this one from last weekend. Firm, with a tiny mole next to the nipple."

"Stop it, your moustache is tickling. God Pepe, that is nice."

"You concentrate on the ceiling, I can manage down here."

The phone tune woke them up.

"OK. I'll be with you in two minutes." Pepe rapidly dressed, kissed her on the forehead and said

"Stay here. Go back to sleep if you can."

He vanished through the cabin door.

After another ten minutes the yacht engines reduced power. Lindsay dressed again, planning to go up on deck in the night air and see what was happening from a secluded place. The engines went down in volume to a gentle rumble.

Fortunately Lindsay's clothes were also in dark colours. She left off her white socks and crept out of the cabin, along the corridor and up the stairs. She had to go carefully as all lights seem to have been switched off. At the top of the stairs, peering left and right, she stooped and went across to a place in the shadow behind a curtain.

There was a lot of movement along the side nearest

to her outside the glass partition. She peeped around the curtain and through the glass separating her from the main deck. The rope she had seen before was wound around a big wheel and then out through an open gate in the rail. One of the crew had a torch and with its light she could see Pepe and another crew member, dressed in black as well, climb down out of sight.

After a short delay the rope began to wind out from its reel. Lindsay's night eyes could now see the big black thing was an inflatable rib with at least one person in it paddling vigorously away from the Rosario. The rope seemed almost at its end when it stopped unwinding. She strained to see into the distance when the door opened and two more crew members came in. She hid behind the curtain. One sounded like Lucas. She couldn't understand what they were saying as it was in either rapid Spanish or Portuguese. They left again and she saw two piles of blankets that they had put against the far wall.

There was a squeak and the reel began turning again bringing the rope back to the ship. The rib bumped against the hull and the same scrabbling started as Lindsay had heard before when she was locked in her cabin. One of the crew opened the glass door beside her and ushered in two shapes which began whispering, followed by another, and then two more. Lucas reappeared and started talking gently to the newcomers.

'It's people. He's moving people. My God, where are they coming from?

Another two came in, then a mother with a crying baby that sounded quite young. Lindsay could stay hidden no more. She came out in the dark and joined Lucas giving out blankets. Lucas accepted immediately that Lindsay would help and asked her to take over the blanket distribution while he went back to the galley.

There were nine in the room, all women and children. Some were sitting and some leaning against the walls. The baby was in its mother's arms and crying pitifully.Lucas reappeared with a large saucepan of something that was steaming, followed by another man carrying an armful of bowls and spoons. Lindsay helped distribute the thick soup to the nine black faces, several of whom were shivering.

There was another bump and scrabbling and six more, all men, joined them. One had a bandaged foot. They handed out more blankets and soup. Pepe was suddenly standing beside Lindsay saying

"Now you know."

"Is there a baby's bottle and some milk in the galley? This little one hasn't stopped crying since she arrived" replied Lindsay.

A couple of minutes later Lucas came in with warm baby's milk and what looked like rusks. The mother smiled her gratitude.

The Rosario was now heading away at around twenty knots, anxious to put as much space between her and the other ship as possible. The crew blew up inflatable beds and lilos and some of the newcomers were asleep in minutes.

Pepe took Lindsay down to his cabin again. She was asking questions all the way down. What was the other ship? Where have they come from? Where are they going now? Are they paying you to do this?

"Come inside and sit down." he said, opening a bottle of brandy that he had collected from the bar on the way. He took two tooth glasses from the en suite bathroom and poured a measure of brandy into each. Lindsay continued firing questions at him, only pausing to sip the brandy.

"Too many questions. Here are some of the answers.They are refugees from the fighting in Mali in West Africa. They are Christians escaping the rebels who are supported by Al Quaeda, who got on the wrong side of the fighting front line. If they had been ten miles South they would have been rescued by French Forces helping the Mali Government. Instead they have effectively crossed the Sahara to try to find safety. They paid to sail from Oran in Algeria to France or Spain but were left stranded by the traffickers on Alboran Island in the middle of the Med. No food, no water. We got the SOS and here they are, on an Uruguayan yacht heading for Spain and they think they are lucky." Pepe paused to take a full mouthful of the strong brandy.

"Where do they go from here? They will be lost in Europe." asked Lindsay.

"We are part of a chain. We leave them in Spain and these people will find refuge in France. They are French-speaking, well 'petit negre', a sort of French patois. France will be their best bet."

"Can you find the first aid kit? The least I can do is patch up the guy with the bad foot." added Lindsay. She returned to the sleeping refugees and woke the tall man with the bandaged foot, persuaded him to let her remove the bandage and re-dressed a nasty jagged cut in his ankle. The young mother was out for the count, obviously exhausted. She took the baby who was awake and chortling and sat on a stool cuddling the little soul and letting it suck on her little finger. She suddenly felt a surge of love for these poor people so far from their homes, and another for Pepe and all the crew who were trying to help them, she was sure, for no reward other than human feeling.

As the Rosario sped through the night Lindsay realised that the entire crew must be sympathetic to what was being done. In their spare time, between ferrying Victor and Maria Carmelita from glamorous venue to glamorous party, they were risking their freedom to help others less fortunate than themselves. She would have great respect for Uruguayans from now forward.

Close to dawn the ship began to slow down. Lindsay was dozing in Pepe's bed. She woke fully and realised that he had already left to go on deck. She followed and looked over the starboard rail to see a faint light flashing on shore. They stood about fifty metres off the beach of a small cove. The first glimmer of dawn made a silhouette of everything. The rib was already launched from its davits and the refugees were lined up to embark. This time the men went first. Pepe and one other paddled the rib ashore through the shallow waves. Two minutes later it returned, helped by the rope connected to the Rosario, only to set off again with nine more, this time holding on to their blankets and a package in silver paper from Lucas' kitchen.

The rib returned, was hauled up at the stern, and Rosario set off back to Marbella to its temporary home against the quayside. Lindsay and Pepe said little more to each other, but each realised he or she had found a contact with similar sympathies.

EIGHT

Jeff and Kate Burrows, Saskia's parents ran a sweet shop in Seaton. They sold ice creams, postcards, newspapers and stationery to boost the takings. The shop was not a gold mine, but it served to supplement Jeff's income as a plasterer. They knew of their daughter's ambition to become one of the Academy students in Marbella with Lucy, her long time friend from Primary School. However they could see no way of ever being able to afford the fees so they steadily tried to dampen Saskia's enthusiasm.

Over the Christmas school vacation Lucy and Saskia had reunited and even played together at Coralie's Sports Hall in one of the final games that Coralie had supervised before driving to Spain. Lucy had realised that Saskia was improving rapidly and set up a meeting between their two sets of parents at the farm before she left for her second term at the Academy.

Helen explained to Jeff and Kate that it was doing Lucy a lot of good to be amongst older teenagers and international ones at that. She told them that she knew Erik well and that he had agreed to take Lucy for half the advertised fees. Both she and George thought they may do the same for Saskia as she was so determined to go to them and knew Lucy and Coralie.

Helen helped Kate enter Saskia for the Under 14 girls singles at two Westcountry Junior Tournaments to be held during the Easter Holidays. Saskia was now being coached by Danny, who had taken over Coralie's role at Ottery Sports Centre and was practising every evening she could, staying on after school and catching the last bus back to Seaton. When Easter came around she won the Plymouth event without losing a set and was in the semi-final at Bristol when the tournament was rained off.

Saskia sat down and wrote her first ever business letter, unknown to her parents:

'Dear Erik,

My name is Saskia and I am going to be your best pupil in your new school. When I am 16 I will be your best champion and make you rich.

My Dad has only a little money and he will have to spend that on my bus fare to Spain, but I can borrow Danny's tent and sleep on the beach if you let me use your tennis courts and tell me how to get better.

I won a tournament last week and it would be two but one was rained on before I could win it. Don't say no or I shall have to kill myself.

Love from Saskia Burrows (age 12)'

A week later an airmail letter arrived addressed to Miss Saskia Burrows.

Dear Saskia,

Thank you for your lovely letter.

Lucy and Coralie and I have been waiting for you to come to our Academy and make it famous. There is an empty bed next to Lucy in the Girls House and the locker has the name Saskia Burrows already on it.

I am coming to Devon again soon and will meet your Mum

and Dad to ask them if they are happy for you to become a Trocadero Girl. I shall also be at Wimbledon in two months time. Perhaps you could meet me there and we could watch some tennis together.

Keep practising with Danny and enter some more events this summer.

Love from Erik

"Mum" said Saskia at teatime that evening "I'll be off to Spain at the end of the summer. Erik says it will be OK. Can I sell my bike to get some pocket money to change into Euros because I may need to buy some things, like food and shampoo."

"What do you mean 'Erik said it will be all right'" replied Kate.

"Don't panic Mum. I wrote and told him I was going to stay in Marbella and he wrote back and said they are waiting for me and that he will come and talk to you and Dad about it soon. Oh! And he wants me to be company for him at Wimbledon in June and go in for more tournaments this summer."

That evening there were concerned phone calls between Kate and Helen and cheerful Skypes between Lucy and Saskia.

"She showed me the letter, so it is all true." said Kate

"You'll like Erik when you see him. He is quite dishy" replied Helen.

"I have to win some more events here, but I will be with you in September" said Saskia.

"Erik told me you were coming if your Mum agrees." replied Lucy

"Course she will. I am going to win enough money so Dad can stop working and coming home covered in white plaster and needing a bath every night."

"It seems we have a sixth girl lined up." Erik told the ladies at coffee break.

"Saskia, friend of Lucy, has written to tell me she is coming after the summer to make us rich."

He and Coralie convinced Lindsay that this was definitely a good acquisition, although there would be a loss in fees due to her parents' limited income.

The term progressed with only minor difficulties, and tennis improvement was shown by everyone except Petra, whom Lindsay thought was only in limbo because she was coming to terms with her maturity.

The Academy broke up for a two week break at Easter. It was good for the students to touch base at home before the busy summer of events around Europe and exams for Kurt, Nacho and Agnieska in May and June.

Lindsay took Soo Jin to enter a tournament in Monaco, rather than send her all the way back to New Zealand as she was not all that keen on flying. She included Petra as well in an attempt to rebuild her confidence.

Inevitably Erik and Coralie found themselves alone at the Academy, accompanied occasionally by Lollo, who unashamedly appeared as before at mealtimes.

"I hate cooking. Knock the cost off my wages." he offered.

"If you keep telling jokes like the last one I really will." replied Erik.

Without the pressures of the Academy routine they were in 'relaxation' mode, rising later in the mornings and enjoying the 25 degree temperature. Coralie spent some time sunbathing and reading.

One night there was an explosive thunderstorm with crashes of thunder again and again almost overhead. It was impossible to sleep through such a racket. There came a knock on Erik's bedroom door.

"Come in"

"Erik, I'm frightened" said Coralie, standing in the doorway in shorts and a T shirt.

"Then you had better come here and we'll weather the storm together."

She willingly climbed into his bed. Erik put his arms around her. It was the only way they could both lie in the single bed. She was shaking. He folded a cover over them both and she rested her head on his chest. Rising to a crescendo in his brain came all the thoughts he had had about her during the last three months. Thoughts that he had valiantly tried to subdue of how attractive was her bubbly nature, her amazing figure and perfect legs, how she was single and not in a close relationship with anyone.

'Was it fair if he took advantage of her in this vulnerable state tonight?'

He kept as still as he could for several minutes. She stopped shaking. He could smell her clean hair – a sort of lemony fragrance. If she stopped moving he would be able to resist her, he thought. Then she moved again and he was acutely aware of her breasts shifting under her T shirt. He had been trying not to become too aware of these when she was on court and especially while she was sunbathing in the 'teeny weeny polka dot bikini' that Freddy sang about in the 1960s.

It was all too much for a red-blooded male to cope with and things he thought he had under control began to start growing in the garden. He kissed the top of her head. She turned to look up at him showing that she was not asleep. His last refuge had deserted him and he began kissing her neck. She kissed his mouth passionately and the next few minutes was the stuff of nightmares for a self-respecting three foot wide wooden bed.

The storm subsided and Erik woke up with pins and needles in his right arm and the shock that he was in a relationship. Coralie sat up suddenly.

"I must go back to my room. I have disturbed your sleep."

She stood up and realised that she had on the T shirt but no shorts, and felt about under the bedclothes until she found them. Then she performed a sort of dance to Erik's amusement that included putting both legs into the same hole in the shorts before getting it right, blowing him a kiss and leaving the room.

At breakfast a sheepish Coralie spent ages at the mini-buffet before joining Erik at the table. She knew he was looking at her but would not catch his eye in her embarrassment. Without looking at him she said

"I'm sorry about last night. I was genuinely scared. I wasn't trying to throw myself at you."

"You must be joking. There I was, innocently dozing in my little bed, and suddenly I am joined by an eminently bonkable female clad only in T shirt and shorts. I was ravished in my own bed. I have never been seduced like that in all my life."

"But I was only looking for companionship in a crisis, not anything else."

"You can't say that it was not a planned operation. Going on court looking like a million dollars day after day, sunbathing in a 'nothing bikini' outside my window……."

"No, no. It's not true. Sure I fancied you but then so does every other female who comes here. Why would you look at me when you could have had hundreds of girls on the tennis circuit. Probably did."

"OK. But are you sure this wasn't a plot dreamed up by you and Lindsay?"

"Why Lindsay?"

"She has been going on about how I spend more time watching you than the tennis playing students."

"Have you?" Coralie looked up

"No. Well, yes, probably."

"So you do fancy me really?"

"Yes, yes I do. Didn't you notice last night?"

Coralie turned a bright pink and took refuge back at the buffet

Returning with a cup of tea, she said

"You don't have to follow it up if you don't want to. We can carry on just as before. No-one else need know it happened"

"I may have to buy a new bed. One of the legs has broken after all the stress it went through last night"

"That was you, not me. I just lay there making gurgling noises"

"Gurgling? You were making more noise than the thunder."

"Let's go off for the day and think about what is going on in each of our minds about each other." suggested Erik.

They made up a picnic in the kitchen and put it and a bottle of wine in the cool box, and decided to buy fruit on the way. Ethel needed a run so they took her with Erik driving.

Lindsay sent Petra home to Zurich after the tournament in Monaco, carrying a large plate as her trophy for winning the Under 16 girls competition. She brought Soo Jin back to Marbella with her for the second week of the Easter break. Soo Jin had met strong opposition and lost in the semi-final of the Under 18 event.

"To be honest, I think Soo Jin did better than Petra against tougher competitors. Petra, however, has gone home with her confidence back up to normal again." Lindsay told the other two on her return.

Coralie could not wait to tell Lindsay about the night of the storm, and about being chased up to her bedroom the next day by a wild Erik and then about yesterday afternoon, when he joined her in a shower space designed for one.

"The Bugger" she said "I knew he was trying to get into your knickers."

"It was my fault really. I came to his room in the first instance" Coralie admitted. "When the thunder scared me."

"Are you sure you want this randy old man disturbing your sleep while you are here?"

"He is not that old, is he? I thought about forty-ish."

"Do you think you could fully love someone over forty? You are only 28 and, don't forget, he has been around the block a couple of times. I mean, God, he has even had me more times than I can count."

"Do you mind him liking me when he is still married to you?"

"No. He is not mine any more. But, be careful, he has a memory of some Aphrodite he fell for years ago, who was supposed to be irreplaceable."

"I won't get too serious. I am just enjoying being desired again." Coralie added.

"Don't be daft. You only need to get out more to be desired by every bloke on the planet. I am amazed you are still single."

"Didn't take you too long to get a piece of the action then?" Lindsay said to Erik admonishingly on the verandah in the evening.

"Aha. Longer than it takes for the grapevine to start vibrating around the Academy. And what evil stories are being told about me this time?"

"You know perfectly well that you have been luring young girls into your cave and introducing them to your best friend."

"One young girl, who found her own way into the cave."

"Yes. And I understand consolation was offered in the shape of the famous Eriksson Viking Blunderbuss."

"It is a rare and beautiful instrument that has hardly seen the light of day for years. Anyway you had more than your share on the beach in the Solomons"

"Legally, it is still mine to take or leave. Though I think I'll leave it to our poor, deluded colleague for the time being, who is no doubt still recovering from being spreadeagled on every surface ever since I left you two alone."

"Before we get too personal about these private matters allow me to remind you which half of this business partnership was the first to discover 'flagrante delecto' with a member of the opposite gender."

"OK, OK. But he is from outside these walls. Your chosen one is part of the team and, if you fall out of favour, it will make a total porridge of our tennis coaching programme."

"We are more mature than to allow that to happen."

"Just don't get her pregnant, that's all I ask." Lindsay emptied her glass and went back inside.

Erik was feeling as if he was twenty again. He and Coralie had sat on the sand in a quiet cove with their picnic. They had bought a melon and some huge oranges from a roadside stall and buried the melon with the white wine in the sand at the edge of the water.

"My Uncle used to do this when he was working in Gibraltar" he told Coralie

"He met a much older woman, who was a customer of his Bank and would come along here somewhere at weekends and stay in her cottage. They would cook fish on a makeshift barbecue and buy oranges and grapes from the beach vendors. Hardly a soul lived along the coast then, he told me. And then, suddenly, wham! Europe came on holiday. Marbella, though has always been here, and then, was a secluded playground for the rich and famous. Exiled

Kings and their families would come to Marbella for the summer and Closters for the winter."

"Now, all it has is the 'nouveau riche' and exhausted ex-tennis players" offered Coralie.

"Not too exhausted to keep you up to speed" he replied and began burying her legs and feet in the sand.

"Look" she cried "Our melon is floating out to sea."

"You can't fool me that easily" he said continuing piling up the sand.

"It really is. Look"

He turned to see the football shape twenty metres off-shore. She climbed out of her sand bed and they both ran down to the sea. It was a shock as they ran into the water and much colder than they had thought it would be.

"Brrrrrr. It's freezing". Coralie stopped as the sea reached her waist.

Erik was swimming strongly to fetch the melon. Eventually she joined him, moving vigorously to keep warm.

"I'm getting goose pimples on my goose bumps" she said

They went back quickly to sit on the sand in the sun and dried each other.

"We are behaving like lovers" she said.

"Worrying isn't it?" he replied, kissing the back of her neck.

On the way home they stopped at Bar Lulu and ordered a jug of Clarence's special Sangria.

"What is different about your Sangria, Clarence?" asked Coralie.

"Trade secret, ducky. One extra ingredient, but a total secret"

"What can I do to persuade you to tell me" she asked frivolously.

"There's not a lot you can do for me, dear, but you could send over that curly haired Swedish person, who may be able to seal a deal."

They spent an hour in the bar holding hands and talking in low tones.

"Forgive me for intruding, but do you two normally sit there like star crossed lovers holding hands?" said Clarence from the bar.

"Maybe you were so busy you didn't notice before" said Erik

"I don't usually miss much from up here. I mean, have you announced this association in the press?"

"Way past are the days that the press were interested in my affairs" said Erik.

"Well. At least we now know it's an affair. May it be a long and happy one!"

Coralie was enjoying being notorious. The lover of the well known Joel Eriksson and the envy of any female who found out. She went up to the bar.

"Clarence, it's my turn to pay. What will you take off for cash?"

"Darling. Everything except my earrings!"

They left laughing and both blew him a kiss.

The summer term began with everyone returning eager to put their winter's practise to good effect in the forthcoming events. Some of these would be together with senior tournaments and some run as separate junior weeks. Torgny, however, had not returned and there had been no message that he may have been delayed.

Erik phoned Torgny's home in Sweden and spoke to his mother. They talked away in Swedish for nearly half an hour. Erik then told Lindsay and Coralie, who were waiting concerned, that Torgny would be on a flight to Malaga the day after tomorrow. It seemed his Dad had left his Mum and gone away without leaving a contact number. Torgny had not seen or spoken to him throughout the Easter break.

His Dad had been the steering force in Torgny's tennis up until now and apparently he is devastated that Dad doesn't appear to be around any more.

"He will need a lot of support from us until Dad reappears. I just hope he does and soon." Erik added.

"What is he down for this summer? I think it is quite a lot isn't it?" Coralie half answered her own question.

"Yes. More than anyone. He has had very little competition on the clay and we have entered him into a lot of events because it is not a big academic year for him." Lindsay answered.

"In some ways that is good. His studying won't suffer and a lot of matches will keep his mind from thinking too much of the need for Dad's input." Coralie responded.

"Is his Mother OK, as far as you could tell? I mean are they well off financially?"

"I really don't know. She sounded all right as she told me. Her sister is staying at home semi-permanently. They have paid promptly, but I couldn't tell you how sound their income is". Erik replied.

Coralie offered to meet Torgny from his Stockholm flight and she met him with a hug and a positive spin on the exciting opportunities he was going to have, to pit his wits against some of the best clay court juniors. Dan was waiting for him in the student sitting room and they spent the evening together walking around the complex speaking in their native Swedish.

After a week there was a mass exodus to a junior tournament in Faro, in nearby Portugal. Faro is in the Algarve in the South and a three hour drive from Marbella. Rather than travel every day they took over a small holiday guesthouse on the outskirts of the town. Only Kurt, Nacho and Agnieska had been left behind because their exams were now quite close.

It was a successful week for their first outing as an Academy and caused the Tournament Referee to tell the Press to watch out for the players from this new tennis school in Spain. Kas beat Nicolas in the final of the Boys Under 14 event, Felipe and Thomas both lost their semi finals in the Under 16 Boys, and Torgny beat Dan in his semi final and hammered his final opponent 6-1,6-1 to win the Under 18 Boys. Lindsay thought he released a lot of anger in that final. The girls also did well. Lucy and Gabriella both lost semi finals, Petra again won the Under 16 and Soo Jin continued her good form to win the Under 18 singles. More trophies came in the doubles and the mixed and a lot of fun was had by all in these doubles matches.

The minibus arrived back at the Trocadero with everyone singing at the tops of their voices.

NINE

Erik had a number of commitments to Swedish TV in the summer months. His contract to commentate and summarise the Grand Slam Events involved three during the period May to September. The first was in May in Paris and it required two weeks away from the Academy. Lindsay was glad to have Coralie on board to cover all contingencies at this time. Lavinia was a star also and oversaw everything in the classroom and examination department. There were two major incidents that put a dampener on proceedings.

Apparently both Kurt and Torgny had crushes on Petra. Both the boys were under pressure at this time: Torgny because of his Father's departure and Kurt, who was about to take important exams. One day a fight broke out in the sitting room and Kurt finished with a broken nose. Torgny cut his hand on a plate that was smashed in the scrap. Petra was in tears and everyone else was keyed up, supporting one or other of the two boys.

Lindsay was furious with them and grounded all the boys for a weekend. However it was Dan who calmed everything down by starting a pool tournament and arranging a barbecue on the lawn outside for Saturday evening with help from Juanita in the kitchen.

Petra obviously fancied Kurt, but understood that Torgny was in the middle of a hard time and didn't know what to do. Dan suggested that she kept away from both until after Kurt's exams and when the next event came along. Then she should play it cleverly and kindly.

"Pepe. Erik thought he saw a small boy on board the Rosario hiding in the bow of the yacht. What was all that about?" Lindsay asked him when they were in his car on the way to a beach just East of Gibraltar.

"That would be Gabriel or Pablo, though they were supposed to keep out of sight. They are a problem of mine. We collected a party of people from Sierra Leone and took them across to the rendezvous about a month ago. In our haste we forgot to count how many left the Rosario and later discovered two stowaways."

"How old are they? Erik thought the one he saw was only about eight."

"Pablo is ten and his brother thinks he is twelve. They have no papers and don't know their birth dates. Parents were killed in the fighting in Central Sierra Leone two years ago and they have been living rough in the forest. They tagged on to a group who had decided that they could find a better life in Europe."

"Are they still on board?"

"We don't know what to do with them. I can't release two kids who only speak their local language into Europe to fend for themselves. They are bound to get caught or into worse trouble."

They arrived at the beach, a fifty metre wide cove between two tall headland rocks. Tucked into the cliff, just below the top, was a small house that couldn't be seen from the roadside; it was more of a trackside.

"This is the drop off point that the yacht came to on each of your voyages with us." said Pepe. "The refugees stay here in this old lookout post until they are collected for the next part of the journey. The men who move them on wait to see whether anyone has tracked the ship and come out here before they bring up a big lorry, usually half full of vegetables, and everyone is shut into the back for the next journey."

"How long do they have to stay inside there?" She asked.

"It is a four hour journey to their village in the centre of Spain, where they are all given a meal and use of a toilet. It is well planned. The village has only 70 inhabitants. They all know what is going on and help, even the policeman. Like us, they believe everyone in the world should have a chance in life"

Lindsay lost herself in thought for a few minutes, imagining the privations that a refugee would have to endure to come all that way across the edge of the desert without an obvious source of food, communication language or any support until they met Pepe and his crew.

They stopped for tapas and lunch in a small bar next to the side road leading from the coastal motorway. Lindsay did not want to drink alcohol this early and asked for tea. The woman looked strangely at her.

"She thinks she has some tea in the back of the kitchen" Pepe translated.

After ten minutes Lindsay was given a cup with tea leaves in the bottom and standing over her was the woman holding a saucepan full of boiling water.

Lindsay stifled a grin and nodded. "Leche?" she asked.

"No leche". "Limon?" "No limon". Pepe was laughing.

"Did you ever drink tea without milk or lemon?" he asked.

"No, never. But I have cooked water in a saucepan for tea before!"

"If we took the two boys from the Rosario and gave them jobs at the Trocadero Academy would we get into trouble with the authorities?"

"Yes. If they found out. You could say they were students and let Lollo teach them Spanish so they had a life in Spain."

"I can't bear to think of two such young boys, so far from home, living in a rope locker on your ship."

"They do quite well. The crew feed them and are teaching them Spanish with a Uruguayan accent" he smiled. "They are getting good in small boats too, paddling off at night and buying chips just before the takeaway closes at the end of the quayside. That is probably what they were doing when Erik was watching."

"I will talk to Erik. Maybe they can come to us and have a future of some sort."

It was May and Erik had just left for Paris and his two weeks at the one tournament that Novak Djokovic did not always win with ease. Lindsay took it upon herself to take in these two skinny disadvantaged lads from the ravages of the once peaceful Sierra Leone. They arrived at 2am looking completely bewildered. Aware that she needed to keep them out of sight and in the background for some time she housed them in one of the old school offices above the kitchen and immediately took Carmen into her confidence.

It was her plan to persuade Erik to agree to a more permanent role for the boys to play when he returned from Paris. To stave off boredom she set them to work cleaning the paintwork and floors of all the offices that had once been the hub of the school. They would eat their meals in a dining/sitting area in the office next to their bedroom. Communication was difficult although Carmen immediately seemed to cope with a mixture of Spanish and wild gesticulations.

"Lollo. In the gaps you will have with your Spanish lessons when the students are away playing tennis please will you try to teach some of your language to these two characters. She brought into the room Gabriel and Pablo dressed in new clothes from the Marbella Saturday clothes market."

"Oh, my goodness. Poor Lollo. Now you give me students with whom I cannot speak or hear!" He took out his voluminous handkerchief and cried into it. The boys immediately relaxed and laughed.

"Sit" he said pointing to nearby chairs. They sat and gazed at his face; the type of face it is impossible not to look at.

Lindsay crept quietly out of the door. She returned half an hour later with a coffee and two glasses of lemonade. The boys were still studying Lollo's face as he mouthed Spanish words to them and they attempted to repeat them.

"Actually they are called Felix and Sink" he told her. "The other names must have been given to them when they came to Spain."

'Or by the crew' she thought, not having yet fully confided their circumstances to Lollo

"Sink" she inquired. "What sort of a name is that?"

"If they come from West Africa, and I think they may, some babies are named after the first thing the mother sees after she has delivered the child"

"No. Surely not. That is not fair. The baby could be called 'stethoscope' or 'underpants' or anything"

"I didn't create the idea. That is just how it is" smiled the good natured Spanish teacher. "His Mum was looking at the sink!"

"What about Felix then?"

"Maybe they had a cat" he laughed.

Initially only Carmen and Lollo knew about the boys staying in the offices. Lindsay took them both out to the Bar Lulu on a quiet weekday evening to explain where the boys had come from. Without saying how, she told them that they were refugees from a civil war in West Africa and had made their way to the North Africa coast to try to find a place to live. Each of her guests was sympathetic to the situation and promised only to tell those of similar persuasions.

"'Ere" called Clarence from the bar, wearing a pink shirt with frills around the neck and white braces. "Where's lover boy this week?"

"Who, pray, is lover boy?" asked Lindsay, and immediately wished she hadn't."

"The Adonis of the tennis world from the last century." Came the reply.

"Do you mean my husband?"

"Well, dear. You had better put him on a shorter lead. He is chasing anything on heat at the moment."

"Did he bring her here then?"

"It was the cheeky one with the big tits."added Clarence "That's the one"

"They were whispering like teenagers behind the school cycle sheds"

"Don't let it worry you. She'll see the light in a few weeks."

"You don't mind him cavorting around in public with other women?"

Lollo and Carmen were all ears to this news. It may almost supersede the speculation going on about Lollo himself and Lavinia.

"No. He is a free agent and it will all add up to a higher alimony when I sort out the divorce. And stop spreading gossip like an old woman."

"Queen, darling. An old queen."

The second problem incident involved Pepe. Coralie had taken four of the students to compete in Liege, a long way away in Belgium. After the French Grand Slam had finished Erik joined them there in a small hotel and they prepared for the main event to be held in Belgium that summer. Lindsay thought she could cope with the remaining students as

Lavinia had three of them lined up for the next exams.

One mid morning Pepe came over to the Trocadero looking serious and refusing coffee, preferring to take her for a stroll around the complex.

"Last night we had a scare" he said. "There were lights on the headland above our cove so the yacht had to motor on past. We tried again and received a warning over the radio from one of the watching villagers, who would be collecting the people. So we came back here with fifteen people on board, and they are now hidden on the yacht. For security the skipper has kept the Rosario out at the end of the jetty. It should be OK because the customs never check her, though I guess there could be a first time."

"I have come to ask a big favour." he continued. "Yours is the only place I know in the area with spare spaces and empty buildings. Is there somewhere that I can bring the people to stay for a few hours until we can fix the next stage of their travel?"

Lindsay wanted to help but was aware of the danger to the whole business if they were found out. She took Pepe inside and they both poured coffee from the machine in the dining room.

"It's a heavy risk for us to do this, and I am now responsible for the jobs of a lot of staff. Also Erik is not here to agree or disagree."

"I will quite understand if you feel you cannot do it" Pepe said.

"How long will they be here?" She asked.

"Until I can bring the lorry from the village. A few hours."

"OK. They can wait in the old chapel. It has been empty since we arrived."

She bit her lip and wondered if she was making a bad mistake.

"Thank you Carina. Show me where it is and I will bring them in my car"

He later roared off towards the town.

During the day the Rosario's Captain moved the yacht to the blind side of the jetty and positioned her stern next to a flight of steps. Pepe parked his car immediately beside the top step. At sundown four people climbed into his car from the side of the steps and ducked down under thick blankets. The windows were of smoked glass so the passengers were obscured from outside eyes as the car passed through the harbour barrier and sped onto the Trocadero.

Pepe hurried the four out and into the old, dusty chapel through the door that Lindsay had left ajar. Waiting there were fifteen string bags of fruit and sandwiches that she had made up during the early evening after Juanita had gone home. Half an hour later Pepe arrived with another four passengers. Then nothing. Lindsay waited patiently for two hours. She called his mobile. No reply.

By midnight she began to worry. There was still no reply from his phone. The only other number she had was that of Lucas, who always called before he came to watch the tennis.

"Lucas, where is Mr Joseph?"

Lucas answered in a low tone. "Policia here. Big problem. Don't phone."

He disconnected. Lindsay felt herself go numb.

'What do I do now?' She collected some blankets and took them to the chapel and pointed to her watch in an attempt to explain that there would be a delay. The refugees seemed to understand. She stayed up fully dressed in the sitting room, half expecting a convoy of blue flashing lights to appear any minute.

At 1am her phone rang and a voice said

"Phone this number, and reeled off 8 numbers twice, then rang off."

Being a Maths teacher Lindsay was fortunate to have a brain that could not only do numbers but retain them. She grabbed a pen and wrote the number down on the corner of one of Erik's old newspapers. She phoned the number

"Hola"

"Habla usted Ingles?"

"Si Senora. Is that Senora Lindsay?"

"Si. I mean yes"

"We have a problem. Call me Carlos. Senor Joseph is with the police. You have eight people, yes?"

"Yes. Eight are here."

"We come for them. Green lorry. One hour. Please look for us"

"OK. Come to the Trocadero Tennis Academy. I will wait by the entrance"

The phone went dead and Lindsay found her hand was shaking with tension.

She waited for 45 minutes before pulling on a thicker jumper and walking out to the gateway to meet the lorry. It arrived ten minutes early and was only quite small. She jumped into the passenger seat next to one of the two men inside the cab. The driver leant over to shake her hand.

"I am Carlos" he said. "You are the brave lady."

'Scared lady' Lindsay thought. "Turn right and down this side driveway."

The van stopped outside the chapel door. The men got out and went inside and quickly encouraged the eight people – six adults and two children – to gather up their belongings and climb into the back of the van. Within five minutes they were all loaded.

"Where will you go?" she asked Carlos.

"To my village and then, I think, Andorra. Thank you Senora. God go with you." The van drove slowly along the driveway and then she heard it pick up speed along the main road.

107

"What on earth have you been doing, Lindsay my girl?" she said to herself in the tone her father used to use.

Later she lay on her bed and wondered what had happened to Pepe, the crew of the Rosario and the remaining seven refugees.

It was not until the next evening that Lindsay began to find out some of what had happened. The evening paper carried a headline

'Immigrants smuggled into Marbella' and underneath it wrote that a man had been arrested bringing four illegal immigrants into the country from a motor yacht moored in the harbour at Puerto Banus. Three others had been discovered hiding on board the yacht and all seven were now in a hostel in Malaga that dealt with people illegally entering the country. The man, a citizen of Uruguay, would appear in court in the morning. The yacht had been impounded and the crew were under arrest and confined to the yacht, which was now moored outside the harbour.

"Poor Pepe" she thought. "How could she get to see him".

She consulted Lollo as to where he may be held and whether she could visit him in captivity. He suggested she should be careful or the police may associate her with the crime. Perhaps wait until after the Court hearing tomorrow and then he would find out where Pepe would be.

The Hearing was fixed for 11am the next day and Lindsay was not sure whether to go to the Courthouse and watch from the public gallery. Lollo came to work and said that he would go and report back to her later. He would understand the proceedings in Spanish better than she could. She waited, unable to eat anything all morning, and tried to concentrate on her maths lessons to take her mind off the subject.

Just after 2pm Lollo returned with Pepe in his car. She was speechless and flung her arms around him.

"Come in, come in. How is it you are free? Tell me all about it. "

They pulled up three chairs in the sitting room.

"Firstly" said Pepe "Can I have a drink?"

"Yes. And what about some food?" He nodded his approval.

Lindsay went to the kitchen and spoke with Juanita.

Lollo said "It is a miracle. This man is a clever planner."

It transpired that Pepe and the crew had made contingency plans in case they ever got caught. The refugees they collected were always on Spanish territories and were being taken to another Spanish territory, so they were not committing any crime.

"I don't understand" said Lindsay "you collected them from Morocco when I was with you, and the other time from a rock in the middle of the Med."

Lollo laughed. She looked briefly at him in surprise.

"The first time we stopped at a small island off the coast of Morocco called Isla del Perejil. It is disputed by Morocco but, as far as the Spanish Government is concerned, it has always been Spanish. We collected your journey's people from there and we collected the ones a couple of days ago from the same place. How they got there is not our concern. We were just moving them from there into mainland Spain."

"What about the others? The emergency ones that had been left on the rock."

Lollo replied this time, bursting to explain.

"That would be Alboran. It is a flat rock, no bigger than three or four football pitches, that only has one house on it. It too belongs to Spain."

Carmen and Juanita both came in at this point and spread cold meat dishes and salads on the table in front of the three of them. Pepe continued :-

"The Court accepted my lawyers assurance that this was all true and granted my immediate release. They also released the ship from the armed patrol and all the crew are free as well. Now, what about my Lindsay? What happened here that night?"

Lollo looked surprised "Here, why here?"

"Not a word, Lollo, but I have been a bad girl too." she answered

"I waited and waited when you didn't arrive with the third load, then tried to call you. Eventually I got Lucas, who quickly said that the police were there and rang off. I then realised that there was a major hiccup. I tried to work out in my mind how I was going to explain to Erik why we had engaged eight African employees while he was away. Then someone called my phone with a number for Carlos."

"It was Ronaldo, on Lucas' phone. He was on part of the ship away from the police whilst they moved her out to a new mooring. You enabled Carlos to put the pieces of information together and find where the eight others were hiding. Did he arrive in the artic?"

"No. In a small van, just big enough for them all. I gave them some food and he said they were going out to his village."

"Mama Mia " said Lollo

"I didn't think anyone ever said that" answered Lindsay "I saw the film."

They all laughed and tucked into the food. Lindsay found a bottle of Spanish fizz to celebrate.

"Unless you two want to be alone together lets go and celebrate properly. I'll see whether Lavinia fancies an evening out and we could all go to a little fish restaurant I know on the other side of the town." suggested Lollo.

They all agreed and visited Casa Fernando, which was a restaurant with a bar and dancing later for all the diners. The perfect relaxation.

"You didn't phone to check on our students' results." said Erik.

"I was a little busy sorting out another matter." replied Lindsay.

It seemed it had not been a good day for their competitors in Liege.

Two were out of the singles and not playing very well. Two more losses in the doubles, both of which they should have won easily. Of the four contenders at Liege only Nicholas excelled. He was a finalist in the Under 14 Singles and won the mixed doubles with Lucy.

"The competition was tough, but not that tough." Coralie explained to Lindsay when they had arrived back. "It was a disappointing week overall."

TEN

"Everything all right back at the ranch" asked Erik on the verandah.

"Yes, fine. No more fun rides on the Rosario though."

"Not this month?"

"Not ever" she replied. She went on to tell him the story of the arrests and the later release of Pepe and the crew. "Their little jaunts will have to be on other vessels because the Rosario will be tracked all the time from now on, after this fiasco."

That night she was late going up to bed and passed Coralie heading the other way towards Erik's bedroom.

"Don't chase him. Let him find you." laughed Lindsay.

"I only have a single bed " she joked back

"So does he."

"Not any more. He now has a small double. We broke the single."

"Oh. My God. Just don't bring down the ceiling."

Lindsay remembered the early euphoria of sexual exploits with Erik on their island with no-one to see or hear. She wondered if it would have lasted if the mosquitos had not got between her and her insatiable lover all those years ago.

On Saturday the minibus took all those who wished to go out to the stables that Agnieska now knew well. They had booked the horses not in training for riding lessons. This was a new sport for most although Thomas showed a deal of competence from when he rode as a nine year old. Coralie and Agnieska jointly took them for the afternoon, ably assisted by the grooms at the stable.

Lindsay used the quiet time to corner Erik again. This time to take him to meet Felix and Sink in the confines of their office block. She explained as she went along what had happened and how she would like to give them a chance and sort of adopt them as pets of the Academy. Erik met and liked the two bright-eyed lads and agreed, at least for a few weeks trial.

"I am too soft for this job" he said. "We will soon have twice as many staff as pupils and a massive overdraft. I have to take another two weeks out to cover Wimbledon next month. This will probably be the biggest refugee camp in Europe when I return."

She poked her tongue out at him as they walked back, but resolved to change nothing whilst he was away this time and therefore not test his patience too much. She didn't want to lose her reliable friend and confidant.

Kurt, Nacho and Agnieska had now finished all their exams and the results would not be announced until August. They were immediately earmarked for the next tournament in order to have a chance to try out their winter training and improvement. This was to be in Madrid and Lindsay saw no reason to leave anyone behind. Torgny's hand had healed and all were fit and tanned from the early summer sunshine. It would mean that there was a good chance that some may be drawn against their own friends but that was the luck of the draw and something that would happen again and again over the next years.

There were six established tennis colleges in Spain and

two of them specialised in juniors. Erik was keen to see how his charges compared with the students at the others. In addition there were many competitors who had no allegiance to a college or academy, and yet others from outside Spain entered at this prestigious event. They all stayed at a hostel in downtown Madrid. The courts were familiar to Erik who had experienced a number of battles on them during his career, not least when he and his partner had won the Davis Cup doubles for Sweden here in 1996.

The tournament began well for Trocadero with everyone winning through to the second round. Kurt and Petra had resumed their friendship and entered the Under 18 Mixed Doubles together. Lindsay knew that playing together like that could make or break a romance. Torgny was surprisingly uninterested in Petra, or anything except his tennis, and concentrated like a demon possessed in each match. Dan commented that, in their doubles first two rounds, he was almost scary. Lucy and Gabriella had become great supporters of each other, probably because they were the two youngest in the party. Unless they were playing at the same time they were always to be seen courtside cheering on the other. Usually doubles would not be uppermost in the thinking of an Under 14 coach but these two insisted upon playing doubles together and had informed Coralie that they were going to kick butts all over Europe this summer. Coralie thought this had come from a film they were both avidly watching last week. These were the future of the tennis academy and she wondered what it would be like when the determined Saskia joined them in the same age group.

Everyone was doing so well this week that the three coaches had to spend a lot of time keeping the lid on their enthusiasm and deflecting taunts to the players from other colleges. They weren't too worried at Torgny's aggression but spent time trying to get him to wind down between matches. Agnieska was continuing where she left off, scorching through matches using her topspin backhand to great effect. Erik hoped she would soon come up against an opponent who could cope with this shot and give her a close game.

As luck would have it Kurt was drawn to meet Torgny in the semi final of the senior boys. They had a close match with Kurt having to work hard to beat his younger opponent 7-5 in the final set. This served to make Torgny more morose and determined and, together with Dan, they slaughtered all opposition in the doubles leaving Erik dreaming of another future Swedish doubles team that could play Davis Cup. They won the doubles without losing a set in the tournament and Kurt was only narrowly defeated in his Final.

Further success came with Felipe, Nacho and Thomas all becoming semi-finalists in the Under 16 boys and Nacho winning the event. Aga won the girls Under 16 singles easily and Soo-Jin was a finalist, losing to the same girl who beat her in Monaco. The Under 14s did not fare so well, except that Lucy and Gabriella became the doubles champions. The last trophy was carried off by Kurt and Petra, sealing their friendship for a little longer.

"This has been such a successful week" said Erik on Sunday morning before they left the hostel in Madrid "that we now have a major new task. Over-confidence. The biggest curse in the sport. Without dampening enthusiasm we have to tread the delicate pathway between ambition and conceit. These kids have now tasted success but we three know that success and confidence are balloons that can burst all too easily. They are NOT the best in the world and we need to remind them of this if they one day want to be."

"Yes, boss". Lindsay and Coralie chorused.

Erik grinned, drained his café solo and told everyone he

would meet them at the bus in ten minutes. The singing started before they had left the outskirts of the big city.

Erik left from Gibraltar this time to return to England. He set off a few days before the start of Wimbledon fortnight in order to travel back to Devon and meet the Burrows family and check on Saskia's progress.

It was one of those cold Junes that occasionally thwart the early summer holidaymakers in England, and Erik wished he had packed the extra sweater as he drove his Porsche down the M3 towards the Westcountry. No chance of lowering the hood today, so he listened to Dire Straits on CD and Mark Knopfler's brilliant guitar playing. Erik had played bass guitar once in a tennis competitors' rock group when he was in his twenties. They only got together at major events because the four of them often found they were playing different tournaments in the same weeks. They were not amazing but it was fun and he recalled once, at the Spa Formula One Grand Prix, comparing notes with Eddie Jordan, who had done the same thing on the Formula One circuit and was always in demand at post race parties.

He arrived, again unannounced, at George and Helen's farmhouse in time to use the brass knocker on their front door and demand coffee. Helen answered the door with hands covered in flour and a mouthful of something she was cooking.

"Good morning, Farmer's Wife. Have you fed the hens and milked the cows?"

Helen beamed a greeting and threw her arms around him in the way that was becoming a pleasant habit.

"Gamma wum dinna nilfone" she said with her mouth full, whilst trying to dust the flour off his jacket. "Cwum in, cwum in."

Erik cwame in.

"Callum will be thrilled you are here. He talks about you non stop and wants to sail the boat down to the Mediterranean in his holidays"

"Any chance of a coffee? I am as dry as a camel's armpit" said Erik.

"Where is Farmer George this morning?"

"Farmer George is in the top field spraying slurry. He will return for lunch smelling distinctly unpleasant."

"You have really got into this farming lark, haven't you? Serious cooking, learning all about crops and spraying and harvesting. All credit to you. George is a lucky man."

Helen ran upstairs and brushed her hair, throwing off the apron and changing her shoes.

"Lucy is having a ball out in Spain with us" Erik greeted her return.

"I know she would like to continue next year if you are happy with the situation. She is competing well, improving all the time and making friends wherever we go."

"We miss her but she is absolutely loving it. She tells us about every match she plays and how she and Gabby are going to wipe the floor with everyone in the doubles" said Helen proudly.

"Tell me about Saskia Burrows. You know she is keen to join Lucy after the summer?"

"Her Mum, Kate, phoned me in a panic a few months ago and said you had told Saskia she could have a place at the Academy. She thought there was no way they could afford it and were scared it would devastate Saskia. I am afraid I told her not to worry and that you had given us a concession. I hinted that you may do the same for them."

"Saskia wrote me a great letter that I have kept, telling me that she would be coming to join us and would make the academy rich and famous. It was brillIant from a 12 year old. How could I say 'no'? Coralie had hinted that she has a lot of determination and quite some skill. I have to see her parents on this visit. Do you have their phone number?"

Helen gave him the number and he left a message asking Callum to meet him on the boat at 6pm. Callum was due back from school at 4.15pm.

Erik called in at the Seaton Sweet Shop at 1pm and met Kate Burrows during her lunchtime break when the shop was closed. Husband Jeff had been working in Beer, only two miles along the coast, and was able to join them. Before Erik could say anything Kate burst out

"Mr Eriksson, we could never afford all your fees and all they tennis rackets and sweatbands and things they have to use. Jeff's not a rich farmer like George and we can't usually afford a holiday every year."

"This is only an idea. Can I call you Jeff and Kate?" They nodded

"And I am Erik these days. I need still to talk to Danny at Ottery Sports Centre and to some contacts in London during next week. Would you like Saskia to join us and train to be a competition tennis player?"

"Yes" They cautiously replied in unison.

"Sometimes they are good enough, but other times they are not. Just in case the students don't make the grade we give them the same schooling that they would have had if they had stayed at home, so there are other careers they can follow if they wish. They stay with us in a boys' or a girls' dormitory and usually eat with us. There are only sixteen maximum at any one time; thirteen at the moment. All food and tournament travel and entries, plus accommodation when away, is paid from the fees"

Kate added glumly " But we can't pay those fees"

Erik continued "If we are able to grant Saskia a scholarship to the Academy then all fees will be covered. All you will need to do is get her to us and back and forth in the school holidays and give her some pocket money."

The two apprehensive parents looked at each other. Jeff said "Sounds pretty good to me. We bought her a racket and she has a tennis dress for tournaments, so that should last a while."

Erik laughed and they both looked at him in surprise.

"Give me a couple of weeks and I may have a Sports Equipment manufacturer who cannot wait to give her any new equipment she needs for practise and competition"

"Why would they do that?" asked Jeff in all innocence.

"Advertising. It's all so they get their name in the public eye. People will be watching Saskia wearing their kit. She will have to wear their jackets and racket covers for any prize presentation or press photographs. It is how they get sales against their rivals. So what is the verdict? Can I steal her away from you for a trial term after the summer? I can assure you she will be in good hands, with Coralie, whom you know and her friend Lucy."

They both nodded enthusiastically.

"Now, I am going to see Danny to check her progress and what tournaments he has arranged for her in the summer holidays. Would you consider putting her on the train at Axminster early on Saturday week, so that I can meet her at Waterloo? I would like to show her a few things at Wimbledon. She can stay with us in our house nearby overnight and I'll send her back on Sunday. Swedish TV rent a house and there will be meals and a bed for her. I promise she will be in good hands with Annika, one of the producers"

"You are being very kind to us Mr Eriksson…..Erik" said Kate.

"Of course. I want to make your little star into a bigger star."

That evening Erik changed in the car. This was not an easy feat in a cramped sports car and he received some strange looks from two passing ramblers. He joined Callum on Viti Levu, which had been put back in the water in April and was on her mooring in Seaton Harbour. Callum was keen to show how well he could handle the sailing boat that they had done up together, and so he took them out and along the coast towards Lyme Regis. It was bracingly cold but they both wore yellow oilskins, which caught the spray as she cut through the light channel waves.

"I prepared her well this winter. Her keel is smooth and clear and the frayed jib I replaced with a new one from Frank Rowsell in Exmouth" said Callum.

"That must have cost a bit." Answered Erik.

"He gave me a discount and I paid for it with the money I earnt cleaning at the Pilot Inn in Lyme over Christmas and Easter."

"What is all this about you sailing her down to Marbella?"

"Just a little trip to come and see my sister bashing tennis balls around"

"That is the sort of trip that needs a professional sailor on board."

Callum said "I have got one in mind. Haven't asked him yet though. Mr Edworthy, my Biology teacher, once crewed in an ocean race from Rio to Capetown and he used to help deliver new yachts to the Med and to the Caribbean. I was going to ask him to come along and take two of the sixth formers from school who sail a bit. They can pay for the trip and that would buy Mr Edworthy's whisky"

"Likes a drink does he?" asked Erik warily.

"I think so. He keeps a half bottle in his desk."

Erik made a mental note to try to check this out before releasing his young co-owner to the ravages of the Bay of Biscay.

Two days later the Television Sports Team from Gothenberg met up at the same house in SW19 that they had used for the last seven years. With one exception it was the same team that had covered Roland Garros a month earlier. The weather had brightened and warmed to a tolerable 17degrees and practise was in full swing around the eighteen immaculate grass courts of this much-awaited event.

"I read that your lot cleaned up in Madrid" greeted Soren, the Director.

"They were good" answered Erik "Three or four of them are going to make some seniors sweat in a years time."

"Why haven't you entered any for the Junior events here?"

"I nearly brought Kurt, but he has been taking exams until a couple of weeks ago. The others can wait until I have introduced them to grass. We will blood a few of them on the hard courts at Flushing Meadow to see how they handle real crowds."

The usual crop of seeds dropped out of the first week, a few surprises amongst them. Erik commentated on some selected matches and summarised the day's play at 7pm every evening live for the 8pm audience in Sweden, which was also broadcast to Norway and Denmark. On Thursday he was invited with others to join The Duchess of Cambridge in the Royal Box and enjoyed much laughter with her at tea during her visit. He had never before actually a eaten a famous Wimbledon strawberry, although he had competed and visited there for years, and the Duchess made a number of remarks about this. With them was another retired competitor, who was heavily pregnant, and the Duchess told them how she had laughed when she went into the Maternity Wing of the hospital to deliver her first baby and a sign on the entrance door said 'Push, push, push.'

Saskia was a little scared, but determined not to show it, as she sat in the train on the way from Axminster to London on her own on Saturday. Erik met the train at Waterloo and Saskia sat next to him in the taxi to the Wimbledon house holding tightly on to her small pink grip with her nightclothes in it.

"Are you hungry?" Saskia nodded

They went into the dining room and attacked the four plates piled high with sandwiches that had been left for the TV crew.

"Hi. I'm Annika, said a very pretty blonde lady who had come in behind her. Come and find me today whenever Joel is busy"

"Who is Joel?" asked Saskia

"Ah. That's me" said Erik

Annika and Saskia looked mystified and Erik told them it was a long story that he would finish another time.

After lunch and a drink Saskia went with Erik into the Wimbledon Club area through a special entrance and wearing a blue badge around her neck. His friends and old adversaries goaded him as he walked around the courts and walkways.

"Is this your daughter, Joel. You never told us about her?"

"Look. At last Joel has got himself a girlfriend."

He showed Saskia all around the outside courts and the display stands, the catering for the daily visitors and the engraved winners boards. Then he explained about the two show courts and how there was seating all around each of them as well as lesser seating for the No 2 Court. As they passed the Nike Stand a man dashed out and grabbed Erik's arm.

"Joel, I have been hoping to catch you all week. Need to talk."

"Hi Charlie. OK, talk away."

"Can we go somewhere and sit down – out of this melee?"

They chose a corner of one of the catering units and Charlie bought two coffees and a gigantic strawberry milk-shake for Saskia.

"Look mate, you've got about a dozen useful kids down there in Spain. I mean, Christ, you shook the junior world in Madrid. How about we do a major deal that we can sponsor every one of your pupils, students, or whatever you call them, and we'll give you something you really need down there"

"Like what, Charlie?"

"I don't know what you need. How about a grass court? Ha,ha,ha.

Seriously though, we could do a great deal for, say, three years of your kids wearing our kit."

"I like the idea, Charlie, but most of the students are already stitched into contracts with other companies. These were fixed before they came to us. Two of them, I think are with you already."

"What if I come down and stay a couple of days and offer you a deal you can't refuse for when all the contracts run out?"

"You can come down and try to twist my arm on one condition."

"Go on."

"Saskia here is blind."

Saskia looked at him, and blinked her eyes to check they were still all right.

She said nothing and read the label on the tablecloth. She blinked again.

Erik went on "On my recommendation give her twelve months rackets, full kit and back up and you can come down and talk turkey when we are all there together."

"Deal" said Charlie "what is your full name Sasha?"

"I am Saskia!Saskia Katherine Burrows."

"I'll get the papers to you on Monday. You in the Press area?"

"Thanks Charlie. Yes, with Swedish TV. See you"

Charlie left and Erik looked at Saskia.

"I'm not blind. How can I play tennis if I am blind?" she asked,

They walked towards the No 1 Court.

"It's an expression in the sports world that means you have no agent and no sponsor." explained Erik.

"What is a sponsor?"

"A person or a Company that pays for some or all of your expenses when you compete. They may pay your travel or supply your clothes and balls, rackets and shoes. Nike are going to pay for all this for you for a year, so you had better not let me down."

"I am going to make you rich and famous." she replied.

It was only half an hour away from Erik's first scheduled broadcast of the day, so he was heading towards a rendez-vous with Annika when they bumped into someone Saskia thought she recognised.

"Hallo Joel, I haven't seen you for ages. How are you and how is everything down in sunny Spain?"

"Hi Judy. Everything is going swimmingly. Aren't your boys doing well?"

"Yes. Quite well, but I know the best is yet to come. I am just away to see Jamie in a tough doubles on Court 2"

"You wouldn't like a pleasant companion while I do a broadcast would you?"

"OK. But where will you be when we finish?"

"Swedish TV box. This is Saskia from Devon. Coming to us in September. You sure you don't mind?"

"I am sure she will be great company. Come along Saskia."

Saskia followed Judy Murray not quite sure who she was and, together, they watched Jamie, who was a doubles specialist, play in a close four set match which he won. Judy was delighted and had kept Saskia interested, explaining how doubles was played and how the players didn't get in each other's way. Erik came over to the court and they thanked Judy.

"Was that Andy Murray's Mum?" asked Saskia.

"Yes. I should have told you."

"I didn't want to ask her because it seemed rude"

Erik explained that Judy Murray was now coaching the Great Britain ladies team and would remember Saskia's name in the future if she ever became a candidate the selectors would consider.

They looked at some of the things that were being sold and Erik bought her a peaked cap and a box of balls that had been used for just 9 games at this year's tournament. They then took seats at the back of the players' enclosure on Centre Court to watch Anna Ivanovich play Eugenie Bouchard. Again it was a close tussle and Saskia noticed a number of things including the concentration, ignoring anything in the crowd, and where they stood to receive service.

Erik said "Don't be afraid to choose a good player and try to copy her."

Annika took over in the evening when Erik compiled his summary for TV and her assistant was organising the production. They stood at the back in a small studio whilst Caroline Wosniaki was being interviewed after her earlier win. It was all in Swedish or Danish, so Saskia couldn't understand what was being said. Then they all went back to the house leaving cameras and lots of laptops in their broadcasting area. A delivery man brought a huge box of takeaway food from a Thai Restaurant, which they shared out and drank with cans of beer. Saskia enjoyed being an adult for the evening, drinking her can of Sprite in the same way and eating strange things from the Thai box. She practically fell asleep at the meal table until Annika steered her towards the staircase and they both said 'Goodnight'. Her bed was in Annika's bedroom and they both slept deeply until 8.30 in the morning.

The next morning Erik took her to catch the train home, having fixed with Jeff to meet her from the train at around lunchtime. She read the Wimbledon programme from cover to cover and wore her new cap for the whole journey. If she was not already convinced she would be a tennis star she certainly was now.

ELEVEN

With Wimbledon over Erik returned to the Trocadero where there was an end of term atmosphere. Although most of the students would still be around for some weeks the academic lessons had only two weeks to run and the sun was relentlessly beating down to make everything stiflingly hot. Whilst away Lindsay and Coralie had taken the minibus of ambitious competitors to Milan to try to make a similar impact to that in Madrid.

Lindsay thought that it was time for Kurt, now almost 18 years of age, to compete in the senior event. She remembered tales of his fellow German, Boris Becker, winning Wimbledon at 17 years. He played well and reached the quarter final, only losing to local favourite Fabio Fognini, who had been around for a long time and was a wily opponent. In the junior events Agnieska excelled again and the doubles pairings proved their superiority once more, including the mixed doubles specialists Kurt and Petra. Agnieska was sweeping aside all Under 16 opposition with ease, so Lindsay decided that she too must step up to the Ladies division at the next tournament.

On the 1st July Juanita went down with a sort of flu bug that was becoming an epidemic in Spain and France, followed two days later by Carmen and kitchen assistant Luciana.

"Erik, can you cook? I have too much to do to spend time messing about in a kitchen. It's an emergency." called Lindsay through his bedroom door.

Erik spat out his toothpaste

"I come from a long line of hunter gatherers. We don't do cooking." came the swift reply.

Lindsay grabbed a cup of tea and headed for the kitchen. There she found Coralie and Soo-Jin preparing vegetables. Soo-Jin was wearing an apron, marigold gloves and snorkelling goggles while peeling onions. Lindsay roared with laughter.

"What's on the menu today, team?" she asked.

"We were hoping you had come to tell us" answered Coralie.

"You look as if you know what you are doing. Can't you create something? Soo-Jin, have you cooked lots of things before?"

"I once made a flat Victoria sponge" the goggles replied.

"Shall I put out an SOS in the students sitting room?" suggested Coralie.

Not receiving a reply, she set off and found six of the students in their sitting zone.

"Can any of you cook? We are without kitchen staff today."

Thomas replied. "No problem. Open all the packets, throw them in a big pan and curry them. We always used to do that on camping expeditions in the hills. It was all right until we added chocolate pudding mix on one occasion."

"Thanks Thomas. Anyone else?"

Dan said "I'll give it a go" and set off back to the kitchen with Coralie.

Dan immediately took over.

"OK everyone. Let's start by finding out what stocks we have. Coralie, please tell me what vegetables there are and Lindsay, is there any meat or fish?"

They reported back and Soo-Jin finished her pile of onions. Dan made a large fish stew and two dishes of green vegetables, followed by fruit and yogurt. He washed all the pans and left the kitchen like a professional.

"You are going to make someone a wonderful wife one day." said Lindsay.

A 'Tennis Board Meeting' was held in their adopted office in Bar Lulu that evening as they left everyone to enjoy pizzas cooked by their new chef back at the Academy

"Who stays and who goes is the main question. We need to inform and advise parents in good time for next school year. Can we decide now or should it wait until later?" Erik asked his two tennis colleagues.

Lindsay volunteered that she thought everyone had been excellent. Most of the time they had all worked hard on court and at their fitness although there was room for improvement in the classroom.

Coralie thought that Kurt may want to move on into the seniors and wondered how much more he could get from them and would he not be better employing a private coach now.

Erik summarised their feelings and his own.

"This has been a fine start and I have been very impressed with the standard of behaviour and dedication at most times with everyone. There is no disruptive element, though I am not quite sure where Torgny is in his head yet. Financially, everyone pays almost on time and comments from parents seem always to be helpful. Kurt is the only question mark. He may well want to set up on his own but he may be better spending a little more time using us as a base, and winning some cash."

"He will also want to stay because of Petra." added Coralie.

"So, we have just three places to offer. Assuming they are all going to return and their parents are keen to pay for another year." Lindsay said.

They contributed that there were two part subsidised places and one full subsidy to come, and Felipe's bursary would need to be confirmed for a second year.

Coralie yawned.

Lindsay quipped "If you weren't up all night performing nocturnal gymnastics with a pensioner you wouldn't be constantly tired."

"Must be time for you two lovebirds to go back to bed. It's nearly nine o'clock" added Clarence pointedly from the bar. "And where is the Uruguayan answer to James Bond these days. Can't he stand the pace?"

Both Erik and Coralie now looked at Lindsay as they too had been wondering about that. No answer came from Lindsay as she studied her Campari and soda.

More success came from the tournament in Zurich, Petra's hometown and where her school friends turned out in force to cheer her to the Under 16 title. Although many of the trophies would be returned for next year's tournaments the permanent mini cups and plates would stay. The Trocadero's cabinet in the foyer was looking impressive.

Applications began to arrive to join the Academy for the next academic year. They decided to despatch the students who had not yet gone home, and look at these applicants at their leisure during August. One place had gone to Saskia, so only two remained to be filled.

The Skype text that stirred Erik the most arrived on August 12th. It was from Oman, from his close friend of over 15 years ago Sally Shaunessy and her husband Chris. On the face of it the message merely asked how he was progressing with his new venture. Sally and Erik had corresponded a few times in the last two years but they discovered that they no longer had much to say to each other. The memory of their passionate love affair ran too deep within each of them that 'surface' chat was somehow irrelevant. The message was obviously written by Sally and, almost as an afterthought, she had added that her daughter Padmini had just won the Omani tennis title for Under 16s and was competing in Abu Dhabi for the UAE cup this week.

Maggie, having called in en route from India to England, had told him that their, then 10 year old, daughter was a keen player and had been coached at her orphanage by his ex-partner and Maggie's husband Sammy, before her adoption into Sally and Chris' family. Now it seemed as if she was progressing well in the sport in her new home in Muscat, Oman. Erik realised that this was a feeler to see whether he thought Padmini may be a candidate for the Trocadero Centre.

He waited a couple of days before discussing this with the ladies. Their planned scrutiny of all the applicants was due. They met again in the unofficial office at Bar Lulu, sat at their usual table within earshot of Clarence, who pretended to polish wine glasses, and they had to accept that he was an uninvited additional member of the committee.

Lindsay was extolling the virtues of Dan, who had covered for Juanita for three days in the kitchen although Luciana returned for the last day to play a part.

"That boy is amazing. He is an accomplished cook and a born counsellor of his teenage peers as well."

They all agreed and discussed how they could reward him for baling them out.

"You should have called me, sweetie. I would have dropped everything to have been able to cook for Erik." said Clarence.

"It would have been too much like the naked chef"

replied Erik "and we would probably have been responsible for the Bar Lulu closing for three days."

"Would Rex have done the cooking for you here?"

"Rex. That's a joke. He has trouble boiling water. He once thought Coq au Vin was a legover in a dormobile."

"Are you eating this evening, my treasure, because time is getting on and the poached salmonella is nearly all gone?" continued Clarence.

"That sounds delicious. I'll have one of those with some boiled potatoes please Mr Bartender, waiter, chef, entertainer." said Coralie

"I suppose, with a voluptuous body like yours, you can get away with being a cheeky sod" Clarence added.

"Voluptuous. I've never been called that before."

"Erik, stop looking at her chest and order something." said Lindsay

Erik studied the blackboard "Just a steak please Clarence. Medium"

Lindsay preferred one of Clarence's avocado salads, for which he was famous with all the vegetarian visitors.

Lindsay had brought all the application letters with her for them to discuss.

"This is what has arrived so far. I think a few titles won in the summer has made some parents and coaches look seriously at us for the next step for their kids. There are eight altogether. One from the Russian Tennis Federation, one from a twenty-five year old man and six from teenagers – well, one is twelve."

They began by deciding that the man should go to one of the academies for adults, and that Trocadero was to remain for younger players. They read through the applications for boys, three of the seven remaining. None looked outstanding and, anyway, it was unlikely that there would be a boys vacancy yet. This left four girls. Erik read them out loud. The RussIan application had to come through the National Federation or the government in Moscow would not grant a visa, so there was nothing unusual about that. She sounded promising, having won in Kiev and then moved to Russia to live, winning again twice in and around the capital. She was only 16 but had also appeared in a Ladies Final in an event that Lindsay thought was quite well ranked. Of the other three it was Padmini who stood out, having won an Under 16 event when she was only 12, albeit in a country not well known for tennis. Erik said nothing because he didn't want to influence the decision through his knowledge of the family.

They agreed to offer places to Oksana from Russia and Padmini, if that is what her Mother's letter had intended. Reserve was Marianne from Romania.

The next day at breakfast, when they were alone, Lindsay said to Erik

"Was that not your special person writing from Oman?"

"Yes. That's why I kept quiet."

"Are you sure you want to open an old wound unnecessarily?"

"I'm not certain she intended Padmini to come. It shouldn't cause any problems for the business."

"No, but it could test your emotions. For us it will be terrific to have four girls under 14 who could be here for the next four or five years."

She left Erik to reply to the Skype text from Sally.

As before, the places offered depended upon an interview and a chance for the coaches to see the candidate in action on court. As both lived a very long way away they agreed to view videos sent by each of them and have a short Skype conversation with the teenager. Sally replied to Erik that she and Chris would love Padmini to have the chance to have proper coaching at the Trocadero. Hers was the first video to arrive and showed the little girl giving an excellent account of herself in the Under 16 final in Abu Dhabi. She spoke to Lindsay and Coralie together on Skype a day later and they immediately told her to come and join them in September.

Oksana's video was of a practise session with one of the club ladies. She had very strong ground strokes but needed work on service and what net work they could deduce. They too spoke to her on Skype and offered her a place at the beginning of the next term. Oksana was 16, so would be one of the older girls. She was so delighted that she jumped up and down and effectively disconnected the laptop.

Erik and Coralie left for a week on the Algarve in a friend's apartment

Lindsay invited Pepe to come to stay at the Trocacdero and help her look after the premises that would be almost empty until early September.

"Did Victor know what you have been using Rosario for since you have been here?" Lindsay asked Pepe one evening.

"Let me tell you a story. In the 1980s we were living in a suburb of Buenos Aires in Argentina. My Father was a baker and we were quite poor. After the defeat of Argentina in the battle for the Malvinas things were not good politically."

"The Malvinas are called the Falkland Islands sometimes aren't they."

"Si Carina. It was a bad time for the people of Argentina. These islands were their hope of oil and gas discoveries that would make the country prosperous, and then the British came down and won the fighting. In the civil unrest the Uruguayans living in the country were often victimised later because Uruguay had let British bombers use their airbases. So my Dad took us back to our homeland. Victor and I were boys at school. The family had to start again. We were like refugees in our own country for many years. Father died and Victor became head of the family. He did not continue the bakery but began to import and export goods from Europe and America. Lindsay patiently listened.

"Then my wife died and I cracked up for two years. In that time my nephew, Diego, Victor's son took over the business operation. Victor retired and kept half the shares. He gets a big annual income from this and gives me 20% if I help other people who are refugees, like we were, to find a way to have a better life. So, yes he knows, and with my effort and his money we do some things that are not always legal."

"I don't know whether I should feel sad or happy" said Lindsay. "Happy maybe because you are making a constructive attempt to even up the extremes of wealth and poverty in the world. In a peculiar way levelling up the differences, piece by piece, person by person."

"I like you and love you because you understand." said Pepe. "Many would report me to the authorities or grumble that my activities are just making them poorer by sharing with outsiders."

Carmen and Juanita took turns to come into the complex and keep the kitchen and houses ticking over, making food for Lindsay and later for Erik when he took over so that Lindsay could spend a few days in the South of France with Pepe.

Some of the students were due to return early in September to prepare for flying to New York and entry into the US Open at Flushing Meadow. Three boys and three girls had qualified, four of them in singles.

The first to arrive was Agnieska. A big Toyota Land Cruiser drove into the entrance towing a horsebox. Aga climbed out of the car carrying a huge silver trophy with rosettes attached. Erik and Lindsay, who had just returned, looked amazed.

"Aga, what have you been doing?"

Kas, who also emerged from the vehicle answered

"She has just won the three day event at Córdoba on Lowca"

"That is incredible. We had no idea you were competing."

"The Stable entered me and my Father brought us and Lowca down from Poland last week. I didn't expect to win because I have done so little training with my horse since I came here"

"You clever girl" added Lindsay, throwing her arms around Aga.

Her Dad came forward from behind them and explained that he must find a hotel to stay in and take Lowca to the Stable for the night. He began to unload his children's bags and tennis gear for them to stay behind.

Erik said "Stay here for the night. We have beds and I am sure we can tether Lowca to a tree and look after him as well"

Aga laughed. "No, he has to have special feed and will be better in a stall at the Stables. Father though doesn't need special feed except a glass of vodka"

Father and Aga took the horse off for the night stop at The Stables, who were waiting to shower her with champagne after the success, which would raise the profile of the Stable in the South of Spain.

Aga's popularity was emphasised by the delighted response of each student, as they arrived, to see her riding trophy. It was the largest in the cabinet and enhanced by the colour of the rosettes. The US competitors had now all returned and Coralie joined them in a dust covered Ethel.

"I took a short cut and found myself on a dusty track in the middle of Spain"

Lindsay felt she needed to stay at the Trocadero to greet the other returning students and the new ones, some of whom would arrive before the New York party returned. She also wanted to finalise their first year's accounts and begin the new school year up to date with office work.

"I'll go next year" she said to Erik, Coralie and the six teenagers as they caught an internal flight to Madrid prior to the long haul trip to Newark in the States.

Although they were only in the Junior Events the atmosphere at Flushing Meadow was unlike anywhere any of them had competed before. They had practised on the hard court back in Marbella for this tournament, all of which was played on that type of surface. Their matches were all on the outside courts but there were always two or three hundred spectators. Petra and Soo-Jin were fazed by the crowds that stood close to the courts and made a lot of comment, sometime not so nice if they had an American opponent. It didn't seem to worry Aga at all and she progressed rapidly to the semi-final of the girls event. Kurt was the only boy from Trocadero in the singles and lost a close quarter-final to the eventual winner.

Aga and the Doubles pairing of Dan and Torgny were now into the last half of the second week of the competition and the changing rooms were less occupied as losing players returned home or watched from the stands. Erik noticed that, the more intense the competition became the more Torgny seemed to love it. He carried Dan with his drive and determination. So far they had won every match in the final set and had played twice as many games as any others. They were now well used to the pace and bounce of these courts.

Finally, after a full year of friendly and tournament matches, Aga came up against an opponent who could handle some of her topspin backhands. This girl had already competed in Ladies events in several countries and great things were expected of her. She was Canadian and had brought a lot of support with her from Edmonton. This was a first big test for Aga and she lost 7-6 6-4. Erik was thrilled, for reasons that he planned to explain to Aga on the plane home. One win, however, stole headlines in the tennis press. Dan and Torgny showed a doubles maturity that the specialist doubles fraternity recognised as a major future challenge to the established couples that made a good living from the events around the circuit. They won semi-final and final without losing another set or a service game, both against American pairings and to a large extent the audience.

In the airport departure lounge waiting for the flight to Madrid the four singles players were not sure whether they had done well or badly. Erik borrowed a small room from a friend in Qatar Airways and conducted a sort of de-briefing session. He praised them all for a great effort in challenging surroundings. A big cheer was given to Dan and Torgny, then a warning that every junior doubles player would be after their scalps next year. He then gave them the task of working out why he was pleased that Aga had met her match on Thursday, and they would talk more about it in Marbella.

Erik sat next to Aga on the Boeing 787. She was angry with herself for having lost.

"Now my girl" said Erik. "You have relied on that one winning stroke for a year to carry you through each match you have played. Emily found an answer to it on Thursday. Others will do the same in the months and years to come. So we have to concentrate on improving all the other aspects of the Aga game. You will then be able to win a few special points with that weapon but win other points with service and the full range of other strokes. Understand?"

"Yes. I understand"

"I will now begin to make as good a tennis player of you as you are a horse rider."

TWELVE

The US Party returned to a semicircle of applauding friends and staff members, with much praise heaped upon the doubles champions and a blown up photo of their presentation on the wall of the students' sitting room. Erik joined the applause and turned around to come face to face with Sally!

It was quite a shock to suddenly see before him the face that he had carried in his dreams for more years than he could remember. It was totally inadequate to just say

"Hallo."

"Hallo" repeated Sally.

They just stood looking at each other for all of a minute, not knowing quite how to continue.

"Er……er….this is Padmini" said Sally, pulling forward a small pretty dark girl with short wavy hair, who had been standing beside her.

"Hi Padmini. Now I know how to pronounce your name properly. We have been calling you Padmeeeni." Erik replied in a daze. His mind was a whirl of past times with Sally, painting her portrait, the little noticeable aging differences her face showed since they last met.

The mingling students had drifted off towards their rooms with Kurt and Petra walking across the grassed area hand in hand. Lindsay was watching Coralie watching Erik and Sally, hoping that this was not the beginning of a difficulty. Pepe had asked her to marry him whilst they had been in France. She had hesitated to answer him then and had been enjoying seeing her friend Coralie so besotted with Erik and almost dancing to work every day.

"When did you arrive? Come inside and we can talk. I'll just fetch my bag from the minibus. Ask Lindsay to look after Padmini." he spluttered.

Coralie decided to go to her room and sort out the mountain of luggage she had brought back in Ethel, but had not yet a chance to unpack properly.

By the time they had reached the dining room and Erik had make a hot drink for Sally and himself he had pulled himself together.

"If I had thought about it I would have realised that you would travel with Padmini and probably be here today, but I hadn't and so I didn't."

Sally laughed nervously.

"I was not sure how you would receive me after our rather dramatic parting." she said. "I came yesterday and Lindsay has been looking after us famously. I must go again this evening and leave my baby with you."

"She will be fine here. We have three other under 14 girls, two of whom are lively and have had a fun year here already."

They drank the coffee and just looked at each other.

"You are happy aren't you?" asked Erik

"Yes, very." she replied "Have I scarred you too much?"

"It took about fourteen years to come to terms with, and then I found myself ready to move on after I convinced myself that the principal outcome I wanted was for you to be happy and content. Whenever I reminisce I look at your portrait that is still in my bag."

He opened his tennis cum clothes bag that he had just taken from the minibus and pulled out a painting that was in a sleeve at the top. It was crumpled around the edges. A large tear crept down the side of Sally's face and dripped on to the back of her hand as she held the painting and looked at herself in a red dress.

Coralie agonised about Erik's meeting with his 'special love' and could not concentrate on unpacking. She just sat on her bed and looked at the wall.

Lindsay showed Padmini around the three tennis courts and asked what sort of surface she had mostly played on in the Gulf. All the time she was thinking of the two women, having tasted a little of each of their likely emotions herself when Erik married and loved her and later, after their island world fell apart, when he left her in New Zealand.

Erik took Sally to Malaga airport for the short hop to Madrid and then a Qatar Airways Boeing 777 to Doha and connection to Muscat. They hugged each other in silence and she wondered how she was going to endure the long journey home without breaking down in tears. Fortunately she recognised the name of the Captain. Toby came from East Devon and was an old friend of her husband Chris. They knew each other from Chris' days at the Royal Marines Commando Training Centre near Exmouth and later kite surfing in the Gulf off Muscat and Doha where Toby lived. Toby was able to come back into the cabin and chat with Sally. His humour took her out of herself and made the journey tolerable.

Coralie joined Erik for dinner and looked for any signs that his feelings for her had changed. He was very quiet and later spent an hour sitting on the verandah watching bright Jupiter climb into the night sky. The love jewel, that seemed so bright yesterday had temporarily folded back into its padded box inside his heart. He was not now sure of its future home.

George and Helen drove in through the archway of the Academy after a long journey down through France and Spain. The boys had been more of a pain than last time and Lucy and Saskia were pleased that the end of the journey had arrived. Even in the GEC truck it had been cramped in the heat of summer with the windows open one minute and then the air conditioning blasting out a few minutes later. The four young ones had sat together across the full-length rear seat and all the luggage was packed in the open truck section with a shutter-style cover.

Lucy had been able to advise Saskia what to bring and, more importantly, what to leave behind. En route this time they had cut inland to stay with an aunt near Bergerac, who had inherited a farmhouse and had converted the barns into holiday accommodation. This had given the boys a chance to let off some steam and swim all day in the pool and play with the dogs.

Helen brought some messages to Lindsay from Kate about all the food likes and dislikes that Saskia had. Lindsay took the list and put it in her pocket. Saskia would learn that everyone ate the same things at Trocadero and she would have to get used to this in the same ways as the others. Poor Ignacio had been spoilt beyond imagination before he came and had not seen a piece of smoked salmon or a Beef Wellington in the whole of the last year at the Academy.

Oksana arrived in a limousine with chauffeur and Mother Valeria. They had stopped on the way at three different four and five star hotels. Although they had talked to her on Skype, Coralie and Lindsay had not seen this coming and had no idea of the family's wealth up to this point. They offered accommodation to Valeria and the Chauffeur. It was politely refused as they used Lindsay's phone to book into the Andalucia Grand Hotel. The Chauffeur was already washing down the car whilst he waited for Oksana to ensconce herself in the Academy.

Oksana appeared quite aloof and the other girls were whispering about her. Lindsay hoped it was just nerves that caused the stand-offish impression. Erik welcomed the three new arrivals at dinner and went through the short list of rules that they had created in the first year. Erik was not a believer in rules, preferring a self-discipline approach to teenagers and a quiet chat with the offender about anything unsociable. However there were a couple of places that needed to be kept out of bounds and a ban on drink, smoking and drugs from a fitness angle.

Thomas had returned with pink hair and was obviously in the middle of a 'wanting to be noticed' teenage phase. Carmen grumbled to Erik that, whatever he was using on his head was coming off on the pillow cases and making her job more difficult.

"What are you using" he asked Thomas. "Strawberry ice cream?"

"It's only been on for two days. I don't think any more will rub off."

"If it does I have told Carmen that you will do everyone's washing."

Helen and George had driven along the coast and arranged to stay for a few days in the area so they could get some sunshine on the boys backs after a miserable wet school holidays.

"I'll get into trouble with the school headteacher when we get home" she told her husband, because we are not supposed to keep the children away in school term time."

They called in at the Academy to check that the girls were OK and loaded into the truck some of Lucy's belongings that she did not need and had left behind when she flew home for the summer break. There were already several ornate flower pots and a variety of fresh fruit in the back of the truck for the journey home. The new route back took them along the south coast of Spain, through the

144

Costa Brava, across the border and up to Carcassonne, then North through France. George, an Exeter Chiefs rugby fan, wanted to watch them play Toulouse in the group stages of the Heineken Cup on Saturday.

It was after 8 pm on the same Saturday that the tennis trio met Lollo and Lavinia at the inevitable Bar Lulu. They were relying on the seniors to get all the students into the dormitories at a reasonable hour. Erik and Coralie were not communicating at all well, and Lindsay was glad that Lollo was his usual cheerful self. Lavinia had spent a deal of August planning a project on the Moors for the students, having discovered that none of them knew anything about this advanced civilisation that had occupied North Africa and also the South of Spain and Portugal seven centuries ago. She told them some of her plans and outings connected to this whilst they sipped their drinks and watched Clarence's outrageous antics.

"A little bird told me, Mr Viking God, that you had taken everybody into a room at Newark Airport after the tennis last week and de-briefed them. Well, I think the authorities should stop all this. Corrupting a young cheeky English tennis coach, who should know better, is one thing but leading the kids astray is a disgrace." said Clarence when he had finished serving another party of guests.

Lindsay followed Coralie into the Ladies.

"Is this just 'fall out' from his meeting with Sally?" she asked.

"I don't know what has happened. It's ages since the thing they had together and I thought he was serious about me now."

Coralie confided that she was sleeping in her own room again, or actually not sleeping at all. Dark rings were beginning to show around her eyes. Having agreed to talk about it tomorrow they both returned to the table.

"How are Felix and Sink getting on with their Spanish?" Lindsay asked Lollo.

"Famously, and I have been teaching them some English, though Felix was not there yesterday. I don't think he gets on well with our food."

The next morning Carmen stopped Lindsay and asked whether she could have Felix back to help clean out the vegetable store.

"Back from where?" she asked.

"Sink said he was helping in the gardens."

"Ah. Yes. He is probably with Jorge somewhere. If I see him I'll send him to you."

At lunchtime she bumped into Carmen again who reminded her about Felix. After lunch Lindsay set out to find Jorge, who was sitting in his gardening outhouse gnawing like a Labrador on a meatbone.

"Mutton" he said, pointing the bone at her.

He had not seen Felix today or yesterday. Lindsay went back to the dining room and asked everyone to send Felix to her if they saw him.

The next day Lindsay remembered Felix and checked with Carmen that he had been to help her.

"I haven't seen him yet." Carmen said.

"Sink. Where is your brother?"

"No entiendo"

"Felix. Where?"

Sink shook his head.

"Lollo. I am sorry to interrupt your lunch but please could you quiz Sink about his Brother. No-one has seen him in the last 24 hours"

Lollo returned looking as though he had been rushing.

"He won't say but I am fairly sure he has gone."

"Gone. Gone where?" Lindsay felt a panic because she was responsible for this vulnerable young lad. Together they

146

went back to Sink and sat him down. Eventually Sink admitted that his Brother had taken his bundle of clothes and left. He didn't know, or would not say where. Erik joined the two of them and they debated calling the Police, but decided that, if he was found, he would be sent away as an illegal immigrant. Erik thought that he may return when he was hungry and suggested that there really was nothing they could do unless a clue turned up leading them to him.

Cameron had no interest in tennis. Other outdoor activities yes, but not tennis. He spent his free time riding around Marbella on his modified mountain bike. His accent speaking Spanish seemed to be a magnet for girls, who followed him trying to get him to say anything to them. He had become fairly independent, attending school lessons but doing his own thing while his Mum ran the affairs of the Trocadero. He had a number of secrets that he had accumulated during the year since they had arrived in Spain. One of the best ones was the ketch moored in the Port Marina that was owned by the father of the amazing Sofia, whose adventurous spirit was akin to his own and who was determined to discover that what she had been reading in books about men and women was true.

Sofia's father was a busy businessman, commuting to Malaga every weekday. Her mother was tied to the house and had no interest in sailing. This left their ketch and its comfortable cabin at the mercy of two fifteen year olds who were determined to explore the most popular age-old mysteries. Cameron could not believe his luck. She had everything that he could want in a girl and was willing to share it with a testosterone driven, good-looking boy from New Zealand.

Each day in the summer break Cameron would walk Sofia to the corner of her avenue, pushing his bike, and then ride home to the Trocadero where no-one ever asked him what he had been doing all day. He took a weekend job in a quayside café to cover the days when Sofia couldn't join him on the boat, and Lindsay was under the impression that he worked a few hours there all week. Sofia's mother thought her daughter was with her school friends on the weekdays, not in the arms of an enthusiastic teenage lover, discovering delights that her parents thought she was reserving for Juan Iglesias, the family's choice of husband in five or six years time.

Unfortunately for them, Father took an August day off and met up with his friends for the promised fishing trip on his ketch, his pride and joy. He discovered his other pride and joy, Sofia, cavorting naked inside the cabin and a boy they had never seen before demonstrating physical intentions, to which he had no plans to introduce his daughter for another five years. Cameron learnt more new Spanish words in the next ten minutes than he had in 12 months with Lollo, and left hurriedly carrying his shorts and trainers along the pontoon.

Cameron also had another secret. He had befriended Felix, taught him some English, and discovered that he had no intention of living in Spain. When they saw George's truck parked outside the kitchen Cameron put some food in a tin and grabbed a bottle of water, folded back the shutter top of the boot of the truck, put a double blanket on the floor of a section nearest the cab and helped Felix and his armful of clothes into the space. He then folded the shutter cover back, whispered "good luck, mate" and rode off on his bike.

George dropped Helen and the boys in Toulouse, arranging to meet them two hours later. He drove to the Toulouse home rugby ground and parked in the car park. Felix waited until he could hear what sounded like a crowd cheering and climbed out of the truck. He found a public toilet on the edge of the car park and sat down nearby listening to people talking. Realising that he was in a country that spoke neither Spanish nor English he decided to jump back in the truck and chance his luck further. The fruit that Helen had planned to distribute amongst her friends at Poppy's Chocolatiere was in bags next to the space in which Felix was lying. He began with an orange and a drink from his diminishing water bottle.

Helen had taken the boys to a Shopping Mall, which had in the centre a playground designed for up to 12 year olds. After tiring them out she took them into a couple of shops and then to have tea in a boulangerie/café.

George got back just in time to meet them at the allotted place and they set off to the pre-booked hotel forty miles North. Luke was asleep by the time they reached the small hotel and George carried him up to their family room. During the night Felix made friends with the Doberman Guard Dog and shared a baguette with him. The baker had called early and left a box of products outside the kitchen back door. Felix also enjoyed a sort of apple tart before climbing back into his hiding place.

It was nearly 10 pm when they reached the port of Dieppe and drove on board the night ferry to Newhaven. It was cold on the ferry and Felix wrapped two of the plastic bags that had held fruit around his feet and folded himself into the big blanket. He had no idea where he was and could not guess for two reasons. He had little knowledge of geography and had no idea where the car owner came from, although he thought they had talked to each other in English when outside the vehicle in Toulouse.

The cursory search of the back of the truck by Customs at Dieppe had not stretched more than halfway along and he was well covered under the blanket and behind the biggest flowerpot. The men searching were speaking in that same odd language that he had heard near the rugby stadium.

Cameron sat on the edge of the jetty at one end of the harbour with his bike laying on the ground next to him. He dreamt of Sofia's lovely smooth skin next to him and hoped she was not in too much trouble. He also wondered whether Felix had made it to England and vowed to spend more time with Sink, who was probably missing Felix and wondering where he had finished up. He half expected Sofia's Dad to turn up at the Academy looking for him, so decided to stay away as much as possible for a week or two.

Felix woke up with cramp in his arm and a pain in his shoulder. The family were getting into the cab again although he could see through the cover that it was still dark. The truck bumped off the ferry and clattered along ramps. Next the vehicle was whizzing along roads again. He tried to peer out of the gap when it stopped but could only see green fields in the dawn light. Felix had learnt to read before the war and tried to make out one of the signs. It said 'Road Works'. He thought about this town and which country it could be in.

They stopped in a car park outside a big café. Felix could smell the cooking and it made him salivate. He tried another bag of fruit. They were custard apples, or cherimoyas as they were known in Spain. His was squashy but delicious. It made a mess of the blanket as he had to eat it lying down, the black pips were now all over the truck. He dare not get out as there were other cars and people about, but he was bursting to go to the loo. Eventually he remembered that the water bottle was now empty, so he found it and filled it up again.

After half an hour everyone returned. This time they were arguing. Felix was sure it was English. He had learnt some English from Lollo and from Cameron and also remembered some words from Sierra Leone when the English soldiers came. The truck drove on for another two hours before there was a twisty road and they stopped and seemed to be sloping downwards. A lot more talking went on and then it went quiet. He peered through the gap. There was nobody in sight at the angle he could see, but it looked like a big cow about 50 metres away. He stretched and climbed out. Every part of his body was stiff and aching. It was colder than in Spain. Felix had heard that England was cold. Maybe he was in England. He leant back into the truck and took the rest of the bag of oranges and his clothes and set off down the lane beside where they had stopped.

George called from the truck

"Darling, I am afraid your fruit has not survived the journey well. Those custard apples that you knew in Qatar have had a bashing."

He talked to himself. 'I thought I had thrown out that old blanket. God, there's even half a bottle of orange juice the kids have thrown in here'.

He went to look around the farm and check that William had cleaned and sterilised the milking parlour properly.

Felix walked down the road, listening for cars. Twice he had to scurry into the hedge in order not to be discovered. He walked past a driveway to a big house and a funny green tower and then on down towards a river he could see just beyond the bottom of the hill. Then there was a village. All the people were white. He moved quickly through the village and out along a road than ran beside the river. After about 400 metres he came to a little bridge over the river which flowed into what looked like a harbour with small boats moored in it and on the bank beside it. The sun had come out. Felix sat down by a wall and ate one of the orang-es, resting his head on his bundle of clothes.

THIRTEEN

The situation between Erik and Coralie grew steadily worse with Erik in a sort of uncertain fog, caught between two strongly repelling sets of emotions and Coralie distraught at the speed she had gone from a scene of euphoric love to one of seemingly irretrievable desolation. Such depths of feeling only served to heighten the senses so that everything between them became data for analysis. Each was looking at the other for signs that the barriers had dissolved, with Lindsay looking at both and praying that the volcano would not erupt and that the love between the two of them would prevail.

School lessons began and the new girls began to settle in and make friends. Erik engaged the PE teacher from the school that kindly gave them use of the science labs to perk up the fitness of each of the students after summer holidays of too many bounty bars and ice creams. Carmen found she had no time for ironing any more with the three extra girls to care for, so it was decided that they were all old enough and capable enough to iron their own clothes. Nicolas quickly managed to burn holes in two tennis shirts and a pair of Kaz's shorts.

In the staff area Erik was looking forlornly at a pile of washed, but as yet unironed clothes that Carmen had left on his chair.

"Why don't you iron them?" asked Coralie, trying to make conversation.

"Are you addressing Erik?" asked Lindsay "He thinks an iron is only something you use on a golf course."

Out on the tennis courts in the afternoons Lindsay arranged a fun tournament with small prizes between the four youngest girls and another between the four seniors. They each played three matches in a round robin. Then, when that was finished, she tried doubles combinations, shuffling the packs within each of the two groups of four. Saskia wanted to play doubles with Lucy and was told to be patient because Lucy and Gabby had proved a formidable duo last year. Padmini had never played doubles before and had to learn from scratch. Petra, already proven in mixed doubles, made a good partnership with Agnieska, with Aga playing on the backhand court to maximise use of her topspin winners. Although they were younger they beat Soo-Jin and Oksana every time. The older two had not yet created a friendship and were still wary of each other, both socially and on court.

On the clay courts Coralie was doing something similar with the boys and trying all combinations in an attempt to give Dan and Torgny some stiff competition. The only real test they managed to create was when Kurt and Erik decided to play together against them. Coralie offered to give Erik a massage after the game to loosen up his now rarely tested muscles, but he declined leaving her quite upset for the rest of the afternoon.

Everyone went swimming in the sea after tennis, racing each other down the lane to the beach and making a cavalry charge into the water. The Mediterranean was still warm after the summer. Few had brought towels so they lay drying in the rays of the setting sun. They laughed as a holidaymaker ladies pink bathing hat floated by.

"It's Thomas' hair. It's come off" called Nacho, grabbing the passing hat and putting it on.

Coralie sat on the sand next to Erik.

"What's happening to us? I can't go on like this much more" she said in a low voice "It's breaking me up."

"I don't know" he replied. "I just don't know"

That evening she ironed all his clothes and then took them up to his room. Erik was probably sitting quietly on the verandah again, lost in thought. She took the clothes into his room and laid them on the bed. On the bedside table was a slightly crumpled painting of a woman. She could not resist turning it around, and immediately recognised its excellent likeness of Sally, whom she had briefly seen the day they had returned from New York.

Coralie made the decision in a split second whilst holding that picture. She strode back to her bedroom, packed the biggest bag she had with a variety of clothes and shoes, and five minutes later was downstairs in the dining room. There was no-one else there. Lindsay was probably in the girls' dormitory with Saskia and Padmini, checking that they were in a happy space. Coralie took out a piece of paper from the computer copier and wrote a long message. She folded it and wrote Lindsay on the other side of the folded paper leaving it pinned under the flower vase in the centre of the table. Taking the bag out to Ethel she threw it in the back and drove out through the archway with tears in her eyes.

Lindsay found the message when she sat down at the table in the morning with her first tea of the day:-

My very dear friend Lindsay,

I am so sorry to do this to you when you have been so kind in so many ways to me, but I just cannot go on pretending everything will change and be all right. Erik has disappeared into the mist with his Sally.

I didn't come here looking for a relationship; only to do my best for you both and our lovely Academy, but the love has become so much a part of me that I just can't stay without it.

I will call you when I get home.

Love from Coralie '

"Oh. Shit! The volcano has blown." said Lindsay out loud.

"Bloody Erik. How the hell do we cope now?"

Almost as if he had heard, Erik came through the door at that moment. She pushed the letter over to him and walked out of the room.

Lindsay returned after giving Erik time for the message to sink in and for her anger to subside enough to hold a sensible conversation. Erik was staring into his black coffee.

"It seems I have screwed up" he muttered

"It's the screwing that has caused all the trouble. I knew this would end in tears. That poor girl idolised you from the first day you put your shaggy head into her Sports Centre two thousand miles away. I just hope she can drive safely across Europe. God knows what she will do when she gets there with no job, no flat and all her hopes pinned out here in our business and on you, you inconsiderate shit."

Erik didn't answer. He was beginning to see that his morose behaviour had hit Coralie much harder that he had realised may happen.

Lindsay poured milk on a bowl of cereal.

"You are going to have to work your butt off now to keep the coaching on programme because I have meetings with the Bank and our Accountant in the next few days. Do you realise that that girl was working about 70 hours a week to support us? A bloody site more than your darling Sally living the life of a princess in the Gulf."

"That's not fair" Erik responded. "They are completely different."

"Anyway, what has she got that Coralie hasn't in bucket loads? And me! I'll bet you didn't walk around like a zombie for years after you sent me back home in New Zealand after our months of whispered devotion"

"You were great and I missed you for longer than you knew. I didn't test the water with anyone else for a long time. I think I need to get my head together or go and get drunk or something"

"You, Mr Viking God (as Clarence calls you) need to get down to rearranging our tennis schedules, and then work on getting our best coach back here and happy, even if you have to jump on a plane and fetch her."

He picked up the daily paper and then put it down again, wondering why he couldn't put Sally out of his mind. There was no future in re-enacting a few weeks of a perfect union when she was now in the arms of her first and loyal love. It had been a mistake to have taken on Padmini. Without her he would never have seen Sally again, now it may be several meetings every year.

However he couldn't blame the little girl for his behaviour. She had had a tough enough early life already, being one of the thirty or more orphans in Sammy's orphanage in South India before Sally's son Greg had arranged for them to adopt her as his little sister. He could see her head in Lollo's classroom learning Spanish in order to live comfortably in the third country she had experienced in her short twelve years.

That evening Erik went to sit in Clarence's bar. He didn't want to be alone. Just to be there, eat some dinner, and watch the evening entertainment centred around Clarence. The flamboyant owner came across to take his food order.

"The sole is good tonight." he suggested.

"OK. Only a small one with a salad please."

"'Ere. What have you done? The word on the street is

that that delicious female has buggered off and left you in the poo-poo"

"How do you know that, Clarence? We haven't even told any of the staff yet."

"My advice is don't. Just get your skates on and bring her back. She is a cheeky little number and just what you need to keep you young and all the sports reps turning up to give you handouts just to watch her bouncing around the courts."

"Yes, maybe, my friend. Maybe I should."

"We'll get some food inside you first. Bet you haven't eaten today. Can't have you wasting away. Come on, drink up." he said to the next table as he returned to the bar.

Helen's son Callum tried to get up to date with all his schoolwork by Friday evening so that he could spend the weekend on Viti Levu. He studied at home until 9.30pm, put his books in his school bag and his sailing clothes out for an early start on Saturday. The forecast was good. Sunny periods and 15 knots from the south. Could be a good beat out into the channel and a run home. George was out early in the milking shed with his herd of Friesian cows. He waved to Callum as he rode away on his bike, sailing shoe laces tied together and the shoes slung around his neck. He had come back on the school bus yesterday with Penny Thomas from the village. Penny has changed very quickly from a nutcase with teeth braces into a disturbingly shapely sixteen year old, and he hadn't really noticed. In a rash moment he asked her if she would like to crew his boat on Saturday and told her she only could come if she brought the picnic.

He took the tiny dinghy that he had left tied to the rail beside the steps from the pathway opposite the boat park and sculled out to Viti. He tied the dinghy to the mooring buoy and jumped across to scramble up the bow. Most sailors waited, climbed over the lower stern and tied the dinghy at the same time as they released the main craft from the mooring, but Callum was younger and more agile. Erik may not have approved but he enjoyed sailing Viti solo, comfortably securing the rudder with a length of rope and hopping along the deck to adjust the jib. He hadn't yet tried to handle the spinnaker alone though some of the long distance soloists did.

He had arrived an hour before Penny in order to tidy the gear up, having left a muddle when he came in late last Sunday. Nobody locks up a moored boat in East Devon. The locals all trust each other and watch out for each other. In Seaton Callum was well liked and respected for his endeavour. He opened the hatch and stepped into the cabin to be amazed by looking into a very black face with tousled hair.

"Where did you come from? Have you been here long?"

The face just said "Felix"

"Hi Felix. I'm Callum" he had assumed Felix was a name and not a greeting of some sort.

Callum took in the scene in the cabin. A tarpaulin that Felix had been sleeping under, the wrapper from his reserve packet of chocolate hobnobs and the smell of someone who has not had a change of clothes for a while.

"Have you run away from home?"

Felix looked a little bewildered as he tried to understand.

"Home. Where?" asked Callum

"Espana"

"Spain? How did you get here?"

"Car. Many kilometres. Ship big". said Felix

"Family? Mama, Papa?" Callum thought he was only about ten or eleven.

"Muerto"

Callum thought that meant dead as dead was 'mort' in French.

"Crikey Felix, you must be knackered". He noticed his trainers were wet and drying by the small window. He made a swimming motion with his arms and pointed to the boy. Felix nodded.

He said to himself 'You must have been freezing at night'

Callum decided to continue to prepare the boat for a sail whilst he thought what he could do with Felix. He was probably one of those illegal immigrants that the news was often reporting and politicians always seemed to be banging on about.

He was untying the securing ropes from the rolled up mainsail when Penny called from the quayside. He told her to wait there. Having secured the dinghy to the buoy he made the decision to fetch her in Viti Levu, which meant he was going to give a ride to Felix. Felix was looking through the cabin window at Penny and realising that there would soon be another person to discover him. He contemplated jumping into the water again and swimming to safety when he noticed that they were moving nearer to shore.

"Come down the steps and I'll help you on board when we come alongside" Callum called to Penny.

The yacht came in smoothly with Callum on the tiller. He had manoeuvred her on jib only. As Penny stepped on board Felix stepped off and ran up the steps to the roadside.

"Stop Felix, wait" Callum noticed the picnic Penny was carrying with a French loaf sticking out of the top of the Sainsburys Bag for Life that held the food.

"Look, Felix, food."

Felix was very hungry, having eaten only hobnobs and oranges in the two days he had been on the yacht. He reluctantly returned and stepped back on board.

Callum let the jib take her out into the harbour again and threw a rope around one of the unused buoys further towards the sea from his own. He went below and found three life jackets and helped Penny and Felix into one each, putting another around himself.

Penny was dying to know who the extra crew member

was. Callum explained as they moved out past 'the Haven' and out into the sea swell. He beckoned Felix and together they pulled the mainsail up the mast and secured it, feeding the sheets through cleats on each varnished side and back towards the steering well.

"Fishing?" Felix asked.

Callum shook his head. "Just sailing".

He noticed Felix was shivering and took him back into the cabin, removed his life jacket pushed him into a warm oilskin, and replaced the jacket. Felix nodded his thanks.

Callum took the tiller back from Penny who had just had her first taste of steering a boat in a straight line and the three of them all made themselves more comfortable on the wooden seats behind the cabin. They were heading out to sea on a broad reach.

"I need your help with ideas about what to do with Felix" Callum said to Penny.

"He only looks about ten." said Penny

"I am doce years of age" said Felix gravely

"He says he is ten" said Callum

"No, replied Penny. That's twelve. Diez is ten"

"Espanol?" asked Penny.

"Sierra Leone"

"Is that a mountain range in Spain.?"

"No, you twit" she said. "It's a country in Africa."

"I thought he looked more African than Spanish. But he told me earlier he had come from Spain. Maybe he came over from Africa before."

The sun suddenly came out and the wind dropped. They were sailing parallel to the coast and Penny noticed that Felix was spending a lot of time looking at her bag.

"What had he had to eat today?" she asked.

"A packet of chocolate hobnobs that I was going to give to you in exchange for a kiss later."

She blushed. "You wanted to kiss me"

"Well, I did, but I don't have anything to trade with now he has gutsed all my biscuits. Mind you, you will have to pay a forfeit for calling me a twit."

Penny brought out the picnic that she had spent an hour carefully making before she set off this morning. Her father had been pulling her leg about the trouble she had taken.

"That's my special gala pie going in that tin. He must be good looking or rich for you to be allowed to give him that for lunch."

Felix was now concentrating very hard on trying to be patient until he was offered some of the food. He smiled as he took a sandwich. Penny passed one to Callum and took one herself. Neither of them had put sandwich to mouth before Felix had finished his. They caught each other's eyes and Callum nodded for her to give him more. He ate the entire Gala pie, another two sandwiches, two pieces of Dundee cake and half of a large cantaloupe melon that she had cut into slices. He also drank a whole bottle of orange and mango squash. Penny and Callum were quite happy to eat what was left and to see Felix's face breaking into a smile every two minutes.

"I am afraid all the cold drink has gone, Callum. Would you like tea or tea?"

she grinned, unscrewing the top of the silver thermos flask.

"Felix, what are we going to do with you?" asked Callum.

"Let's break the law and keep him with us" said Penny "He is our secret."

"You mean keep him on the boat and bring food every day. I suppose he could stay on Viti until she comes out of the water, but there is no heating. No loo either. He will have to do it over the side."

"Is that what you do? I'm never swimming in the harbour again." said Penny.

"No. We will have to tell someone so that he can find a place to live and go to school and get a job and stuff. I thought I would go and talk to that vicar who makes the chocolates and ask her."

Penny said. "Yes. I like her. She even swears sometimes. She won't get him sent back to one of the bad countries like they sometimes do."

They pulled up the sails again after the picnic and ran before the light wind back into Seaton Harbour, moored and cleaned up Viti Levu. Penny tidied up Felix and combed his hair and they all three walked back to Axmouth pushing Callum's bike.

"So, you came to see me on a Saturday because you think I only work on a Sunday, did you?"

The Rev. Penelope Duguid stood at the vicarage door looking from one of the visitors to the other. You had better come in. They told Felix's story, as much as they knew, and asked what they should do now, and made her promise to think of some solution that didn't mean he had to be deported.

"I'll try my best to think of one but, if I can't, we may have to enlist the help of the authorities. He can stay here with me in the vicarage. There are lots of bedrooms and I only use one of them. Leave him with me and come back and see him tomorrow, if you can in the morning, when I have to take a Church service.

The three of them, using a mixture of English, Spanish and sign language, managed to explain to Felix what they had planned. He just nodded.

Callum took Penny home.

"It wasn't the day I had planned. We were supposed to sail along the coast and eat the picnic on a beach. Maybe Branscombe or Salcombe Regis." said Callum.

"I loved it. We had quite an adventure with Felix. I'm going to keep quiet about him for a few days until we know he is OK."

"Do you want to go out with me again? I mean, you still have to pay that forfeit for calling me a twit"

"Of course I do, you twit. Anyway I'll see you at the vicarage tomorrow morning." Penny ran indoors because she could see both parents and her brother pretending not to watch them through the window.

FOURTEEN

The Viking was not feeling very Godlike this morning. He had drunk too much of the single malt whisky that Nacho's parents had given him for his Birthday and had a headache. He very much wanted Coralie back but did not feel it fair to chase after her if he couldn't promise 100% of his love. He still could not calculate how much of that resided elsewhere.

As he sat at the breakfast table nursing his head there was a scream and Gabby rushed by the window followed by Nicholas brandishing a tennis racquet. Lindsay walked in shortly afterwards.

"Gabby offered Nicholas the boiled egg she had cooked and changed her mind about eating. He carefully buttered a piece of bread and sat down to his egg in eager anticipation only to find that it was the shell of the one Gabby had just eaten turned upside down." she laughed. "Sometimes I love these kids."

Erik cheered up a little.

"I overhead the four mermaids (this is how Erik referred to the four youngest girls, who all swam like fish) discussing which country they had decided to play for in a few years time. Padmini was going to represent Oman because they don't play a lot of tennis and she would be No 1. Gabby decided she would choose Vatican City for the same reason and because everyone there wore long skirts all the time, and therefore couldn't run around the courts as fast as she could. Then Lucy remembered she used to live in Qatar, so she would be their No 1. Saskia told them all not to be ridiculous. She was going to play for Great Britain because she already was a good friend of Judy Murray who picked the team. I had to creep away for laughing."

"Does she know Judy Murray?"

"Yes. Judy looked after her for a couple of hours at Wimbledon when I went to do a commentary on the first Saturday this year."

"Did you take her up there for the day?

"Yes. I thought she deserved a reward for her determination and for writing me that letter."

"You are a nice man sometimes. I'll bet you gave her a great day out when you could have been meeting up with all your old mates"

"They all thought she was my secret daughter! I did manage to wangle a sponsorship package for her in the blink of an eye. Which reminds me, we will have a visit from Charlie Mills who is keen to pick up all the students as soon as their current contracts runout" added Erik.

"Charlie Mills has been trying to get his hands on my contract for years. I always wear thicker underwear when he is around."

"Then you are the one to entertain him. Use all your charms to get the most out of Nike. It will also keep Pepe from taking you for granted. Charlie will wine and dine you at the best restaurants in town. He may even offer you a naughty weekend at a five star on the Costa Packet."

Charlie didn't call, he just turned up in an Audi he had hired at the Airport. He liked to arrive unannounced to see that his Company's money was being used to its best effect and, rumour had it that he kept a book of notes as to who wore what and when. He produced this when the player's agent was trying to negotiate a better deal.

"I have come all way to see you Lindsay and to offer you something to make your life much sweeter."

"You can keep all that inside your pyjamas, Charlie, and then tell me what Nike has to offer."

"Let's have a look around and me have a small break in the sunshine, whilst I see what is left in the budget"

That evening Charlie and Lollo struck up an instant friendship and enjoyed a hilarious evening with Clarence and the first recorded appearance of Rex. Clarence left the bar to Rex and joined the two of them at the table.

"Hun, bring me a gin and tonic will you? I am going to relax for ten minutes after slaving over the cooker for half the day."

"Hun, Hun? Do you call him that all the time?" asked Lollo

"It's short for 'honey' isn't it? But nobody else uses that expression." added Charlie. I'll give you this twenty euro note if you can tell me one other person who calls his partner 'Hun'"

"Mrs Attila" said Clarence and snatched the note.

Callum decided he would tell Helen about Felix. He doubted they would do anything hasty.

"Mum, George" he called when the boys had gone to bed "I have a problem I want to run past you". He told them everything he knew about Felix. They had no suspicion that it was they who had brought the lad 1500 miles across Europe.

The adults asked all the expected questions. How old is he? How did he get into the country? Where are the grown ups that must have been with him? Where has he been before he came to Seaton? Callum was unable to answer much of this as he had not managed to find out more than Felix's name and origin.

"I think you have done the best thing by taking him to Poppy. She is the most level headed person around these parts and will know what to do." George remarked. There will be a way in which he can stay in the UK if he wants to. The Government won't send a twelve year old back to another country unless his relatives are looking for him and want him home.

"His Mum and Dad are dead he told us, so he is an orphan."

"All the more reason for the authorities to keep and care for him" said Helen.

Because it was Sunday Poppy had not been able to make any progress and come up with a solution for Felix, but she had raided the boxes of a forthcoming jumble sale and found some different clothes for him to wear. He was looking clean and happy and his trainers had spent the early morning in the washing machine.

On Monday Helen went down to join her friends at Poppy's Chocolatiere and sat with Bronwen whilst Rachel served behind the counter and Poppy put her head around the kitchen door. Helen was not sure whether to bring up the subject of Felix in front of the others, but it seemed that Poppy had already sworn them to secrecy when she asked Helen if she had heard anything strange from Callum in the last 24 hours.

"Do you mean Felix?" she whispered

"Ah. You do know. Good. I have told the others on pain of a chocolate ban if they speak a word outside these walls. Felix has just finished his breakfast here before we opened, and now gone back to the vicarage. He stayed the last two nights and is doing well, though I think he is a little mystified by the bathroom and the toilet cistern."

"What are your plans for him?" Helen asked.

"First, try to find a Spanish speaker who can gather some more information about him. We don't know whether he is one of a group of refugees or whether his family members are looking for him"

"How will you do that?"

"I phoned Julio Mendes from the Grammar School. He is Spanish, although he teaches Chemistry. He will come over after school this afternoon and talk to Felix."

Julio came and was rewarded with a plate of assorted chocolates and cakes with his coffee. He spent nearly an hour with Felix and then sat down with the four ladies who had re-convened their meeting at five o'clock.

"He actually doesn't speak a lot of Spanish. We threw some English into the conversation and even French because, where he comes from is surrounded by small countries that have a French base to their languages."

"Great" said Poppy impatiently. "What did he say?"

"He thinks he is twelve years old but doesn't know his birth date. He was caught up with the civil unrest in Sierra Leone around the diamond town of Makeni and lived amongst the rebels with his brother"

"What happened to his brother?" enquired Bronwen. "-Did they travel together?"

"I'll tell you later. He and his brother found their way to Spain, up the west side of the Sahara and, with others, on to an Island called Parsley Island and then by ship to Spain. Then he was taken to live and work in a house where they played tennis all day."

The four looked at each other, shook heads and frowned.

"He befriended an English boy who, one day bundled him in the back of a car. He travelled for days without any idea where he was. Then on another ship still in the back of the car or van. The car stopped finally near here and he got out and decided to hide in a boat in the harbour. He doesn't know where he is and was delighted when I told him this was definitely England. For some reason everyone seems to want to come here. I think it must be to get some of these delicious chocolates." He put a fourth one into his mouth.

"Thanks so much Julio. Now we have something to work on. We know he is alone and no-one is currently looking for him. So much for the border checks at the ports."

"Callum said his parents are both dead. What happened to his brother" asked Helen.

"I didn't ask him that, but he probably is still in the house where no-one works and they all play tennis every day." replied Julio.

"Julio, can you keep our secret until we can do something helpful for this poor lad?" asked Poppy.

"My lips are sealed." Now I must go home and mow the lawn. It's going to rain tomorrow."

Sink was lonely and frightened. He and Felix had always been together since they had arrived home and found the hut ransacked and their parents lying dead outside the back door. Felix had made all the decisions and found him food. Now he was alone and in a place where people did strange things. They only seemed to go to school in the mornings and ran around outside for the rest of the day. The food was good and they were kind to him, especially Cameron who brought him sweets and crisps. But Felix was the only one who understood his language and he could talk to for more than a few words.

Cameron quickly realised that Sink was in trouble. He came up to his room one morning and looked into the tear-streaked face of a worried little boy. He was only nine or ten with no Mum or Dad and now his brother had gone. After school each day when Sink had finished his cleaning job he took the little boy around the town with him. Nobody seemed surprised to see them together and no-one asked where Sink had come from. Cameron told Lindsay what he was doing and she just told him to be careful and tell anyone, who asked, that Sink was a friend who was staying on holiday. Cameron found him a bike that was being thrown out because the boy had been given a new one for his birthday. They began to ride around the town together.

Jorge also began to look out for Sink and asked whether he could help in the grounds instead of cleaning the office area. Sink became an enthusiastic gardener and began to care for one particular part of the grounds as his own. Jorge encouraged this and left this part entirely to the little boy, teaching him the names of the shrubs and flowers. One day he told Lindsay that he was going to take him home for tea. Jorge and Maria's children were now in their twenties with children of their own. It was not long before they asked whether Sink could come and live with them. Lindsay and Erik decided to put extra into Jorge's wage packet each week to cover the costs of feeding their newly adopted son. Sink began to show that he had the same infectious smile as his brother. Maria began to teach him to read and write Spanish because it didn't seem possible to arrange for him to go to school without birth documents and lots of people asking difficult questions.

Whilst the Felix saga occupied the thoughts and concerns of an increasing number of the residents of the small village of Axmouth a small red Peugeot called Ethel drove down the nearby main road towards Ottery St Mary. Coralie didn't know what she was going to tell her parents, who had been delighted when she landed such a good job in her beloved sports world, and even more pleased to hear that, at 29, she was in love with a well-respected man. Although he was thirteen years older they didn't see that as a problem.

'Better than some of the long haired wallies she used to bring home when she was at College,' thought her Dad.

Coralie had run out of tears and tissues by the time Ethel had crossed the border into Western France. She stopped at a café where there was no milk and drank a black coffee, which only reminded her more of Erik and all the hopes she had pinned on the future of their magical affair. She was cross with the waiter for spending more time peering down the front of her blouse than serving the 'croque monsieur' that she had ordered. She was not in the mood to flirt in return and wondered if she ever would be again.

It was not her day, or even her week. She missed the fast catamaran ferry at Cherbourg by 20 minutes and had to book on the Barfleur with Brittany Ferries to Poole in Dorset. She would land nearer home but the journey would take longer. She took a blanket on board with her and curled up on one of the reclining seats to sleep off the long drive from Marbella.

Coralie and Ethel arrived at Poole Harbour at 8 am. The sky was overcast and threatened rain. She felt much the same herself, overcast by cares that did not exist a few short weeks ago. She had filled up with petrol in Cherbourg as it was twenty per cent cheaper than in the UK so Ethel was able to trundle home without another stop. She stopped in Lyme Regis to draw some money out of a Bank ATM. The machine paused and asked her to repeat the PIN number. This she duly did and it paid out the £100. She was dividing the money to put half into her bag and half into her jacket pocket when a police squad car, complete with blue flashing light, came to a halt beside her.

"Good Morning, Madam" said the tall policeman as he stepped out of the car and donned his hat at the same time. "Have you just used the cash machine here?"

"Yes"

"Please come and sit in the back of the car"

"But….but I was only parked for two minutes to get some money"

"We are not concerned about your parking. What is the problem?"

"No problem" answered a bewildered Coralie.

"No-one is making you draw the money?" his colleague continued.

"No. I am alone with Ethel"

"And this Ethel is not putting you under any undue pressure?"

"No. Ethel is the car" she added sheepishly.

"Tell me then. Why did you use the emergency pin code?"

"I don't know anything about an emergency code"

They confirmed that everything was normal and she was only drawing cash to spend in the normal way. Then they explained that she had put in her PIN number backwards and that was known as a call for help when the cardholder was under duress to pay money to a stranger.

"Oh. God" she said. "I have been in Spain and haven't used the pin for months. I must have put it in the wrong way around."

"Well, at least we know the system works. It's the first call out we have had at the station for this reason. Drive home safely"

They drove away and Coralie went towards her own car feeling like a crook under the gaze of half a dozen shoppers.

'Whatever else is going to happen to me' she thought as she drove the last miles to her parents' home in Ottery.

Her Dad had recently retired as an official in the offices of East Devon District Council. He and his wife sat with a cup of tea and listened to their, once again tearful, daughter tell her tale of woe.

"What will you do now?" asked her Mother.

"I really don't know, Mum. Everything seemed to be so good when I came to see you in the summer. Maybe I can find something in one of the care homes around here."

She lay out on their sofa and closed her eyes whilst her Dad pottered in the garden and Mum prepared some lunch for the three of them. She thought of her lovely quartet of 12/13 year olds that she had hopes of steering towards great things in the future, and mothering them at tournaments around the globe. She thought of Clarence. Would she ever meet anyone again who was so rude about her figure. She thought of Erik and the fantastic feeling of being held in his strong arms. Then she took her phone out of her bag and called Lindsay.

"Madam" Carmen said to Lindsay, who knew this must be serious because Carmen only called her that on formal occasions.

"Madam, do you know what I have just found lying on my new clean towels on the bottom shelf of the linen cupboard?"

Lindsay thought 'cockroaches' 'tabby cat' 'two kilos of tomatoes'? She looked up from the Invoice File and shook her head.

"Luciana and that Swedish Tawny!"

"You mean they were…….they were……..inside the cupboard?"

"I told her you would dismiss her and that I would tell her mother."

Lindsay put down her pen and reluctantly stood up

"OK Carmen, leave it to me."

"What is it with these bloody Scandinavians?" she said over lunch at the prestigious Marbella Club with Charlie.

"They just cannot seem to keep their trousers on"

"What's has Erik been up to this time?"

"Not Erik. One of the randy students has lured the cook into the linen cupboard and has been exploring her dumplings"

Charlie burst out laughing so suddenly that a piece of bread escaped his mouth and nearly landed in the massive hair of a mature lady sitting at the next table.

"I suppose that will be the end of another promising sports career. He is not one of mine is he? If he is, I think I'll increase his money on account of using his initiative"

"It's serious, Charlie. I need to do something about it. Luciana's parents will want to think she is pure and untouched by human hand when they take her down the aisle to be welded to the latest downtown heartthrob."

"Not much chance of that these days. They are all on the pill at 14 where I live."

"It's still different in some places in the world." Lindsay ventured. "In India, Samuraja once told me, they lock their daughters indoors when they come of age and only let them out on their wedding day."

"How is Sammy these days? He did well for my Company in the nineties when I was just a grasshopper"

"Married, with a dozen kids. Our youngest girl here came through his orphanage in India. Padmini. She would be a good candidate for you"

"She's one of mine already. Bill collected her somewhere in the Middle East when she won something."

"Oman. She won above her age in Oman." said Lindsay.

"So, do you think I should sack the cook and send home the student?"

"No. They were only following nature's rich legacy. Doing exactly what you and I would have liked to have been doing twenty years ago if we'd had the chance."

Lindsay told Luciana to keep her knickers on in future and, if there was one repeat, she Lindsay would go straight to her house and inform her parents that their daughter was a trollope (although she had to look up the Spanish for 'trollope' in the dictionary). Torgny was sentenced to iron Carmen's sheets and towels for a week and not to take advantage of the innocent locals, who were brought up to reserve their talents for more permanent relationships later in life.

"Coralie, love." said her Dad at the lunch table. "Why don't you take a couple of weeks off, jump back in Ethel, and go down and stay with David in France. It will be easy now you are used to gadding about Europe. He called last evening and said it was lovely down there now. The flowers were all out and most things are shut down until the ski season begins in the middle of December."

David was her brother, who from a small boy always wanted to ski. He worked now as a ski instructor in the village of Les Carroz in the French Alps and stayed on painting and decorating houses in the summer. Les Carroz was near Chamonix and the tunnel through Mont Blanc into Italy. It seemed David was looking after and living in a large house whilst the owners, whom he had taught to ski, were spending the summer in the West Indies. There was plenty of accommodation.

Coralie agreed to go provided her Mum and Dad came too. Neither of them had been out of England since her Dad was sent to Cyprus during his nine years in the army after he left school.

This time Ethel carried a heavier load all the way up to Dover and chose the sea crossing rather than the Channel tunnel because Mum thought it would be claustrophobic. Dad drove some of the way, his first time on the right side of the road and found the French habit of tailgating a little annoying. They skirted Paris and followed the map to within spitting distance of the border into Switzerland. Coralie took over and they found Cluses and then began the steep climb up the road towards Sammoens, Les Carroz and Flaine, three of the popular ski resorts in the French part of the Alps.

"This piece was the last climb on one of the stages of the Tour de France in 2014 " said Coralie. She negotiated another hairpin bend. "The winner rode up here to Les Carroz almost as quickly as we are getting there in Ethel. Those guys are incredibly fit."

"They are all on those diabolical steroids aren't they?" said Mum from the back.

Coralie thought that it was a shame that the sport and the clean competitors had been tainted with this drug tag.

"Actually, Mum, the word is anabolic, and they are not all on them."

From fairly bland and uninteresting buildings down in the valley they suddenly found themselves surrounded by chocolate box wooden chalets, large and small, bedecked with flower baskets. Green meadows stretched away from the road and small forests of conifers. Delicate flowers were growing amongst the trees and in the gardens of the houses. They passed a petrol station and a small supermarket and then entered a village of mainly wooden buildings with a stone set of offices in the middle of a triangle of roadway. There was a variety of shops selling food and ski equipment, bistros and restaurants, property agents and two bars.

Coralie parked Ethel in the village centre and called David. He appeared in two minutes from behind them and greeted his family warmly.

"This is going to be a great holiday for you all." he said.

At exactly the time Coralie was hugging her big brother, Erik was strapping himself into seat 12k on the Easyjet Airbus A320 to London Gatwick to try to persuade her to return to Marbella.

FIFTEEN

Having twice refused Charlie's offer to join him in his room at the Pearl Hotel for dessert, and having a good guess at what that dessert may comprise, Lindsay began to push him for what he was prepared to offer to let them persuade the students and their relatives change allegiance to his Company. With the exception of Kurt, who had now turned 18 they all needed parents to sign any contracts.

"I know you are only wining and wooing me for economic reasons and not for the irresistibility of my stimulating company." said Lindsay "I was not born yesterday."

"Maybe not. But you look as though you were born a few years later this evening than you are claiming."

"Bollocks you creep. Come on. What is on offer?"

"Three years. We pick up all travel bills for the kids and two supporting staff members. You all stay free of charge in our nominated hotels. I want a minimum of fourteen on my books, that is eleven more than now. We pay a coach to fill in for Coralie until such time as you find a replacement, providing you start looking tomorrow. After three years of uninterrupted devotion to my label we pay for you to build a practise grass court. You will have to maintain it. Oh, And you have to sleep with me for a week like you nearly did twenty years ago when we were both green round the gills."

"Get stuffed, you old ram. Anyway I am a happily married woman."

"Never?"

"Yup. I have been married to the same man for over twenty years."

"Who? When? You're kidding me."

"Erik. I am Mrs Lindsay Eriksson. And that is the truth."

Maria Carmelita came across the room to greet Lindsay as Charlie digested this latest piece of news.

"Lindsay. How good to see you relaxing a little. And my Nacho, how is he this week?"

Charlie muttered "Eating a banana half an hour ago."

She turned and looked down her nose at him

"And you are?"

"Totally pissed off, if you must know" said Charlie.

Charlie spent the evening with Lollo and they both got embarrassingly drunk at Clarence's bar. Rex had to pour them both into a taxi and then go along himself to almost carry each of them into their separate accommodation.

Lollo arrived in the school staff room the next morning clutching an ice cold bag of rice, that he had taken from the freezer, to his head.

"That Charlie is a bad influence on me, a sober upstanding citizen of Andalucia". The rest of the room nodded in agreement, not altogether agreeing.

On the way to breakfast in the Pearl Hotel Charlie looked pale and drawn.

"Are you sick, Mr Mills?" asked the Receptionist on duty.

"It's the Spanish teacher from the Trocadero. He's a bad influence on me. Introduced me to the local brandy. He is a menace."

He walked on towards the restaurant and she smiled knowingly.

Twenty minutes later Charlie was holding his head and talking into his iPad.

"I've got a big fish almost hooked here in Spain. Can you find a good coach who has just been offloaded by one of the top players and needs a holiday near the beach? Male or female. Get them to call me a.s.a.p. Thanks Jill."

Lollo was sitting on a bench in the Trocadero grounds at 1pm talking to Jorge about Sink. Although Sink could not go to school, between them Lollo and Maria had him speaking good Spanish quite quickly. He would leave his gardening job and join Lollo's class every time Lollo took the youngest students. Gabby was learning fastest, probably because the language used the same Latin roots for many words as did Italian. They all enjoyed Lollo's class because he was funny, although today, every time he laughed he held his head.

Charlie arrived and Jorge moved back to his gardening.

"You are bad for me, Charlie Mills. I will have to take you to the Bar Lulu this evening to teach you a lesson."

"Not again, Lollo. I think I was put to bed last night by a seventeen stone gay docker."

"Did he stay?"

"No, he bloody didn't."

Saskia and Padmini appeared and began knocking balls across the net to each other.

"Those two are both mine" said Charlie.

"They must have been by different mothers" Lollo had managed to keep his eyes open enough to notice that one was very black and the other very white.

"Idiot. I mean they are both Nike girls. Saskia, where is your cap with the Nike tick on it?"

She called back "In my bag."

"Try to always play wearing it, my treasure. You are a Nike girl now. Everything you do has a tick on it, like your schoolwork."

"Ha, ha." said Lollo and Padmini together.

179

The weekend outings that Lindsay and Erik tried to arrange through the winter months to inject some variety into the lives of the children had to be put on hold as they struggled to do everything on the complex without Coralie's input.

"You only fully appreciate someone when she is no longer around" said Erik one evening. "I think I have sorted my head out now. I am going to find her and bring her back."

"She'll only return if she thinks you are sincere and it will become the dream she thought she was living before." said Lindsay.

"She went straight home to the UK didn't she?"

"Yes. Where else was there to go?"

Erik booked himself on a flight for the next evening.

It was raining in Gatwick as they landed and he caught the Gatwick Express into the centre of London and went to collect his car.

"We serviced it last week and it's purring like a pussycat" said one of the mechanics at the garage that stored the Porsche.

Erik thought better of driving down at night and booked into a Premier Inn halfway to Devon.

Coralie had taken David's advice and turned off her mobile for all the time she planned to stay in Les Carroz. She went for a long walk around the village each day and then further afield up the hill to Flaine, and later down the hill. She hired a bike from one of the few businesses that were open and used it to reach further, enjoying the air which was much fresher than the sea breezes in the south of Spain.

She wondered what everyone was doing back at the Trocadero and how they were coping without her. She missed the children more than anything. Lindsay had been very understanding on the phone and not very complimentary about Erik.

Sitting on a grassy bank on the side of the road she had an intuition that Erik may come looking for her. Her personal tutor at school always told the girls to listen to their intuition. Mrs Carnegie used to say that she thought it was better developed in women than in men. It had been a part of women's protective mechanism over the centuries in a male dominated world.

Coralie's intuition was spot on that day as Erik was heading West expecting to be able to apologise and be able to persuade her to return with him to Spain. He did not know Coralie's parents address and, being unable to get her to answer her mobile, he had to work out how to find them. Arriving in Axmouth at coffee time he called in at Poppy's to an enthusiastic welcome. The four friends were meeting again to gossip but, principally to further discuss their new young refugee. They knew Erik well from his times staying in the area. They were all in love with him and broke out in hot sweats every time he appeared. He, in turn, liked them all and was surprised to catch them together this morning. In a trice Rachel produced his black coffee.

After some initial small talk Erik explained why he was there. There had been a misunderstanding with one of his staff members and he had come to take her back, but he needed to track down her parents address. Poppy responded by producing a telephone directory. No joy.

"Many people have only mobiles these days or prefer to stop cold callers by staying ex-directory."

Only Helen knew Coralie, from the days she coached Lucy, but she had no idea where she had lived or where her parents were.

Erik left to try Ottery Sports Centre where Coralie had worked before. He thought she may even be there looking for her old job back. They had not seen Coralie and only had the address of the flat she gave up fifteen months ago. Danny, her replacement, had not realised she was back in the country. He asked for an update on Saskia and whether she had settled well so far from home.

Erik was trying Coralie's phone every hour and was now hoping that she was actually in the area and had not high-tailed it off to apply for work a long way away with one of the contacts she had made during last year. His only remaining route of enquiry was her old flat at the back of Ottery. He knocked on the door and a woman answered with a small child hiding behind her skirt.

"I never knew her. She had gone before we moved in. Try the agent.

Erik went to the offices of the agent who let the flats. They knew Coralie's forwarding address in Marbella but nothing about her parents.

He drove around Ottery looking for Ethel, weaving around road after road and turning in and out of cul de sacs. By lunchtime he was tired and fed up. He went into the London Inn for a pint and a pasty. Whilst he was finishing his first Devon Pasty for more than a year he noticed a postman further down the bar and it registered that he was likely to know all the Matthews in town. In return for a pint he asked about any family named Matthews in Ottery or the surrounding villages.

"I'm not supposed to tell you" said the postman. "You could be the jilted husband come back to commit murder. Why do you want to know?"

"Girl I knew abroad and am serious about. I let her go without realising I wanted to keep the relationship open."

"There's an old lady in a bungalow in Longdogs Lane, single Mum with four kids out at Wiggaton and a middle aged couple in Canaan Way. I think that's all. Apart from a nurse in the doctor's surgery who lives out of town."

Erik took the number of the house in Canaan Way and,

leaving half his pasty behind, jumped in the car and drove along to see if it was the right house.

Five minutes later he was ringing the doorbell. No reply. He rang again. Still nothing. As he walked back down the pathway the lady pruning a shrub in the next door garden called across

"You looking for Jackie and Ted?"

Erik nodded.

"They've gone on holiday with their daughter."

"Do you know where?"

"Abroad. France I think they said."

"Thank you. How long for, do you know?"

"Sorry"

Erik climbed back into the Porsche and made his way slowly back to the pub in Axmouth, where he booked a room for the night and called Lindsay. He still tried hourly to call Coralie's phone. She had probably turned it off deliberately, expecting him to call her. Now she would look at all the missed calls from him and keep it turned off.

Scott Percy met Charlie Mills in the foyer of the Pearl Hotel two days later. He had finished his contract coaching a Brazilian doubles pairing two months ago and was taking a break before looking for another full time coaching post.

"It's probably only a short term thing, Scott, but dead easy. They've got about eighteen kids here in a coaching academy that does school in the morning and tennis after lunch. Five days a week, afternoons only. One of their coaches has buggered off without notice. They need you until she comes back or until they realise you are the answer to all their problems and offer you a million euros to stay on. In the meantime we are paying you to help them out. It's Joel Eriksson and his business partner Lindsay. Some of the kids are useful and they come from all over. I think they all speak English. I'll take you up there right away."

They climbed into Charlie's smart hired Audi and drove up to the Trocadero Tennis Academy.

"Thanks Charlie. You do move fast. Scott will be a great help. Let's go inside and I'll fill you in." Lindsay led the way into the dining room and the coffee machine. Cameron showed Scott to his allotted room.

Meanwhile Lavinia was bending Lollo's ear

"Has she left then? That would be such a shame. She is a lovely girl and it was a great opportunity for her to get into top tennis coaching. What was the problem?"

"Lovers tiff, I hear. You know what you women are like. One setback and you rush off back to mother."

Lavinia smacked his arm.

"Where's Erik then?"

"How do I know? I am just the hard pressed Spanish teacher "

"Hard pressed. You make me laugh. We only work in the mornings and for the nicest people. You're a big fraud."

He gave her one of his beaming smiles that lit up his whole face.

"Give me a kiss, my beautiful princess"

"Oh. Get off you devil"

She went off laughing.

Having spent an evening in the public bar of the pub with some of his old acquaintances Erik slept a disturbed night. He went across to Poppy's Chocolatiere for breakfast of croissants and coffee.

The same four ladies gathered together again.

"Do you waste every morning in here scoffing chocolates?" asked Erik

Rachel answered "No. We have a particular problem we are trying to solve this week. Can I tell him, Poppy?"

"Yes. We can trust Erik, as it involves his boat."

Erik looked up, suddenly more interested. They told him about the young refugee boy and the quandary they had.

"Dismiss what you can't do for him and then see what you can do to help. Go through each option systematically." suggested Erik

They started by eliminating all contact with the authorities, listing that as a last resort, and went through all the illegal employment and educational possibilities, deciding that they were all in the 'No' category. Then they looked at the positives. They could adopt him unofficially. They could go to Africa and try to find other members of his family. They could find an orphanage that may take him.

Erik joined in "Helen, you and George keep him at home, teach him to become a dairyman and a capable farm worker. It will be cheap for you and great for him, learning a trade. After a few years apply to adopt him legally. You can then tell the whole story and they will give you custody and him citizenship."

"I don't know that George would want another family member just yet. He has only recently gained three new ones."

"Go on, ask him." chipped in Rachel with Bronwen nodding.

Erik tried Coralie's mobile number for the first time that morning. Again unsuccessfully. He couldn't leave Lindsay any longer running the Academy on her own and felt he had to get back quickly. Coralie could be anywhere. She had probably booked a holiday at short notice and taken her parents to any one of the resorts in Europe. He berated himself for having been short sighted when Coralie had been there at arms length and trying to understand what she had done wrong or could do to rectify the situation. Love was such an ethereal thing. Perhaps it was only women who ever really got close to analysing it accurately. After all they spent an enormous amount of time discussing it and placing 'love' on a pedestal above all other things. Most men everywhere seem to have been taught that love is too 'girly' to discuss and rate highly. Football, beer and fast cars, of course, are much more important. It must be very good on Mars; though Venus would be amazing if Coralie was there too. 'Coralie, Coralie.' The sudden realisation hit him between the eyes. All his thoughts are around her now the mist was blowing away from his brain, not Sally or anyone else. It was Coralie who dominated his thoughts and feelings.

Lindsay was racing around for 16 hours a day trying to hold the business together. She was meeting visitors, supervising school lessons, supervising tennis sessions, paying bills, making up wage packets and living on cheese sandwiches. Her love life was on hold while her business partner and her new best friend were either chasing or running away from each other across Western Europe. Her own lover had proposed to her and then disappeared. She had asked him to give her time to decide, though it was really a way of saying 'no' without hurting him too much. She loved being seduced by his fit brown body and being taken to restaurants and told she was still attractive and desirable, but a full time commitment, no way!

Cameron was already 80% independent and learning about the world and its personnel. Lindsay did not know quite how much he had been taught or had discovered during his Marina exploits in the summer or that he had dispatched one of her prime responsibilities in the back of a truck to a far distant land. However, Lindsay had tasted family life – well two years of family life and thirteen years of juggling her finances as a single Mum. She now enjoyed her freedom and was not prepared to give it up easily. Male company she felt she still had the opportunity to have on her terms.

Pepe granted her time to 'think'. He and Victor had flown

back to South America to spend time with their Mother, who was having an operation to remove a tumour from her neck. Maria Carmelita and the Rosario had stayed moored to the Marina in Puerto Banus. The Marbella Club was a magnet for Victor's wife, who was unashamedly a social butterfly. Always there was a celebrity in the Club or in the vicinity nearby and this gave her a chance to pitch her social skills with the rich and famous. Royalty had spent hours enjoying the sumptuous facilities at the Club over the years and photographs adorned the walls of many current and exiled members of royal households from around Europe and the Middle East. The visits had not been so frequent in the last decade but you never knew who would sail into the harbour and pay the exorbitant harbour dues to secure his or her 'gin palace' to the Marina.

Ignacio (Nacho) was enjoying some independence too. Until he came to the Trocadero it seemed his every move had been monitored by his ambitious Mother. His only escape had been on a tennis court. He had attended a boarding school for the sons of the wealthy over in Argentina and had felt trapped in their large house in Montevideo during the holidays or taken to places in which he had no interest in the Rosario. All he really wanted to do was to mix with normal people and have fun. He had lost contact with his girl at home who had probably been snapped up by another admirer who could give her more attention. He really enjoyed the camaraderie of the Trocadero teenagers and, for the first time in his life, felt like a normal child.

He had decided in the last fortnight that he would earmark Padmini as a future girlfriend and ask her to play mixed doubles with him in the next year's tournaments. His olive skin was much lighter than hers but he loved her chocolate colour and her ready smile. She was quite surprised when he brought her a flower that had been broken from its stem in the garden. Neither of them said anything. She just took it and kept turning back to look at him as she walked to her next lesson. Running out of things to say to Sally on Skype that evening she said

"Oh Mum. Nacho gave me a flower today."

"Who is Nacho?" asked Sally

"A rich boy from South America"

Sally was suddenly aware that her daughter was rapidly approaching maturity and would soon be having boyfriends. She made a mental note to discuss boys and love in more detail in the next school holidays.

Skype had become an important ally in making the students feel less homesick. One or other seemed to be online and exchanging information with relatives and friends whenever Lindsay walked through the students' sitting room. She made a mental note to ask Dan, the self appointed counsellor, whether there was anyone who didn't have that all-important contact with home.

SIXTEEN

Erik landed back at Gibraltar after his abortive attempt to find Coralie feeling totally fed up and frustrated. He had not changed his clothes in two days and needed a haircut. Instead of walking across the border into Spain and catching the bus to Marbella he decided to go into Gibraltar Main Street and get his haircut. The barber shaved his face at the same time and gave him a head massage, something he had not experienced since playing a tournament once in Calcutta. He came away feeling much better and treated himself to a new sweatshirt from one of the shops on the way back to the border.

He had just missed a bus and had an hour to kill, so he sat in a café and looked out along the coast and out to sea. He remembered his Uncle Sven and another of his reminiscences from his days in Gibraltar at the Bank. His transfer there had been a reward for passing his Bankers exams earlier than most others. During his time there he was asked on every Monday morning to go to the Manager's office, on the first floor of the building, and count money that had been brought in a suitcase by one of the customers. He sat counting the cash whilst the Manager and the customer chatted about the weekend activities. Each week he overheard the discussion of the dangers and adventures of smuggling whisky from Gibraltar into the coves along the coast. Each of these coves was patrolled by policemen carrying rifles to stop this same smuggling. This was during General Franco's austere regime and the country was poor and short of many of the imports that it enjoys today. The policemen used to be bribed to ignore the boatload of contraband that would arrive on the moonless nights and be unloaded and driven away into the heart of Spain. Erik thought of Lindsay and her refugees pursuing a similar activity and delivering into these same coves.

Erik arrived in Marbella looking tired and dejected. He promised Lindsay at lunchtime that he would become the principal tennis coach for the foreseeable future and let her concentrate on all her other responsibilities. She was able to ease his guilt a little by introducing Scott and explaining that Charlie Mills had arranged quickly to find and pay a replacement, hopefully temporarily, for Coralie. Nike were going to pay Scott, thereby pressurising them to agree to the sponsorship deal that was on the table. Scott went off to prepare for the afternoon tennis while Lindsay said that she had secured what she thought was a good set of promises from Charlie and still managed to keep her clothes on. Erik agreed that it sounded good and he would begin to compare the individual deals, already enjoyed by some students, to see that it was better for each of them to change allegiance.

Scott was enjoying his new job. He had not taught juniors before and began to admire the standards and, in many cases, the determination to learn and improve. He was intrigued by the elegant Oksana, who gave the impression that it was her God-given right to win each game she played. He admired the intense concentration of Torgny that was reminiscent of his childhood hero Bjorn Borg. He loved the constant banter between the four young girls, who were unable to stop talking throughout every session.

Kurt was showing that he had the making of a future coach, and helped a lot by taking groups whilst Scott, and now Erik, could take one to one periods with individuals who needed to change or improve specific techniques.

Sink was missing his brother still but was happier than he could ever remember. He loved making his plants grow and would check the ones in pots each day to see whether they had grown a little since the day before. Maria was like a mother to him and gave him the love and care he had not had for years and could hardly remember. She made delicious meals and there was usually some tasty addition just for him. His bed was comfortable and he slept all night. So often his and Felix's beds were the ground or a wooden floor in the forest or during the 'long walk', as he called it, into North Africa under the hot sun.

Sink decided to work hard for Jorge so that he wouldn't be sent anywhere else. He was trying hard to be good at Spanish to please Mr Lollo and Maria. He also wanted to play this game that they all did, bashing balls at each other over a fishing net, but didn't quite know how to ask where to start, so he just watched them in his lunch break. Cameron took him out occasionally on their bikes and they each had a fishing line to dangle over the jetty wall. So far he had only caught a crab and one tiny fish that he had given to Maria's cat.

Coralie was missing the Academy and her friends more than she had believed possible. She put her love for Erik in a sealed casket in the back of her mind and walked through the summery Alpine hills imagining what each of the children would be doing and wondering whether Lucy and Gabby still thought about her. She had so wanted to help them further to enjoy the 'magical game' before they become embroiled in love affairs and babies and mortgages, to meet dozens of interesting people and make their mothers proud of their daughters.

On the second Tuesday, halfway through a baguette full of cream cheese and sitting on a bench overlooking a green valley and a herd of Jersey cows with the big eyes, she reckoned she had had enough looking back and it was time to think of the future. She could find a job and start afresh. She didn't need Erik if he didn't love her and, anyway, there were three and a half billion men out their looking for a partner. Maybe it was only about two billion if you took off children and old men and those who were gay or happy with their wives. There would certainly be one or two amongst those who thought she was worth a try.

That evening she persuaded David to take her into one of the Les Carroz bars. It was quiet. So many villagers had gone away and closed their businesses in the two months before the start of the new ski season and the first snowfalls. In the corner were two guys from the parasailing business that did a roaring trade in the winter. They were passing time cleaning all the gear ready for December and spending the evenings in the bar. One was looking at Coralie all the time as she sat opposite David sipping her lager that they had ordered by the jug and poured into small glasses. He looked nice with his tanned face partly hidden by long curly dark hair and designer stubble.

When David got up to go to the loo Coralie boldly went over to the other table and gave him a napkin, on which she had written her mobile number. It was the first time she had ever done anything quite so bold since she had posed topless for a boy at school, who was going to study photography at university and claimed he needed some glamour photos for his portfolio.

He called her later that evening and they agreed to meet and walk in the mountains the next day. Although Coralie was anxious to restore her confidence and re-confirm her desirability to men she still wanted to be respected by a normal fairly slow burning relationship. She had admired Carlo's attractive, but huge hands, but had not expected to find one of them inside her jumper as she was pinned against a conifer and being kissed vigorously by a spiky face so early in the walk. She fought him off and breathlessly told him to go. Having misunderstood her intentions and having his Italian pride shaken, he stomped off back to the village. Coralie put her left breast back into her bra and continued the walk on her own.

She had left her phone on after receiving the call from Carlo and it rang again during her walk. It was Erik. She had answered the call at the same time as looking at the display showing who the caller was, too late to stop.

"Hallo" she said

"Coralie…." said the familiar voice.

She rang off. And then looked at the phone and half wished she hadn't. She switched off the phone and carried on walking. Now her brains had scrambled again and she couldn't think straight. She wondered why he had called her. Were they up the creek without paddles at the Trocadero? Were the students complaining to their parents that there were not enough coaches to justify the fees? Maybe he was missing her in his bed. Perhaps he was concerned that she had jumped off a cliff in a distraught moment. Now she wouldn't know. He had opened the wound and all her deepest desires came pouring out and making her cry again. It wasn't fair. Why has God got a sadistic side to his nature as well as a wonderful loving one?

Steeling herself not to be easily taken in she switched on the phone and rang the number back. It was engaged. Huh! So much for his concern. He was already talking to someone else. She switched off again. She berated herself for nearly falling into his trap and strode off down the hill.

Erik was, in fact, calling her again. Each time he tried

it went into the answerphone message. He kept on trying, at ten minute intervals, all the afternoon. He concluded, from her recognising the call and ringing off, that she didn't want anything to do with him now. She may be back at her parents' home now or still on holiday somewhere in Europe. He went back to assist Scott with his own assessment of the needs of each student, that he had built up over the last fifteen months.

David cornered Coralie in the garden the following day.

"Why don't you take Mum and Dad home, leave the car and come back here for the winter? There are some good jobs going. They often come with accommodation and food. Spend the winter partying with the skiers, meeting loads of new blokes and getting Erik out of your head. Then, after the snows melt, go back to a sports job for the summer months. Here you can learn to ski, mug up your French, which is pretty crap as far as I can tell, and relax. Dad is quite worried about you and you know you were always his favourite."

"It sounds a possible" she replied. "And you will be here so I know someone to begin with. What could I do?"

"Work in a bar, in a shop or super market, clean chalets. There are jobs doing any of those here or up in Flaine or Sammoens. You won't need the car and you probably won't want to drive on snowy roads anyway. Fly from Bristol and I'll meet you at Geneva Airport."

"I'll think about it and call you when I get back with Mum and Dad."

It was another week before they left. Their parents had bought a fondue set to use at home and some ready made packs of fondue mix. They had enjoyed cooking in the house that David was minding whilst he decorated a chalet down the road. They spent three evenings in Bistros and watched their dinner being cooked on an open hearth surrounded by jacket potatoes wrapped in silver foil. Coralie had enjoyed buying the bread daily whilst it was still warm in the Boulangerie and packing her lunch for the daily walk or bike ride. After two weeks she felt fit and had explored most of the area. She tried to imagine it all covered in deep snow if she decided to return. Ethel did them proud and, by the time they reached Calais, her Dad was enjoying being a continental road user.

"George, if we don't take him in, he will be taken to an orphanage up country and put in amongst a load of other children who don't know him. He will be miserable and probably the only black boy. Certainly the only one from Africa. He will be cold and lonely" said Helen passionately.

"And George, you know you hate getting up so early, especially on Sundays to milk the herd. William won't be here any more. He was only helping out while you took Lucy back to Spain." added Callum.

"All right, all right. I'll probably get thrown in jail for harbouring or trafficking illegal immigrants. I'll give him a tryout. Just for a month to see if he is any good. I can't pay him, not officially, because there is a fine of £10,000 for employing someone here who shouldn't be, but he can earn his keep. Where would he sleep?"

"In the house, with us, as one of the family." Helen said cheerfully, now looking forward to returning to Poppys with the good news.

They tried to explain to Felix what had been decided by the unofficial committee of the ladies of the Chocolatiere. He nodded at everything they told him in English, in schoolgirl French and in 'holiday in Majorca' Spanish.

His only reply was a sad face which said "Sink".

"It's all right dear, they have a bathroom and they will let you use it" Bronwen tried to console him "And a western toilet with toilet paper."

He replied "Sink. Ou est Sink?"

"In the bathroom. She has just told you." said Rachel helpfully.

He got into Helen's car with a large bag of mainly jumble sale clothes and they drove up the hill to meet his new family.

Poppy shook her head "I hope this works and he doesn't freeze to death in one of the fields in mid winter."

"We could always ferry up a mug of hot chocolate every hour" added Rachel.

Padmini and Saskia, though forced to play together, were now giving Lucy and Gabby a hard game in their weekly match organised by Lindsay. Much of the coaching for juniors concentrated on the skill of the singles players, leaving doubles as an afterthought. Trocadero, however, started to look at this branch of the game more seriously. Erik and Lindsay recognised that all club teams played only doubles and that there were lucrative doubles and mixed doubles events at every tournament. To a certain extent this emphasis had been driven by the recent success in the US Open Junior Championships by Dan and Torgny, who were now ranked as the No. 1 junior pairing in Europe.

Erik thought that, unless one of their number had outstanding singles potential, they could all learn to excel in doubles. If a player achieved a rapport with another there was a good living to be made on the doubles court for a specialist and many, who may never achieve a ranking high enough to qualify for entry into a singles draw, could find their way into a lucrative doubles programme. They would also have more energy to devote to their specific event than the singles player who played in both. There were other advantages in doubles play, training and practice. There was more pressure on accuracy of ground strokes because of the marauding net player and also on service, and particularly not wanting to let down your partner.

Lindsay agreed with this, especially as the Brown Brothers had successfully forced the Professional Tour in 2008 to look more favourably upon the doubles events and now the prize pot had doubled. She also reckoned she has an academy of good doubles prospects. Only her two senior girls were showing signs of being loners. They had good baseline technique but their net play was in its infancy. They also had not yet gelled with a partner or showed any serious interest in doing so. In contrast Petra and Aga were showing signs of a great future understanding on the court, it didn't look as if any of the four youngest would ever want to play with anyone other than each one's current partner. There was already a mini war going on for each pair to claim supremacy.

The unexpected bonus that had just dropped out of the sky was Scott, who had been a specialist doubles coach for the last five years and guided both his last two employers to significant wins and a respectable income.

The PE teacher from the local school was getting involved with the positive responses of the Trocadero students against the average enthusiasm he experienced from his pupils at school, and he was giving some of his own free time to helping the older boys with some early weight training. He worked with Kurt for two evenings a week. Kurt was now 6ft 4ins tall and a solid thirteen stones in weight. Erik still had plans for Kurt in singles. He was fit and had good stamina and his forehand was catching up the good backhand he brought with him. The next tournaments were at the beginning of January leading up to the Australian Open. A good performance in these may earn a qualification or a wild card in the Open.

Carmen came to Lindsay.
"Madam. Where is Felix gone?"

"We don't know Carmen. We cannot find him. He will be somewhere in Spain."

"I worry him. He only small boy. Maybe no food. I no sleep last night."

"What can we do? We have been looking everywhere and asking the people in Marbella.

"Jorge says Sink wants brother."

"If we find him we will bring him back to be safe here."

The first thing Pepe asked when he arrived back was about Felix and Sink. Lindsay was embarrassed to have to tell him the story about Felix, but she was able to temper it with the good news about Sink. He was very happy with Jorge and Maria and his work in the garden at the Academy. Pepe shrugged as he realised there was nothing they could do for Felix at the moment.

"And Carina, what about you? Did you decide to love your Pepe for ever?"

"Maybe I will love you forever, but not with marriage."

Pepe looked sad but not devastated.

"I have too many commitments that I should not be loading partly on to you. The business here and my teenage son. And I have had my freedom for so long that I would be bad company if I had to change"

Lindsay watched him closely to see his reaction, not wanting to hurt this kind man, whom she knew she loved in no small way.

There was a pause in which she refilled their coffee cups when Pepe said

"I knew all the time that this would be your reply, and so did my Mother. I told her about you and how we dreamt the same dreams for the world, how you were a good person who helped others. She was still very weak after the operation, but she said you would not marry me or grace our name."

"How is your dear Mother progressing? You only said in your text that the medical people thought the operation had removed all the tumour and that there was no more cancerous tissue."

"She is doing well for one of 77 years. We have employed a nurse and housekeeper to care for her in her own home and promised to bring her here with us on the Rosario next year."

"I look forward to meeting her. By then we shall have been close friends for two years" Lindsay used this opportunity to emphasise her desire to continue their friendship and not let her decision break them up."

Pepe nodded and came across the sofa to kiss her softly on the lips.

"I wanted to see you first. Now I must talk to the crew of the yacht about my next plan for some refugees. Would you like to come to the village where all the people have been helping us? I must go there tomorrow."

She saw him to the door, beside which he had left two suitcases and she realised that he must have come straight from the airport by taxi to see her.

"I can come with you if you make the village visit on Saturday"

"I will collect you at 8am on Saturday and we will take breakfast on the way." he said as the new taxi drew up.

Christmas fast approached and the next batch of examinees began to study harder at their school lessons. Kurt, Agnieska and Nacho had received quite good results from their subjects taken the previous summer, reinforcing a theory Lindsay had sometimes voiced in her teaching career, that small classes will always reap greater dividends for the participants. The costs of providing full time schooling for a Government is high, even for classes of 30 or more. Most teachers feel they can teach well classes of a maximum of 12 if they are all doing the same work. Any larger and the needs of some pupils are missed. In a 40 minute lesson in most subjects there are likely to be 6 or 7 pupils who grasp the topic of the day easily and need to be stretched to keep their attention. There are another 6 or 7 who struggle and need to be helped through the work again to sufficiently understand it.

The rest muddle through. They don't make a fuss. They demonstrate an apparent understanding of the topic and leave together with the others for the next lesson on the programme. The teacher later discovers that, hidden amongst these 18 or so pupils are more that fall into each of the two other categories. The discovery can be through cleverly set homework or perhaps not until end of term tests. With only 12 pupils there is time to monitor each one at the time the topic is being covered and no-one slips through the net.

If her theory proved correct then the small classes they ran at the Academy, and the school operating for weekday mornings only, will not disadvantage the students in any way. In her experience many children were falling asleep in the classroom in the afternoon and would gain more by being outside having gainful exercise. However, they would have to rely on the flexibility of the teachers to cope with some classes having pupils of different ages studying often widely differing syllabuses.

SEVENTEEN

Although Clarence frequently told his customers that he didn't do Christmas and it should only be for children, he was a big kid at heart, and spent a large slice of the Bar Lulu's November profits on decorations. The Bar Lulu became a Christmas Grotto and even more of a magnet for the locals as well as the many holidaymakers, who arranged to leave the winter weather in Northern Europe and enjoy their non-working days in a more ambient climate.

Clarence was an accomplished clothes maker who used to make all his own outfits during his career as drag artist. Now he ran up a variety of exotic Christmas items to wear behind the bar. They were all completely 'over the top' garments designed to cause comment and stimulate the repartee upon which the place thrived. When he bought the rundown café three years before his neighbours were very wary of Clarence and thought his extrovert nature would cause problems in this suburb of Marbella. He spent his savings creating a new kitchen, an upgraded café into a restaurant and added the bar as a feature that could been seen by every customer.

The entire accommodation was on a terrace floor high above the road with a balcony that looked over the nearby houses as they stretched out towards the sea. Rex had arrived a year later and, being built like one of the docks he had been working on in Valencia, acted as a deterrent to anyone who became aggressive and to the occasional unpleasantly homophobic customer who discovered he had come into the wrong establishment.

Most of the students had gone home early for the Christmas holidays because they needed to be back immediately after New Year to prepare for the tournaments in the Far East that led up to the Australian Open. Erik guessed that someone would travel to fetch Padmini and take her back to Oman. He imagined that the person accompanying her would want a full breakdown of her progress and how she had settled from the Academy's point of view, and he almost dreaded that that person would be Sally. The lid he had clamped on to his feelings for her was already beginning to wobble under the heat of the engine driving his heart, even just at the prospect of another meeting.

Jennifer from Manila in the Phillipines had been helping Sally with all the household chores in their large house on the Exxon Compound in Muscat. Her sister was working in Malaga and they had not seen each other for more than two years. Because she was very capable Chris and Sally bought Jennifer an air ticket to combine a meeting with her sister and the collection of Padmini. The two ladies, who were both supporting their children back in Manila by taking jobs far away, met and spent a happy weekend together at the Trocadero. Lindsay took them to watch Clarence in action and to enjoy a good spanish paella on the Friday evening.

A much-relieved Erik agreed to supervise the remaining departures by road and air whilst Lindsay was collected by Pepe and taken up to the centre of Spain and the little village of Cremona. She was amazed to see a banner suspended above the road that said 'Bienvenido Pepe y Lynsey'.

"I told him the correct spelling over the phone" said Pepe. "But still he gets it wrong."

They stopped the car in the centre of the village and it

was immediately surrounded by 18 or 20 people who were smiling and laughing and tapping on the windows. As the two occupants emerged they began chanting 'Pepe, Pepe, Pepe' which some changed to 'Lynsey, Lynsey'. They were led up the steps to the patio at the front of the village church where a microphone has been set up with a loudspeaker box. An oldish man in a black suit and wearing a trilby hat tapped the microphone and the usual squeak emitted from the loudspeaker. He spoke in Spanish for a few minutes, interspersed by bursts of applause from the, now around 50 members, of the listening crowd standing on the lower church steps and beyond. Then Pepe took over and thanked them all, praising the good people of Cremona for the fine gestures they were making to help poor refugees to find a future in Europe.

They walked back down the steps through a tunnel of clapping villagers and were taken into one of the smartest houses in the village, given a glass of wine and told to sit and enjoy their meal. They were served a meat dish made of lamb or goat meat with cooked vegetables called 'cuchifritos', followed by a delicious dessert 'tortell', which was a kind of pastry with marzipan and dried fruits. Brandy followed and five or six toasts.

During the afternoon walk around Cremona Lindsay met Carlos again and his family and so many others, who wanted to shake her hand. One mother asked her about Felix and Sink. 'So they even knew about the two boys who missed the connection on the beach' she thought. Carlos told both of them that the eight refugees that he had collected from Trocadero had been taken by lorry to Andorra and then into France. They were now living with families near Cannes, many of whom had also been people displaced from French-speaking territories as well. He had heard that one man already had found work in a print works and two of the ladies were cleaning houses. He told Lindsay that, like

Pepe, she would forever be welcome in his home and issued an invitation to come to stay whenever she needed a holiday from all that strenuous tennis.

They had been in the Province of Castilla-LaMancha and drove back into Andalucia and back down to Marbella. Lindsay walked into the Academy carrying a huge bunch of mixed flowers and a basket of three bottles of red wine.

"I have had the most incredible day, amongst the loveliest people" she announced to Erik, who was sitting in his usual armchair, having been pampered with food by Juanita and had Luciana doing all his ironing.

"Oh. That's all right then. The highlights of my day were coming around the corner and witnessing a passionate farewell of the two lovebirds from the linen cupboard. Which led to Luciana offering to do my ironing, presumably hoping to blackmail me into secrecy."

Erik entered Soo-Jin and Oksana into Ladies Singles Events in Hong Kong and Singapore. It was the time to see how they performed against the journeying lady professionals, who were hoping to kickstart the new tennis year with some strong results. They each performed well, one making a semi final in Hong Kong and the other also the semi final in the Singapore event. Soo-Jin particularly wanted to succeed in her home New Zealand but was given a tough draw and lost in the second round to the capable Heather Watson from England, who eventually won the title.

Lindsay and Erik had decided not to attempt to enter most of their charges into the Australian Open qualifiers for the Senior Events and to concentrate on the Juniors. Agnieska made the final of the Girls Junior Event and only lost 7-6 7-6 to a nervous opponent ranked way above her. The other stars were Dan and Torgny, who had qualified for the Men's Doubles. They had learned much more from Scott during the Autumn and beat pair after pair of ranked male doubles partnerships. They became favoured by TV channels for commentary and became the youngest doubles combination to reach the last four of a Grand Slam. They could hardly believe their pay cheque or being interviewed on Swedish TV by none other than Erik, who had been able to update the viewers upon the prospects of both they and other promising Swedish youngsters.

Kurt had a wild card entry but lost a first round tie to one of the seeds in the Men's Singles and he and Petra were runners up in the Junior Mixed Doubles. Kurt qualified to play as a Junior by virtue of being born three days after the deadline date. The long flight back with Qatar Airways from Melbourne was a happy one, helped by Qatar now offering flight concessions to the Academy for all their long haul journeys, and Business Class to the coaches. Scott, Lindsay and Erik shared a bottle of the Rose Champagne from the wine list, congratulating themselves on a good start to the year.

They all arrived tired and needing showers to find that there was no water at the Trocadero because the Water Board were repairing a major leak at the filtration works beside the reservoir. Carmen had ordered bottled water to keep them going until the supply was restored. The local Club de Tenis willingly opened their shower facilities to everyone and there was a crocodile of students carrying wash bags and towels seen walking down the road for the next two days. In return they arranged a fixture with the Club to test the younger doubles combinations against stronger adults.

It was a rather embarrassing mistake. Although the Marbella Club had both Ladies and Men's teams in the top local divisions they were slaughtered by the pairings at the Academy. The youngest four and Petra and Aga represented the Academy. Dan and Torgny were banned from competing despite protesting vehemently, as was Kurt. Erik put the five youngest in the team and included Rubio from the secondary school, who had been impressing their PE teacher recently. Every pair won every match and Erik spent the evening trying to compensate by laying on a feast for the Club Members.

"It certainly showed them the quality of our kids. They will go around the area telling all the other clubs that this is no tinpot setup and that some of ours will make a dent in the tournament circuit." Lindsay enjoyed telling Charlie on the phone that evening."

"Babe. You stick at it. There was some good tennis being played by a couple of the ones I saw and they were only just out of diapers. That skinny eight year old from the Gulf was sending down serves that would have put me on the toilet"

"Charlie. What a delightful turn of phrase you have. Actually she is twelve."

"I don't care. She is one of mine and I am going to keep her under a special 'Mills protection blanket'"

"Heaven help any girl who gets under your blanket. Now, ring off because I've got to make up the wage packets or nobody eats this weekend."

"So long Lindsay."

"It says 'Manuel Iniesta and Lavinia del Rey will welcome your attendance at the Church of St Xavier, Marbella for their betrothal and later at Bar Lulu for their celebration on January 31st at 12 Noon.'" Cameron read.

"That's next week" said Lindsay. "I need a new dress."

"They kept that quiet" said Erik.

"No they did not." commented Carmen. "Everyone knew."

"Friends, yes, but not the whole nuptials."

"This is Espana. We do things properly. Not in the linen cupboard" she replied.

"Poor Luciana. You will never let her forget that, will you"

"No. I will not" answered Carmen emphatically.

It was a beautiful day on January 31st and it seemed that half the town had turned out to witness the wedding of two well-loved local characters. Lavinia had taught at two schools in the town and Lollo had been both teacher and private tutor to three generations of the district's children. They arrived in a wooden trap towed by a haughty black horse and under the reins of the owner of Aga's stable. The Priest, another drinking buddy of Lollo's, had some difficulty keeping laughter at bay when he took the service, especially when he had to announce Lollo's full name:

'Manuel Joaquín Rudolfo Jair Vicente Boavista Iniesta-Paladio'

Lollo's face did not help. He was showing horror, sadness, surprise and delight at intervals according to the content of the service, handkerchief in hand like a shorter image of Pavarotti.

Lavinia was grace itself, wearing a simple aquamarine dress with matching hat and shoes and carrying a posy of freesias and white carnations. Although a large lady she gave the impression of being an innocent and slightly embarrassed maiden. Clarence was Lollo's best man and spent much of the service in tears and Lavinia's assistant was her stick-thin best friend of forty years. All the Trocadero students were there in the Church and they received an admonishing frown from the Priest as they led a spontaneous applause as the couple came back down the aisle as Senor and Senora Iniesta.

Clarence had made a hasty departure from the Church to get back to the Reception, for which he was responsible. He had been cooking for days and stayed up most of the previous night to make certain the buffet was worthy of his good friend. Nicholas spent too much time at the adult end of the drinks table and was sick in the street gutter before being taken back early to the Academy to sleep off whatever was preventing him from standing up. Sink formally presented the couple with a banana, a coconut and one kilo of rice. Cameron had told him that this was a tradition at all weddings in Sierra Leone and brought good luck on the newlyweds. Lindsay, knowing her son too well, for some reason doubted this.

Earlier, in the general melee of friends greeting each other and photographs being taken, Cameron had noticed Sofia in the crowd with her parents. He had managed to scribble a note and put it in her hand as he walked by trying not to be recognised by her father. When he saw her across a group of guests later she caught his eye and nodded enthusiastically. It was over a year since their catastrophic discovery in the boat on the Marina and he still dreamt of her amazing silky skin and wild abandon. They met outside her school on Monday afternoon and walked along the cliff path in the opposite direction of her house. She told him that she had had two boyfriends since they had been together, but he was still the best. They kissed again and Cameron decided that he had to see her and spend time with her again.

Lollo and Lavinia postponed their honeymoon until the Easter vacation and just went away for 24 hours in a car provided by the Trocadero to the La Manga Country Club. Lindsay and Erik returned happily to their complex and shared a glass of wine on the verandah.

"How different from our wedding" she said recalling the copious quantities of palm wine and the buffet of Guinea fowl and fruit cut into a dozen shapes. "Will you ever marry again, Erik, or will no-one ever compare with me?" asked Lindsay.

"Never again, my beautiful bride. You have spoilt me for any other. Actually, we were pretty damned good together. I was a young male virgin and you were the experienced lover who taught me more than I imagined it was possible to do."

"You rat. You had been rutting your way around the tennis courts of Europe leaving a stream of innocent females distraught in your wake. From what I can remember you had me on my back as soon as the ferry had gone around the headland, and before we had made a shelter or piled our belongings together."

"You were completely irresistible then and I hadn't made a habit of resisting any pretty girl on the tour. Come to think of it you still have the wherewithal to make a man happy." He moved towards her.

"Get away from me, you oversexed husband person, and go and find the second great love of your life and exercise your charms on her".

"Have you heard from her yet?" He asked, suddenly serious.

"Nothing. I left a message on her answerphone to call one of us"

"I wish I hadn't lashed up a good team. I didn't appreciate the bad effect it was having on her just having a pause in our frenzied love affair. I certainly had not expected her to throw all this up and go."

"You men will never get close to understanding us, and some of you spend a lifetime trying."

George had discovered that Felix was resilient to the colder weather that had caught up with Devon in the winter. He had got up in time every morning to milk the Friesian herd with George, learning quickly how to do the work. With demonstration and gestures George was communicating quite successfully with the lad. He looked at Felix. Today he would go down to Mole Valley Farmers and buy him some thick winter clothes and gloves and a balaclava type hat because you can lose a lot of heat through the head. Indoors, at breakfast, he said

"I reckon your Felix can do this job in his sleep. He is talking to the cows already and they used to tell us at Agricultural College that that was a sure sign of a good dairyman. He seems to understand the importance of hygiene and is washing and sterilising everything properly, even when he thinks I am not looking."

"Is he warm enough out there? It's been bitter at 8.30 when I take the boys to school so it must be very cold, especially for an African, a couple of hours earlier."

"I'll get off to the shop later on and buy him some thicker gear as he's shown he is good enough to train." answered George, taking his mug of coffee out into the yard.

Helen reported to the Chocolatiere Committee later that morning that George was pleased with Felix and she thought he could be persuaded to keep him on. She also thought, if Felix could cope with the winter, he would be happy in the summer. The Devon climate was a lot warmer than some of the places he could have ended up. Poppy was pleased that they had saved Felix from an uncertain future, probably institutionalised for several years. She was winding down her daily chocolate output ready for massive effort during the week before Christmas when she had dozens of orders to be put into fancy boxes as Christmas presents. This coincided with a heavy church programme leading up to and during Christmas Day.

Coralie caught the 6.30 am flight from Bristol to Geneva two weeks before Christmas to join a chalet cleaning firm that mainly employed gap year students and worked from the more central Les Carroz resort. She found the Go Massif minibus that David had booked for her and, an hour later, was back in the village that she had left in sunshine and amongst green fields and forests. Now it was a winter wonderland with a metre of snow having fallen up on the Grand Massif, which comprised the three resorts and their surrounding hills. An impossible depth of snow stayed suspended on wooden chalet roofs and icicles a foot long hung beneath the eaves. Every branch of every tree carried its weight in snow.

"It is just like a Christmas card" she said to her Brother as he met her in the square at Les Carroz .

"Good you could come, kid." He said "Time you had some fun."

Coralie checked in with the Alpina Chalet Company and was attached to Elena from the Czech Republic, who was returning for a third season. There was a uniform and, as Coralie tried hers on, Elena said

"You will have a problem, Chloe."

"Coralie" she was corrected.

"You are pretty with good shape. Apres ski some men will be chasing you. They get tired from the skiing and the drink has big effect. Many will want you. You decide now you going to sleep with all of them, one two every week like some girls, or not with any."

"None is best for me" said Coralie. "What is the best way to stop them?"

"Don't go to parties or tell them you are lesbian."

"First year I am here I sleep with one man. Next week his friend stays and he has told him about me. One day he didn't go skiing and I am making beds, he jump on me and try it on. Big problem, I run to kitchen and he trap me by the cooker. I hit him with saucepan. It was induction saucepan, very heavy. No more skiing for him. Two days in hospital and then he go home."

Coralie laughed.

"The Company say it my fault and next time don't lead them on. I angry but I stay. Now this third year in Les Carroz."

Every day they had to tidy 12 chalets and make the beds whilst the guests went skiing. On Saturday they started earlier and worked until late changing all the bedding and taking it to the central office which had a laundrette at the back. A van delivered the fresh set of bedding to each chalet just before they needed it. On Sunday they were on call to deal with any queries. With the exception of Saturdays there were apres ski parties every evening, Saturday being the arrival day when everyone was tired after a journey and had not yet found their way around. Because there was a majority of men the chalet girls were always welcome to join in the fun. Ski instructors too joined in, usually standing at the back and listening to novices telling the room how to do this or that manoeuvre. The experts said nothing and let them have the floor. David took Coralie to her first party on the Sunday evening and she tried the gluwein which would flow copiously for the next four months. She began to recall her French from school and was surprised at how much she understood, although it was a little different trying to actually speak it herself.

She quickly found that the exercise seemed to have an effect on many of the men, making them more randy than usual. Two glasses of gluwein and a few beers and they became even bolder. The smoothies were smoothing, the gropers were groping and egos were blown up to bursting point. Coralie watched the atmosphere reach a certain level and then she would slip away before she became cornered and pressured into the sort of close relationship that she was trying to avoid.

David kept a protective eye on her, checking from time to time with Elena that she was OK with the work and relaxing in the evenings. Sometimes she and Elena were sent to assist with a chalet in one of the other two resorts. Neither had a car so they caught the local bus and, afterwards, they would take a ski lift to one of the cafes further up the slopes and joke with the skiers and drink steaming hot chocolate.

Christmas was one long celebration. Coralie was given a pile of presents by chalet dwellers who liked her or had drunk too much and thought they had fallen in love with her. This included an enormous teddy bear called Reginald and a heart pendant. None of her boyfriends had ever given her the traditional heart before, so it was a surprise coming from a shy Swiss guy whom she had hardly noticed all week.

EIGHTEEN

New Year arrived on the ski slopes where the snowboarders almost outnumbered the skiers. Celebrations continued well into the night and the morning of January 1st as French, Swiss and British in the majority hugged everybody and made unrealistic resolutions for the year that stretched before them. Coralie and Elena had no break from the daily bed making and kitchen clearing. In every chalet there were dozens of bottles and cans, unwashed dishes, and clothes strewn across most surfaces.

It snowed sometimes for two or three days and everyone cheered at the newly covered slopes. Then the sun appeared in the clearest of skies and reflected so brightly from the pristine white panorama.

It was a surprise when her Swiss admirer returned for another two weeks early in January. He had come more for Coralie than for the snowboarding that had been the objective of his original Christmas break. She obliged by spending evenings with the group from his chalet. Thomas was not a groper or a jumper, a heavy drinker or a noisy orator. He was not spectacular to look at, but there was something warm and attractive in his gentle nature and undemanding company. He had brought his car across the border from Lucerne and took Coralie down to the wide valley and along the toll road to Chamonix. He insisted on paying for their lunch and for every one of the coffees and hot chocolates they drank whilst watching, with amusement, the beautiful people who belonged in a Chamonix environment and the pretenders who thought they did.

Coralie had scooped back her emotions relating to Erik into the sealed casket and lodged them into the 'no go' cavity at the base of her brain. She enjoyed immensely the meal at a small Bistro. Thomas had chosen her favourite claret to compliment the meal and she had been hungry enough to eat every morsel. They returned to his chalet to join the other inmates for coffee to find that they had gone on to a party further down the road. Coralie let this gentle man kiss her properly for the first time. She felt happier than at any time since before she decided to leave the Trocadero. Knowing that this was one of the chalets she would have to tidy in the morning she let Thomas take her to bed. He was due to leave in two days, and although it was never a good reason to do it, she felt he deserved a loving response for all his kindness and unobtrusive company.

Thomas left two days later to return to work in his Father's ballbearing factory in Switzerland having stolen two weeks from this year's holiday quota to find Coralie again. They promised to meet up as soon as he could escape for a long weekend. Elena worked on the opposite side of the bed helping Coralie change the duvet.

"You like him a lot, don't you?"

"Yes. He is different from most of the other guests, who are just looking for a holiday experience before they return to their steady girlfriends at home."

"Did he tell you about his wife and kids?"

"You have to check them out. Look for photos in his wallet when he is in the bathroom. Catch him making phone calls back home when he thinks you are not around. Play the game. The odds are in the man's favour to begin with, so you have to play dirty to even it up."

"Oh. Elena. Where is your romance?

"I left it in a field in Czechoslovakia when I was 17. It turned into my baby son who lives with my Mother every winter whilst I do this to buy his new shoes."

Erik sat in the same seat - No.12k - that he had been allocated on the last flight he had made to England. He was relentlessly not superstitious, but he hoped the outcome of this journey would be more successful. As he stared into the contents of the onboard meal in front of him he wondered whether he was chasing Coralie again because of his needs and desires or whether it was for the benefit of the Academy. Lucy and Saskia had been the ones to finally push him into trying a second time. They had come to the bench, from which he was studying the forehand grip that Oksana had on her racket, and told him that the Academy was not laughing any more.

"What do you mean?

"Coralie laughed a lot and made the tennis fun. Now you don't smile any more and Scott is quite serious." Saskia always had spoken bluntly and to the point.

"I know we are meant to be serious about some things, but now it is everything. Lindsay doesn't have a friend to talk to and is always looking stressed." added Lucy.

"The only person who is happy is Mr Lollo and we all love him" said Gabby, who had now joined them.

"Mr Erik" Padmini's voice now came from behind him "Go and bring our Coralie back". He turned and looked into her deep brown eyes and then at the other three, who were all pleading with their expressions.

Erik muttered to himself as he tried to find a clean shirt to add to the few other garments he had thrown into his trusty grip.

'Why am I listening to the 'string quartet', (as Scott called them because they had managed to break more strings in the time he had been there than their older friends who hit the ball harder.) None of them is even 14 yet.'

Of course he knew perfectly well why he was listening to them. They were voicing the thoughts of everyone who worked at the Trocadero and had not had the courage to tell him. They were also telling him what he had been putting off for weeks, the only remedy for the ache in his solar plexus.

"You are making a lot more trips back here than I had expected" Georgiou told him as he handed over the keys to the Porsche. "I put two new tyres on the rear for the MOT, so you owe me a few quid more this time."

Erik was unable to open the roof because it was a cold week in February. He had debated taking the little car down to Spain to get more use from it, and to be able to use it more as it was intended, with the wind blowing through his hair. Today he knew where Coralie's parents lived but could not phone them. Knowledge of their phone number may have saved the flight to the UK.

"Come in Mr Eriksson. You have had a long drive and must be ready for a hot drink" said Jackie Matthews.

"Please call me Erik. And I would love a black coffee if it is no trouble."

Ted joined them from the garage and washed his hands in the sink.

"Coralie said you may phone us or call in one day because you often came down to Devon."

"Is she here with you now?" he asked optimistically

"No dear. She has a job a long way away these days, almost as far as the one in Spain."

"When I saw Ethel parked in your driveway I assumed she had come home to live"

Ted answered "She doesn't need a car where she is"

Erik thought 'Cruise ship. I'll bet she is working on a cruise ship. She would need a car anywhere else'

"Where has she gone?" The couple exchanged glances.

"Look Mr Erik ...... Erik. She is making a new start and it took her a while to get over what happened in Spain. She didn't say much so we guessed that she wasn't good enough for the high power coaching you all needed. I know she missed everyone very much, especially the two girls she had been coaching here in Ottery. Now she is with her brother and doing something completely different and she made us promise not to tell anyone, even you, where she was" Jackie said slowly and thoughtfully.

Erik's tried to think on his feet. 'How could he persuade them to tell him where she was?'

Jackie poured him another coffee and he decided to come clean with the whole story.

"Coralie was terrific as our coach. She is competent and everyone loves her. She has helped several of our kids to settle a long way from home and has helped them improve beyond their wildest hopes in just a year."

"Then why did you send her away?" asked Ted, taking a bite out of a digestive biscuit.

"We didn't." He was not sure how much they knew of their daughter's friendship with him, but he took the plunge:-

"She ran away because of the way I treated her. I was inconsiderate and totally unfair to her feelings"

"Were you lovers?" asked Jackie

Erik nodded. "We were very much in love, and I still am."

"I had an intuition that you may have been" she added.

"I knew she was potty about you" said Ted "but I also thought she would be just a kid to someone like yourself with all your experience and sitting in the Royal Box and everything. Never thought you would go for her."

"You have been watching too much Wimbledon on TV" Erik smiled. "I have come here, hoping to find her and take her back to Marbella. All the students are missing her badly and I think it may be having a bad effect on some of them, especially the four youngest girls. I want to go back to how she and I were too. However, if she doesn't want that then I can promise not to disturb her work and leave her alone to move on with other relationships that she may make in the future. The staff are missing her too. She taught them how to make a Devon Cream Tea and they all gather round on Fridays for Juanita's scones and cream. So I implore you to give me a contact with her so I can at least go back and tell them I tried my best."

"Tell you what I'll do" said Ted, taking charge. "I'll call her this evening and ask her to contact you if she wants to"

"Has she bought a new mobile? I have been calling her for months but her phone is always switched off" said Erik

"Same one. She switches it on every day for a 15 minute slot so we can call each other, and then off again so you can't get her. What is your number so I can tell her if she wants to call you? And where will you be?"

He wrote the number down and told them it was the same as before and that he would be in the Seaton area for a couple of days. Then he asked them to call him if Coralie wanted to remain incognito.

After he left, Jackie asked Ted why Erik thought Coralie was in Italy.

"What do do mean?"

"Cogneeto is in Italy isn't it?"

He gently explained that Erik didn't actually think that was where she was.

Erik drove over to the Sports Centre and took Danny out to lunch and told him the latest details of Saskia's progress. He then bought some old fashioned licorice whirls from Kate Burrows' sweet shop in Seaton, telling her the same as he had related to Danny. Next he fetched the key to The Umpires Chair from Phil Mercer, in the process finding that the room was unoccupied, and drove up to park underneath the old tower. He sat and marvelled that the view was still lovely in February. Then he walked across to the Farm hoping that the new farmer's wife was baking today. He was greeted with the customary hug by Helen.

"I am trying to make Lardy Cake"

"What on earth is that?"

"Just something different for the boys. You can try it if you stay long enough this time. It will be ready after teatime."

She called Callum, who was at home studying today on a free afternoon at school. Callum was just coming down the stairs to fetch the two boys from Primary School. He drove these days, having passed his test first time and as early as he could after his 17th Birthday. Erik went with him and, in the car, he told how he had found this black lad sleeping in the boat a few months ago. He was a refugee from West Africa. They had taken him in, probably illegally, to train him on the farm and give him a home. They stopped again at Saskia's Mother's sweet shop for ice creams even though it was in February, but small boys are often unpredictable in their choices of confectionery. Arriving back at the farm Erik was last to re-enter the house and he took a detour to peer into the dairy shed. Hosing down the floor was Felix, who dropped the hose and ran to him.

"He couldn't speak for a moment and then said "Sink, Sink?" and burst into tears. Erik put his arms around him and they sat on the wall. He explained that Sink was fine; about Jorge and Maria and the gardening job.

"I come Spain with you?" Felix asked.

Erik left him to continue cleaning the milking area after the cows had gone back to a distant field. He told Helen and

George, who later joined them, that he knew Felix when he, presumably, was on the way to England. For some time, during their discussion, he had assumed that Felix must have been brought to England by them. However, they did not seem to know much about him and, of course, he had been found by Callum on Viti Levu. On balance it was probably better for Felix to stay on the Farm. If Erik took him back to Spain he would need a passport and he would never be able to enter the UK again. He tried to explain this to Felix, who was bewildered when he said he would arrange for him to talk to Sink very soon.

Callum used an Ipad for his A levels and he had already joined Skype and What's App. Erik planned to get Sink to a computer linked to Callum and for the brothers to talk at least once a week. Felix' prospects were best with the love and care he would receive at the Farm, and it was as near as he was likely to find to family life

Penny's Mother took the call and later, when she came home, passed it on to Penny.

"Callum called and said he was going down tomorrow to scrape Vicky's bottom and would you like to help?"

Penny laughed. "Thanks Mum. I'll call him. Her name is Viti and she has her bottom scraped at least once a year. And it's not another of your weird therapies either" Penny picked up her mobile still chuckling to herself.

"Come down Pen. You can meet Erik. He would have been one of your Mum's heartthrobs if she ever watched tennis on TV"

"Watch tennis! We can't get anything to eat during Wimbledon fortnight. She and Auntie Margaret just sit all day in front of the TV eating nuts and drinking tea"

"Tell her you are going to meet Joel Eriksson then. She will know."

Erik stayed in The Umpires Chair overnight. It always brought back the best of memories of the time his main hobby was painting, and particularly of one of his best works and it's subject. He vowed to resume his art one day soon. There were many new images in Spain that he had photographed in his mind and he would like to try to reproduce on canvas. In the morning he noticed it was not yet light until breakfast time. The water heater had been switched off since the last visitors had been there over New Year, so he had to wash and shave with the water boiled in a small kettle and taken down the steps to the suspended bathroom below.

At the pre-arranged time of 11am he joined Callum and his girlfriend in the car park that Phil Mercer used as an extension of his boatyard. Viti Levu was out of the water and up on blocks and Callum was already working on her stern assisted by Penny. Erik looked around the sturdy old boat that he jointly owned with Callum and then climbed on board up a metal ladder on wheels that he pushed over from Phil's workshop. Every two minutes he caught a glimpse of someone peering between the other boats parked around Viti. Looking more closely now there seemed to be several people walking around casually or peering often in his direction. One particular lady, he could see out of the corner of his eye, had a mobile phone camera pointing in their direction whilst he was with Callum and Penny.

"Are you planning to sell the boat Callum?"

"No. Why?"

" There are people taking photos, I think of Viti. Do you know them?"

"Oh No" said Penny "It's my Mother. She has come to see if it is really you"

"OK. Go and get her. Let's put her out of her misery."

Penny was gone for fully ten minutes, reappearing from the end of the car park with seven ladies of indeterminate age.

"I'm so sorry Erik. This is my Mum, and my Auntie Margaret and I don't know any more names but they come from the Budleigh Salterton Tennis Club and I am afraid they have come to ogle"

Erik laughed "Good morning Ladies. I am Joel, but they call me Erik around here. Have you really nothing better to do on a cold Saturday morning than look at an ancient tennis player?"

There was a titter of nervous laughter, but tongues were tied.

"I have seen as much as I want here. Let's leave these two young people to themselves and retire to a little café I know in Axmouth. Jump in your cars and follow me. This white car is mine and I have one spare seat in it for the journey."

A few hardy ramblers found their way to the Chocolatiere in February, but this was the first time a tennis club had convened a meeting in front of Rachel's counter. The seven ladies drank hot drinks, ate too many cakes and chocolates and asked Erik about everything from mixed doubles partners to who sewed the name on his white shorts. They left with lots of inside knowledge of the tennis circuit fifteen years ago and several souvenirs that Erik had found buried in his untidy Porsche, some of which would later be raffled for funds and one or two which would be pinned up in the clubhouse.

When they had all gone, and only Erik remained, Poppy said

"You are a nice man, Erik. You didn't have to do that. It has absolutely made their weekend."

"When I first joined the international merry-go-round I watched Steffi Graf do that time and again, often long after the rest of the competitors had gone back to their hotels. She was a great favourite and she put herself out to make it a special day for a few supporters, who may have travelled for hours to watch a match or two and spent a lot of money on tickets. She saw me watching once and came over and said.

"They pay my prize money, and their children will come one day and pay yours"

That evening Erik called Ted Matthews.

"Hi Ted. Anything from Coralie?"

"She said she may call you, so I didn't know whether to ring you or not."

"Thanks. I will return to Spain in the morning and keep my mobile charged. It's been good meeting you both. Next time I'll take you out for a meal somewhere nice." He rang off and went over to give a resume of Lucy's tennis plans for the year to Helen and George. Helen told him that Lucy had told her on their Skype chat that the four girls didn't want to travel to any tournaments without Coralie.

"She told me that they would go on strike and withdraw their labour. I nearly cracked up laughing when she said that. Four little scraps holding you to ransom. I told George and he just said it showed guts."

"They have plenty of that. Four shop stewards together" said Erik

Later, in the Tower, he called Lindsay

"Nothing yet. I think she is on a cruise ship, working with her brother. I have asked her Dad to keep trying to get her to call me and at least talk."

"Not much else you can do. Better come back. Scott has done his back and I need you on court a.s.a.p."

NINETEEN

Shortly after settling back at the Trocadero Erik linked his Skype address with Callum and brought the two young lads together for an emotional reunion. Neither Callum nor Erik had the first idea what they were talking about. They laughed and screeched at each other for over an hour. Their joy was a great reward for the two bystanders. Callum told his Mum that it must have been awful to have been separated from the only person left in the world whom you knew really belonged to you and cared for you. He vowed to link Felix and Sink at least once every week and made a date with Erik to set this up.

Pepe came back to Marbella directly from Cremona. He wanted to discuss the latest plan to assist refugees with the only person he could relax with and who would be sympathetic to his aims. He talked about the new crisis in Syria driving families to move out of the country and seek a safe haven and a future for their children. Thousands were pouring across Turkey with only what they could carry. The countries of Western Europe were taking quotas of these refugees and trying to accommodate them and weave them into established communities. A terrific example was being set by Germany who had taken a huge social risk by agreeing to take half a million estranged souls in the next year.

Spain was also playing its part with a quota of new arrivals. The economic bombshell in 2008 that had affected the world had left Spain struggling, like Greece, Portugal and Ireland, with no option but to impose austere economic policies upon the population. Property prices had fallen as many owners reneged on mortgages and loans because their jobs had disappeared. The arrival of outsiders to swell the jobless and stretch welfare payments could become a recipe for civil unrest. Pepe, Carlos and the villagers in Cremona had been meeting to try to make a contribution that may ease this potential problem. They were buoyed by the success of their unconventional actions recently to help many outsiders who had seemingly no chance left in life.

The skeleton plan was to be financed by Victor, put into practical operation by Pepe and run on a daily basis by Carlos and a number of his village friends. Lindsay had listened with interest, pleased that her friend had found another interest to invest his talents. She was bursting to hear what it was they were going to do. Pepe didn't keep her waiting much longer. After she had opened a bottle of red wine and poured them each a glass - they were those vast glasses, two of which almost emptied the bottle – he delivered the magic words.

"We are going to build and operate a chocolate factory and run it with the refugees. They will all stay in our homes until the profits from the factory can be used to steadily build each family a house of its own."

There were several villagers who had had to take enforced early retirement from a similar factory in a nearby city when their business was closed and transferred to Romania. Victor had the business skills and Pepe the organisational practice. These villagers would provide the manufacturing expertise. Lindsay offered encouragement and marvelled at his drive to continue to help even more people. She gave him a long, lingering kiss and watched him walk to his car, happy to have had the opportunity to release pressure by talking to a non-judgmental listening ear. She closed the door thinking that this listening was a part of love too. It was a new experience for her.

The snow still fell in the Grand Massif and the icicles still reflected the sunlight from the clear skies that followed. The visitors still came for their one week crash ski experience or their two week package of lessons and parties. Coralie had felt free. She had cut the ties with her past and the casket at the base of her brain no longer had sharp corners that reminded her that it was there. Thomas was a nice magazine that she could read or leave alone. He wasn't the publication that was delivered every week and you were compelled to indulge just because it was there. She had thought Erik had moved on, had become knee deep in his new business by day and resurrected his dreams of the perfect Sally by night. Then her Dad phoned and told her what she did not want to hear.

'What should she do?' Every defensive instinct shouted "Be strong. Don't do it."

Thomas managed to arranged a free Friday to add to the weekend. He phoned her in the 15 minute window that she had only told him and her parents. His timing was good. Coralie was weakening under the mistaken belief that Erik wanted to talk about something serious that had happened to one of the students. The mind played irrational tricks at stressful times. He met her at the triangle in the middle of Les Carroz and told her to collect her things to be able to spend the next two nights with him in a small apartment that he had rented only two hundred metres from the village centre. He didn't want to rock her job boat because he knew the agencies were beginning to lay off staff towards the winters end, so he told her to still go to work every day and come to him when she finished.

The uncomplicated love he gave her settled her back into the conviction that keeping the past behind her was the best remedy. Erik received no call. He buried his misery and returned to concentrate on the tennis programme that Scott had planned but could not participate in. Scott's third treatment from the chiropractor was due that same afternoon. He seemed to be improving and hoped to be able to resume work in another week to ten days. The last time his back had gone it was OK again inside a month.

"I am sure you have no need to fear anything out of the ordinary, Maria Carmelita. It is not love or anything sordid. It is just the fascination of a sixteen year old for a very pretty girl with a beautiful ebony colour."

"Ee as been told before. No girlfriends. Ee as been brought up to know that del Forlan family only marry to the lighter skin. I ad to pay one girl in Uruguay to stop contacting him"

"I have been teaching teenagers for twenty years and assure you I will monitor everything between them" said Lindsay.

"We know a high class family with daughter who will marry him. It is fixed. Any more problem and I will take him back to Montevideo."

She saw Maria Carmelita back to the chauffeur and her car.

"God preserve me from 'pushy mothers'" she later said to no-one in particular. Scott looked up from a tennis magazine he was reading.

"Hear, hear, to that. What's the crack?"

"Posh South American family trying to stop the natural urges of a harmless teenage son. Back door racist as well." Answered Lindsay

"No teenage son is harmless. They all carry a six shooter that can go off at any time, often out of the control of the owner." said Scott

"This is a good lad who has had a top education and high standards of behaviour"

"No-one educates their 'willies' though. That's where the trouble starts."

"You, Scott, are a cynical bastard" she replied.

"I was once a teenager amongst other boy teenagers in Tazzy."

"Yes. As a nice Kiwi girl I can imagine you lot rampaging around Hobart in marauding gangs hunting down anything in a skirt."

Scott went back to the full-length photo of Maria Sharapova, this months centrefold in the middle of his tennis magazine.

Lindsay brought Nacho and Padmini together and asked them to promise that they would concentrate on school and tennis all the time they were at the Academy.

"What was that about?" Padmini asked Nacho later.

"Someone has told her that I like you. My Mother has been here. I saw her yesterday. She thinks I am going to marry some rich cabbage that she knows in our home city. Maybe I will shock her and marry you"

"Huh. First I have to love you. You should be so lucky."

She walked away, this time without turning back.

Padmini had matured early and was aware of Nacho's eye constantly following her. She thought he was very handsome and said to herself

'I'll marry him one day.' She began to think about her wedding and the flowers she would have and the jewellery she would wear.

Other romances within the Trocadero Complex were further advanced. Kurt had changed his parents' plans and persuaded them to finance a second year at the Academy.

229

This was to be with Petra, who lived not too far away from his Munich home, in Zurich over the border in Switzerland. They were keen to take their relationship to the next level and spent every spare minute together patiently waiting for their freedom to roam the tennis circuit released from adult supervision.

Torgny frequently passed notes to Luciana who watched his tennis practise every day in her afternoon tea break, with Carmen usually scowling at her from one of the building windows. Torgny was constantly trying to find other 'linen cupboards' and planned a close encounter with the assistant cook, who had already shown him that she was not as innocent as her supervisor thought.

The only other pending romance was one that had, so far, escaped the knowledge of the staff gossips. It was Cameron's introduction into the pleasures of the flesh by a pocket tornado called Sofia. He too was actively searching for ways to continue their gymnastics.

Sink had been fishing each time he cycled down to the jetty near the Marina. His line was thin and not very long and he still had only the crab and the tiny fish to his name. Cameron had left him to cycle off and buy them both a can of drink on this hot day. Another man came over and said

"You need a stronger line if you want to catch bigger fish. Here, use mine. You can return it when I come down tomorrow."

He attached a sardine to the hook and handed it over to Sink, who accepted the short rod, line and bait gratefully. He would have been quite happy catching the sardine. It was bigger than his best catch to date. He cast out into the sea and waited to tell Cameron his good fortune.

Ten minutes later Cameron cycled down the jetty to see a crowd at the end surrounding Sink and two other men holding on to the rod, which was bending to almost 90 degrees as the line stretched taut out into the water.

Someone shouted to him

"Your friend has caught a dolphin!"

Cameron threw down the bike and put the two cans on the ground, rushing to Sink's aid. There was no space for another person to swing on the rod handle so he looked over the side. About 40 metres out a huge fish was thrashing around with the line running out towards it from the jetty.

Cameron thought quickly. He must save the dolphin. He could see that it probably was one because a small school were rolling up for air another 50 metres further out. He ran to the other side of the jetty where a fishing boat was just casting off for its daily trawl out in the Mediterranean. His Spanish was good now after nearly two years with Lollo. He explained the problem and they waved acknowledgement and increased motor speed to go around the end of the stone jetty. Five minutes later, with the dolphin still firmly attached to Sink's heavy duty line, two of the boat's crew leant over the starboard side and cast a small net around the creature, who was tiring and near the surface again. They pulled him into the fishing boat. The net prevented him from moving much and he lay on the bottom of the deck. The boat then motored towards the jetty with Sink's line still in the mouth of the dolphin.

It was a bottle nosed dolphin of the species often seen along the Costa del Sol inshore waters. One fisherman held open its mouth as another carefully twisted and tugged at the line and hook inside its throat. After a moment the dolphin seemed to hiccup and out came line, hook and a ten centimetre tuna still attached to the hook. The dolphin coughed and was sick on to the deck at the same time as the tuna spat out half the sardine. The men washed off the tuna and released the line for a grinning Sink to wind it in with the tuna still attached. They took the fishing boat out into deeper water and gently lifted the heavy dolphin over the side.He lay in the water for quite some time, then his tail lifted and dropped back on to the water surface splashing one of the crew who was watching. The last they saw of him was his body swimming strongly away out to sea.

The crew waved to Sink and their boat turned out to sea for the day's work. Sink carried his tuna in triumph back to Maria to cook for their dinner. It was a baby, but too far gone to be able to put back in the sea. He ran into the house shouting

"I caught a dolphin."

Outside, Jorge, enjoying his day off, looked at Cameron who nodded. Cameron cycled home, leaving his friend to tell the unlikely story.

"Why didn't you bring me the dolphin" said Juanita to Cameron.

"I could have fed everyone here for a week."

"No way could I eat them. They are as intelligent as we are." said Cameron

"So are some of the animals we eat. In France they eat horses" she offered as a good reason.

"In the South Seas they used to eat people" said Cameron as he went out through the door "but I couldn't eat one of those either. Well, not a whole one anyway."

Sink had a Skype link with Felix that was even longer than usual. Judging by his hand movements it was at least a whale that he had caught.

Felix was still waiting for one of those warm mornings that George had promised him came in the summer to the farm on the top of the limestone cliffs. His woolly gloves, with the fingers cut out, were OK but it was colder than at any time of year in his part of West Africa. He was standing in a metal bath of disinfectant to clean his wellies before he joined the family for a hot breakfast.

"What an amazing coincidence it is that Felix knew

Erik, and then, of all the places in Europe, he found his way here to our small village." said Helen from the kitchen.

Both she and George were thinking the same but neither was voicing the possibility. They shook their heads at the same time. 'No, impossible.' Callum had already worked out what had happened and was contentedly sitting on the school bus next to Penny, glad that he didn't have to shovel up cow pats from the milking shed like his recently discovered stowaway.

"Did you phone him then, Cory?"

"No Dad. I am very happy here. I have a Swiss friend who comes to see me from time to time and he is very kind. He is an engineer. My job is easy and the holiday atmosphere is always upbeat. I am moving on, Dad."

"Good girl. You have probably made the correct decision. Swiss Engineer is he? Maybe he'll send me a cuckoo clock for my Birthday."

Coralie had kissed Thomas goodbye that morning. They had had a pleasant weekend together in the small apartment and each told the other about their rich life experiences, leaving out the bad ones. She had walked to work feeling good. She always felt good when the spring had almost arrived and summer lay ahead with the tennis outdoor season imminent.

'Oh. God. 'Tennis.' What was she going to do this summer? She needed a job and somewhere to live. Only seldom did they go together in the sports world.'

"Is he the permanent one then?" asked Elena, as they made yet another rumpled bed.

"I was considering that this morning. I don't think so. There was an electric charge with Erik. There isn't with Thomas. He has all the qualities a woman would need in a husband. I don't think he would ever be unfaithful. I can see him changing nappies and ironing the clothes. He has a good job and one day may be boss of the family business, but the spark is only a spark, it isn't a flash of lightening like it was with Erik, and even with Harry whom I knew before in England and nearly married."

"Don't wait too long. Your clock is ticking and you will never find the perfect one. They only exist in cheap books. In reality, the good looking ones are always in someone else's bed and the ordinary ones are not good looking enough. The sporty ones will never cut the grass or wash the dishes and the kind ones have no sense of variety or adventure. Make a choice. Pick one that makes you wonder what he will surprise you with next, or one that will be reliable, cook the dinner and make you dream about being in the arms of the hero in the film you are watching on TV."

Coralie began to write to some of the contacts she had made during her year of coaching at the Trocadero and escorting the students in their quest for tournament success. Several people had assumed that she was the only coach of the player who had just impressed on court and approached her:-

"Here is my number if you ever fancy the idea of teaching/coaching in Las Vegas/Toronto/Melbourne/Rio/Hawaii. Just pick up the phone. We have 4/8/12/25 young players and a good track record. They need someone just like you."

She thanked them and put the cards in her bag, never expecting to look at them again. Now she carefully chose the ones to whom to send her text enquiring about employment. Within seconds a reply came back from Hawaii.

'You the blonde woman with the psychedelic headband?"

She remembered the striking blonde from one of the weeks away and the equally striking clothes she wore.

Coralie thought she was a rep. for one of the sports companies. She didn't reply.

Someone from the first tournament she attended in Faro replied thanking her for the enquiry. There was a new post in the tennis section of one of the large golf clubs. It was to coach a group of four juniors and any sons or daughters of visitors to the Club during the year, who were prepared to pay by the day. There was an apartment with the job about a mile away from the Club.

Coralie decided to wait and see what else came up. She ordered current issues of tennis magazines, from the Newsagent in Les Carroz, that she knew carried advertisements for coaching and management posts.

Pepe had not told Lindsay about one of the advantages in siting the chocolate manufacture in Cremona. It was one of a number of villages in a lush valley in the Province and through the valley ran a picturesque river. It was a dairying area and there had, until eight years ago, been a milk processing plant at the bottom of the village. This was the building that Victor was restoring and altering to create sterile conditions for a food processing operation. Most of the milk being produced in the valley would be used in the manufacture in due course. The launch item was already designed jointly by two experts, each of whom had taken early retirement from Lindt and Cadburys. It was a Swiss-style recipe with a fruit and biscuit centre, shaped as a bar and to be called a 'Zanzibar'. An additional significance was that the first refugee to pass through Cremona four years before originated from Zanzibar in Tanzania.

Progress was rapid. One quarter of the building was complete and stainless steel equipment had been installed into a sealed unit. The bars were being made by a team of workers who had been established in chocolate production or in packaging to a high standard. The launch into a supermarket chain in Spain was planned just after Easter and expansion into the lucrative Arabian Gulf countries to follow, depending on early sales.

Syrian refugee families were beginning to be housed with village families in Cremona. They usually had to be split up to stay in two houses, side by side. The Government Housing Minister was indicating that funds may be available to built temporary homes on the edge of the village and the Employment Ministry was working closely with Victor and Pepe. Usually favourable publicity followed the scheme, which was not draining welfare resources provided from Madrid. Victor realised that a positive press would continue if everything carried on without problems. He had managed to obtain charitable status for the project because it was non-profit and of social benefit.

TWENTY

The Easter Vacation at the Academy was not taken in line with that of the Spanish Education Authority because of the entries to two major junior tennis tournaments held at this time. They were back into the clay time of the year, for which Spain's top players has been known for their skill. A majority of the courts in Southern Europe had red clay as a surface.

By virtue of their birth dates many of the Trocadero competitors were in the last year of whichever age range they were entering. This meant that they should have a better opportunity to stamp their mark on those divisions.

The Under 14 girls collected everything possible in the two tournaments in their age group. Lucy and Gabby each won one of the singles events and beat each other in the finals. Padmini and Saskia were the losing semi finalists in both. Not surprisingly, considering their doubles practise was greater than in other tennis schools, they beat each other in the finals of both doubles events. Padmini and Saskia, surprisingly won both, although they were 26-17 down in matches in their tussles at home. Charlie Mills, back in his office, was smiling almost as much because his two spon-sored girls were on the back pages of the newspapers.

There was great joy in the Children's Home in India, in Oman and in East Devon amongst the knowledgeable tennis fraternity, and in Bologna Gabby's face graced the front page of the city's evening paper. Kurt and Petra continued their unbeaten mixed doubles run and Felipe, to the delight of the Marbella Club won his first Under 16 singles title. Everyone had climbed a few places in the junior rankings that were now issued for Europe. The exceptions were Dan and Torgny. Erik had agonised whether he should be entering them in the Under 18 singles events, but he decided to keep them at home to dedicate his time to bring them further into training for the men's doubles events during the coming summer.

He persuaded his old partner, Sammy, to fly up from Bengaluru in India and take some exercise on a promise of a few evenings out in Malaga and Gibraltar. He and Sammy practised every day for two weeks with Dan and Torgny, in the mornings one on one and in the afternoons a full, 'no holds barred', best of five sets doubles. It nearly killed poor Sammy, who was twelve pounds overweight when he arrived. However, when he found the scales on his last day there, he weighed just two pounds more than his competition weight from years before.

The older pairing won the first matches in straight sets, though not easily and principally through guile, acquired over a decade in the top ten doubles partnerships and as winners of a cluster of tournaments. By the end of the first week Dan and Torgny had won once and taken another to four sets. The last two were won in four sets by the youngsters with Dan holding every service game both times. They all went out to a night club in Malaga on the last evening and toasted each other, and again to a successful summer to come.

Lindsay and Scott returned with the victorious students and Juanita and Carmen organised an end of term celebration party for staff, students, teachers and coaches. It was an outside barbecue and some of the parents, who had arrived early for the next day's academy exodus, joined in. Nacho and Padmini carefully kept apart for the whole evening as Mother was in the vicinity.

Sally had the good sense to send Jennifer again to collect Padmini. Jennifer had enjoyed such a happy reunion with her sister last time that she had worked like a Trojan for the last three months, and so Sally and Chris sent her again.

Sally had noticed the effect her own presence previously had had on Erik and the expression on Coralie's face on the sidelines. A little research had confirmed that the two were lovers. She didn't want to hurt Erik any more than her departure had fifteen or more years before.

Steadily during the next day everyone left. Erik ran two sorties to the airport and put Thomas, Petra and Kurt on a German long distance bus. Lindsay helped Oksana into her limousine, together with Lucy and Saskia, who were going to be dropped off to meet Helen at Lille and return with her on Eurostar. She then took Soo-Jin all the way to Madrid to use the Qatar Airways concession and be flown home to New Zealand via Doha.

On the way home Lindsay diverted to Cremona and was staggered to see the progress made at the new factory site. Pepe showed her around and she was given a dozen Zanzibars to take back to Marbella.

"Doesn't the dust from the building site get into the chocolate?" she asked him. He answered with another question

"Did you never know how white chocolate is made? No. It's actually OK. The seals around the manufacturing area are very sound."

By the next evening all the students and parents had gone and the staff were sent home early with thanks. The newly married couple, Erik, Scott and Lindsay drove off together to see Clarence and relax for an evening looking back on another term.

"Good God, you're early". Clarence was just throwing open the front door. I haven't even had a chance to brush my hair."

"I suppose you and Rex have been having a siesta." said Lavinia.

"Too right, Lavinia. It's the only good thing about this country, the daily siesta. Anyway, Rex is stressed and I needed to give him a massage."

"Mmm. Lucky old Rex". said Lindsay

"I can do you too, if you like. For a small fee of course."

"Actually that could be rather nice"

"Nice? It will be the experience of a lifetime, my good woman"

Lindsay looked at Lollo and Erik.

"Why don't you boys let Clarence give you a massage?"

"No thanks" said Erik "His hands would be everywhere I don't need them to be"

"It would teach you men how it has been for us. Women only have to show a centimetre of flesh and, in a trice, there is a male hand where it shouldn't be. You have had an easy time by comparison." Lavinia told him.

"Are you qualified to grope people in the name of massage Clarence?" asked Lollo. "I mean do you have a certificate from some College or University?"

"No dear, it comes naturally to me. I let the energies guide my hands"

"And that is the case for the defence, Your Honour " said Lavinia

They all laughed.

"What about your drag days. Did you train for that? Is there a BSc in Drag?"

"My degree was exclusive and took three years of hard work to complete."

"Costume design at the Savile Row Institute?" asked Lindsay

"Cheeky. No, I have a 2/2 in Lethargy at the University of Outer Mongolia"

Erik changed the subject.

"Clarence, you know we all hang on your words and base our decisions on your wisdom and advice."

"No" Clarence answered warily.

Erik continued

"Lollo and Lavinia only went away for one day to celebrate their nuptials. They haven't yet planned a proper honeymoon and need your advice."

"Do you mean where to go or what to do when they get there?" said Clarence, attempting to look innocent.

"The Academy is giving them the honeymoon as a wedding present as, between them, they have everything else probably in duplicate. Now is the time for them to relax and make the best of the Easter break in some exotic destination"

"If I was Lavinia I would not relax for a moment with that randy git having a key to my chastity belt" Clarence continued.

"So we are all agog to hear the pearls of wisdom fall from your lips" added Lindsay.

"I'll get your drinks and come and join you as no other customer has been so inconsiderate as to arrive before we were open. Then I shall expect complete silence as I deliver my judgment." He skipped off to the bar.

"Are you really giving us a honeymoon?" asked Lavinia holding on to one finger of Lollo's podgy hand.

"Yes we are" said Lindsay emphatically. "Without you two the Trocadero would not be half the institution it is"

"I'm not ready for an institution yet" said Scott

Lavinia continued :-

"What if Clarence suggests something wildly expensive?"

"Then we shall have to mortgage the students" replied Lindsay quickly because she had been wondering the same.

Clarence brought a tray of the drinks he knew they all liked and two of the dishes of tapas that lay on the bar.

"Are these the leftovers from lunchtime?" It didn't stop Lollo from helping himself with the assistance of one of the toothpicks that permanently sat in a pot in the middle of each table.

"No they are not. I would lose one of my Michelin Stars if I did such a thing"

Clarence looked horrified.

"Now, gather round. Ah! You already have. Right ho then. To be sure you only blame yourselves and not me if it goes wrong I will give you several choices……" Lindsay opened her mouth to speak.

"Silence please whilst the offer is being delivered from the deep reservoir of knowledge within." He tapped his head.

"First option is a course of 10 parachute jumps from 12,000 ft over Dubai."

Laughter exploded around the room. Lollo feigned shock at their reaction.

"Secondly. A day's instruction and race around Brands Hatch in England driving a 200mph Lamborghini"

More tittering from the others.

"Thirdly. A weekend in Las Vegas on the Strip with 500 Euros to spend"

Lindsay could not avoid looking at Erik to see if his reaction was any better than hers.

"Fourthly. The Bridal Suite on the MV Rosario with five star cuisine when it delivers its cargo of Zanzibars to Malta and Sicily, leaving in two days I am told by Mr Pepe."

"Finally. A week in my apartment in Lanzarote, which just happens to be free from this coming Saturday, with dinner served daily on the terrace by my good friend Rupert, who owns the restaurant 50 metres along the road"

There was a silence as everyone contemplated the choices. Lindsay tried to think how they would be financed and Scott was not sure whether Clarence was making it all up as he went along. Erik simply thought that Clarence was a great guy and a terrific showman. Lollo stood up to make a speech, producing another white handkerchief. He mopped his brow and Lavinia noticed that the handkerchief was definitely the same one that had appeared in the Church.

"My dear friends…..and Clarence. It gives me great pleasure to offer thanks to the Thomas Cook of the Costa del Sol for these excellent suggestions. I wish to accept, without hesitation, the day in the Lamborghini. My lovely wife, however, wishes to be strapped to a muscular young instructor and to plunge to the desert on a parachute. There was a long pause. Then Clarence started chuckling, followed by Lollo's serious face beginning to break down, until everyone rocked with laughter. When they had stopped and raised their glasses to Clarence Lavinia said

"Thank you very, very much. With no offence to your lovely offer of your apartment Clarence, I think we would love to go on the cruise to Malta."

Lollo nodded enthusiastically and Lindsay thought 'Phew!!'

Two days later, after Lindsay had been to see Victor and Pepe in the Marbella Club and bought them a bottle of the best Chablis, they drove Lollo and Lavinia, bedecked once more in an array of tassels and scarves, to the Marina. There awaited a dozen well-wishers who cheered as they went aboard the Rosario and threw rice and confetti in handfuls over them.

The Motor Yacht pulled away from the side and purred

over the water at the regulation 5mph until she left the harbour entrance. Pepe and Lindsay held hands as they waved to the pair who were leaning on the rail. The last they saw was Lucas, standing on the stern pointing to, and holding aloft, a huge lobster. It seemed that lunch was already ordered.

At the rear of the crowd of well-wishers on the quayside were two fifteen year olds with an ulterior motive. Papa was attending a meeting in Malaga and Mama was being shown by her visiting Mother how to make the best cheesecake in Espana. Daughter was genuinely spending some time with the Spanish tutor from the Trocadero, thought to be very important as examinations were approaching in June. She had omitted to add that it was likely to be only a few minutes in his presence. Papa had stupidly left the key at home to his boat that was, as before, further out in the cheaper berths on the other side of the Marina. The crowd dispersed and Cameron and Sofia walked separately down the floating walkways until they reached the craft, stepped on board, opened and slid back the entrance to the cabin. Cameron secured the hatch whilst Sofia pulled the little curtains across the windows. They piled the padded bench seats and all the cushions neatly on the floor and then looked at each other. Cameron said in his best Spanish

"Shall we continue from where we left off?"

Sofia nodded and leapt at him. They both collapsed on to the cabin floor

They woke up in the early afternoon. Cameron kissed her passionately and she rolled on top of him looking for more loving.

He said "I am not supposed to be doing this with you. It is against the law in New Zealand and I think it is here too"

She thought for a moment and said

"It's OK. I am 16. It was my birthday two months ago."

"That's good" he replied. "But you are breaking the law doing it to me then"

"You are only 15 still?"

He nodded. "For two more weeks."

"Too bad. Then I shall go to prison. Now you can give me my birthday present."

Coralie was surprised, when she opened her iPad at breakfast time, that two more replies to her emails had come into her Inbox overnight. One from Phoenix Arizona invited her to attend a practical interview at a specific date and time. It had come from another of the admirers of the quality of the Trocadero students that she had met at Flushing Meadow in New York. He was beginning a new school for coaching resident girls only. If she wished to attend she was to quote No. 14 on all the correspondence from now on. This sounded quite interesting, until it dawned on her that the date was one week from now. She opened the other.

The second email reply was from Ireland. She knew Galway was a lovely city from postcards sent her by one of her school friends who had attended the University on a music degree course. The offer was to coach twin boys from a wealthy family who lived on the outskirts of the city. The salary was not great though it included a room in their large house shared with a private teacher. There would also be an interview, but it did not include anything on court. The family had already received a recommendation from Kurt's father, who was a business associate.

Elena was unwell that morning so Coralie was working alone. She thought about the responses so far and wondered which would be the best. If she was No 14 on the list for Phoenix she didn't hold out much hope. It was a long way to go and there was no mention of paying for an airfare. She would wait to see what came from the adverts in the two tennis magazines she had chosen. The problem was they did not appear for another three weeks and the likelihood of being laid off by the chalet company prompted her to reply immediately to the known opportunities. She decided to go for the Faro job and for Galway, both of which included somewhere to live. She liked the prospect of living in either of the two countries having met many nice Irish people and liked the several Portuguese she had met on a day trip to Jersey, where many from the Portuguese Island of Madeira worked; and also from the Faro tournament last year.

She replied to the Golf Club near Faro on the Algarve and was invited to visit during the next two weeks at her convenience. They would appoint on April 30th. The Irish job would not begin until the end of August, after the family came home from their summer vacation abroad, but they would like to see her in May or June.

David told her that his bookings for ski instruction were coming to an end and he would take a holiday before beginning the next batch of houses and chalets to decorate. If she wanted to go to Faro on a specific date he could finish his contract and leave the last clients to Mario, his colleague who lived nearby in Flaine. He could drive her to Portugal and they could enjoy a few days on the beach whilst they were there.

Coralie left the Alpina Company a week before she and Elena would have been asked to finish. The ski season was finishing and Elena was returning to her son in the Czech Republic. They bade a tearful farewell as Elena helped her load her bags into David's VW Golf. There had been fewer 'missed calls' from Erik throughout April and she felt free to begin again. The interim winter's chalet work had kept her quite fit and it had cleared the last of the uncertainties that crept into her mind occasionally. Thomas was concerned that she may move too far away from him, but wished her well at the forthcoming interview.

Thunder and lightening followed them down the mountain around the hairpin bends to the valley and the motorway. David didn't have a SatNav, preferring to rely on his knowledge of France and Spain and reference to a map of both. They chattered for the first two hours towards and through Lyon and then as they continued West towards Brive, before Coralie fell asleep against the embroidered pillow that had accompanied all her dreams since she left Ottery for the adventures in Marbella.

When she awoke they were beyond Brive in the car park of a pretty café, both hungry for lunch. They began telling each other tales of their schooldays when David had been three years her senior at the local Community College. He told her about the time they had put a small dog inside the RE teacher's desk. It was an old desk with an ink well hole in the top corner. The first sign of the dog was a snuffling noise and the appearance of some whiskers and a wet nose through the inkwell. They had been in the middle of a serious debate as to whether 'thou shalt not kill' in the Bible had meant that everyone should be a vegetarian. The discovery of the dog and the ensuing chaos led the class clown 'Traffic Lights' to turn the discussion into a case for eating dogs as they do in some places in the Far East. He was eventually sent out of the class for suggesting that the window sticker on the teacher's car which said 'A Dog is for Life, not just for Christmas' should be changed to 'A Dog is not just for Christmas. There should be some left for New Year.'

"Why did you boys always call him 'Traffic Lights'?" Coralie asked

"It was cruel and it stayed with him all through his apprenticeship. He had one green eye and one blue one."

"The teachers wouldn't allow that now. Or probably us calling the deputy Head Girl, Fiona Burns, 'TD'"

David looked across at her with a frown.

"Short for 'Third Degree'"

They continued all the way past Bordeaux and down to the Spanish Border telling each other amusing things about their schooldays and which teacher they liked and which ones they didn't, and some they liked who were no good at teaching and others, whose classes they hated but always learnt a lot.

"What about Miss Underhill?"

"She was horrible. Straight out of a Dickens tale. Put more people in detention than all the other teachers together."

"The girls all thought she must have had a bad love affair or her parents used to beat her, and she used to take it out on the pupils."

"Once, she kept us all in class for an extra hour and everyone missed the school buses out into the country areas. I think she got into trouble for that. We were only about twelve and got our own back for that. She lived near the school, so three of us went around in the winter and woke up her tortoise."

They drove into Spain and up to Pamplona in the foothills of the Pyrenees. Here they stopped and arranged to stay in a little guest house with only two rooms. One was already taken. The other had twin beds so they shared the room and halved the cost. Before dinner David took Coralie for a long walk in the last of the sunlight. He took her to a rock and sat on the ground in front of it facing a view to the west of fields, cattle and trees sloping down towards the heart of Spain.

"I asked Mary to marry me here" he suddenly said

"Mary Costello?"

He nodded.

"I hadn't realised you were that close"

"Nor did I until about five minutes before I blurted it out. I used to do things on impulse in those days. I did really like her though"

"Did she accept?"

"No. She laughed in my face, got up and walked off. Bless her, she never mentioned it again and we are still friends. She could have told everyone. First time I have told anyone else"

"I am privileged" said Coralie seriously. "I shan't tell anyone else either. Anybody else you have proposed to?"

"Nope. Only one in 33 years."

"Time you found someone to be permanently in love with"

"I have. Me!" He got up and they walked slowly back to their dinner.

"It is really nice spending some time with you, Sis. We haven't done this for years. Probably never talked properly about anything for more than five minutes." David said, from the bed nearest the door.

"Do you snore?"

"Don't think so."

"Haven't any, of the hundreds of girls you have slept with, ever told you?"

"Thousands, please. No none of them. Actually I only ever slept with Mary. Don't tell anyone. It would ruin my 'street cred'. Goodnight".

TWENTY-ONE

"You must not fire it at people because the bow is quite strong and could take out a person's eye". Helen was putting limitations on Luke's birthday present Uncle Erik had left behind for his 9th birthday, a smart longbow and a pack of 12 arrows with suckers on the end. Luke and school friend Kieran were about to set off around the farm searching for suitable targets. Luke had one of those adorable faces that old ladies can't resist kissing and mothers assume reflect a cherubic nature. Reality had begun to demonstrate that inside was a devil genie anxious to reveal itself to the world.

Over the weekend arrows began to appear in strange places. These were arrows that could not be collected for fear of breaking cover and discovery. Felix found himself milking cows with arrows sticking out of their flanks. The guard of honour outside the Axmouth Church, waiting to salute the coffin of the Late Brigadier Roper, was surprised to find the hearse arriving with two arrows stuck to the side. Mrs Bottomley, who would insist on wearing a hat decorated with fruit and flowers every spring, walked along jauntily one morning with an arrow seemingly woven into the design. The situation was not helped by Kieran contributing an additional supply of arrows for the longbow.

By Tuesday evening the sign above Poppy Chocolatiere had registered bullseye arrows through all three of the 'o's.

Road signs, bicycle saddlebags, golf trolleys on the nearby course and a wreath placed at the war memorial all suffered from the accuracy of Luke's misguided present.

Relief for the villagers came via Constable Higgins, who often appeared at the primary school gate with Boris, his German Shepherd Dog. This was a Police public relations exercise and one which had the effect of stopping the cars delivering children from parking on the double yellow lines. He returned to his van with Boris one day to find that the wing mirror of the van had an arrow affixed to it and that Boris, who was following close behind, also appeared to have been attacked by North American Indians. The ensuing visit to the Farm led to a certain birthday present being consigned to the loft when its owner returned from school.

"Just wait until I see Erik" exclaimed Helen as she served Felix his breakfast.

"Have you managed to calm the cows down yet?"

"Now OK" replied Felix smiling. "I find one arrow on heel of my welly".

Helen was about to make some remark about Achilles, but swiftly decided that it wouldn't mean a lot to Felix.

"Did you go around firing arrows at things in your village when you were nine years old?"

He smiled again "No. But I given Uzi Machine pistol when I ten."

Helen decided not to pursue that conversation either.

George arrived and joined them for his breakfast.

"Felix. Today I will teach you to drive a tractor."

Felix's eyes lit up.

"You cannot go on the road until you have a proper licence, but you can drive it around the farm. We'll start with the old Fergie and see how you get on."

Felix was much happier at the Farm now. He was beginning to feel like one of the family and it was a little warmer every day for his early start. The clocks had gone on an hour and he liked the lighter evenings. The policeman saw him when he visited but didn't say anything to him or about him to George and Helen. And his Skype link with Sink made him sure that his brother was in good hands.

Back in Spain the PE teacher from the local secondary school was walking into the Trocadero complex and heading towards the main building to begin work in his second job when he spotted Lollo sitting on his bench, having just returned from his honeymoon.

"You've put on some weight Lollo. Food very good on board I suppose"

"Hola Jordi. Si. Just a couple of kilos. We were needed by Mr. Victor to sample the Zanzibar as official food tasters."

"For the sake of your heart you must come to my gym. Start today, come now."

"No, my friend. I tried that equipment regime once before and, after a short time of immense enjoyment, my rowing machine sank. No, it is too dangerous for me to risk now that I have a wife to support."

"She will be supporting you, if you have a heart attack."

"It's all in the hands of God. Too much exercise can be very threatening. I shall be off to my favourite hostelry soon to take my medicine – my elixir."

Jordi, the PE teacher, was operating a programme to build the strength of each tennis student to peak in the summer when all the European tournaments are played. He had become a valuable member of the team and was enjoying the intensity of the all round training of the students; something he would love to have pursued with the best of his school sports stars.

Coralie and David continued their journey across Spain, through Madrid, where they stopped to visit some of the tourist sites. Then down to Seville. They stayed in Seville, a beautiful city, in a small hotel overlooking one of the garden squares. There was a spring flower procession that evening with dancers swirling and tapping through the streets and open carriages drawn by matching pairs of horses with silky manes. In each carriage sat four people in traditional costume with brightly coloured dresses and cummerbunds, mantillas and open fans. The procession flowed right around the square before moving on to the next one. They stood on their first floor balcony and toasted the dancers with glasses of wine.

The last stage of the journey to Faro began with Coralie calling the Golf Club to say she would be there this evening and asking for recommendations for somewhere to stay, before meeting the officials perhaps tomorrow. David drove the VW to the border with Portugal and along the beginning of the Algarve to the Golf Club a few miles beyond Faro.

They stayed in an annexe to the Clubhouse that was often used by visiting event speakers or celebrity golfers who had come by invitation. The Club had a dining room for members and they ate there so that Coralie could get a good night's sleep before her interview the following morning. Two of the small Sub-Committee responsible for tennis were in Lisbon on business, but the other two and the Club Secretary were available to interview her. David thought she looked fantastic in her new white dress that was not too mini and the red belt and clutch bag contrasting with her 'snow tan' and dark, almost black hair, which she had tied back loosely.

The trio of interviewers adopted the 'good cop, bad cop' technique of interviewing. Coralie had experienced this before and went out once with a police officer, who had explained what the idea was. One interviewer, the man this time, was very aggressive and sceptical of her answers whilst the other two, the lady and the Club Secretary were kindness itself and praising her achievements and references.

She was in a carefree frame of mind and gave clear answers from which she did not waver. When asked if she had any questions of them she confirmed that there was a bedsit available in the vicinity. She also wanted to see courts and changing facilities and a sight of the four permanents pupils of the current coach.

The 'bad cop' from the interview showed her around and turned out to be charming and a keen player in his youth. Only two of the four students were on court and a visiting teenager, who was paying for coaching. She watched them play a double with the coach for a few minutes. The court was the traditional red clay.

Coralie and David left the Club with a promise that an offer would be made, not by April 30th as they had said in the email but, due to another candidate not being available until May 2nd, on May 4th. They moved on to stay a week at the Pestana apartments near the Praia des Roches, which was owned by a friend of Davids in the UK, though not in use in April.

"So it's May 4th now is it? As Luke Skywalker would say 'May the Fourth be with you'"

"Enough, big bruvver. I can't stand a week of that." laughed Coralie

They drove another fifteen miles further on to the apartment. David phoned the owner to tell her they had arrived and to thank her. They walked down to the wooden restaurant on the beach and ordered a meal of fish freshly caught that morning by the brother of the restauranteur.

Pepe reported back to the factory in Cremona upon the first export of the Zanzibar. The second quarter of the building project was almost complete. There had been a few hiccups with the production line. He reassured his colleagues that this was only to be expected in the first year. The training of the first six of the refugees was going well and they would be integrated next week into the full workforce, and this had attracted a grant from the Government towards their wages.

Pepe managed to prise Lindsay away from the books and the courts of Trocadero for dinner at a new restaurant in Marbella that was aiming for an upmarket clientele. Their location was not too good and they had to walk from the car park almost 100 metres. Pepe was carrying an intriguing rectangular box. Lindsay speculated that he had brought his own wine, rather than chance a new cellar.

'At least it is too big a box for a ring, so he is not going to try to change my mind.' Part way through the meal he asked the Head Waiter to bring the box from the refrigerator. Lindsay was even more mystified.

It was a box of tulips in bud, some white, some light brown that he presented to her. The Head Waiter, a colleague and several other diners watched as she went to take a stem from the box. Lindsay pulled her hand back slightly. They were not flowers, but chocolates! She took one out. It was a large strawberry that had been dipped in white chocolate attached to a long plastic stem.

"Go on Carina. Bite into it" said an amused Pepe.

She bit through the cold chocolate into the strawberry. It was a delicious combination. Then she pulled the whole strawberry from its stem and ate the rest leaving the leaf top behind. Two people at the next table applauded.

"What a wonderful present" she exclaimed with her mouth still partly full.

She looked again at the tulips in the box and handed a brown one to Pepe and another to the lady at the next table. They looked so realistic.

"It is a creation of one of the refugees who is training at the factory in Cremona. She used to paint pottery in Aleppo in Syria. We just gave her access to some white and brown chocolate to create something. She bought fruit in the village and I have no idea where the stems came from. Now we have an unique addition to our Zanzibar." Pepe enthused.

"What did you think it was when I brought it from the car cool box?"

"Wine. I thought you weren't going to risk the wine at a new restaurant."

"Enjoy being the first lady to receive a 'Cremona Bouquet'"

"We are too busy, you and I, Carina" said Pepe over coffee "I have no time to spend with you. And you have no time to spend with me. We should both slow down and begin to enjoy life and each other a little more."

Lindsay hesitated for a moment.

"You are right. It is one thing for you to devote your life and energy to helping those too poor and unfortunate to help themselves, and quite another to burn yourself up and restrict the amount you can do in the future. For me, I am only too aware that we need more staff to work on the tennis side. One or two more and one extra on the teaching staff."

The next morning Erik and Lindsay discussed the staff shortage over breakfast and made a couple of decisions. Scott joined them muttering about something.

"I was out with Lollo last night testing last year's Rioja at Bar Lulu."

"Headache?" asked Erik "Take a drug-free remedy"

"Such as?"

"Rosemary is good for a headache."

"Yeah." said Scott "She always had one when I went out with her"

"Here. Try this in a little water."

"Better?" asked Lindsay a few minutes later.

"Yes. Thanks" said Scott

Erik was sitting opposite him.

"Fancy working for us full time, rather than being Nike's lackey?"

"Go on"

"Same job, bonus for wins and finals. Lindsay will talk money when she has had another look in the books. We will stay mainly doubles orientated and you become our main man in doubles coaching."

Lindsay chipped in

"Erik and I continue all singles and support for your doubles programme. We try to find a good additional coach to concentrate on the singles and eventually take over that programme."

"I'll need at least what Charlie is paying, and the 'all found' bit that he pays you for" said Scott

"We can definitely do that. I can say that before looking any further into our finances" replied Lindsay

"Bloody Hell, you're on mate". He got up and shook hands with each of them. "Hey, great."

Lindsay took Padmini to Dr Muller, the Academy's official general practitioner in the centre of Marbella. He diagnosed anaemia, but wanted her to be properly checked with a consultant in Granada to clear the possibility of leukaemia. She phoned Sally to tell her and Sally spoke to Padmini on Skype that evening. Lindsay went through her notes from the meeting with Dr Muller. It is well known that many people from Padmini's ethnic background are often anaemic. There are some hereditary leukaemias. Do you know much about Padmini's parents or grandparents?

"Not much and nothing about their medical history" said Sally.

Sally told Padmini that everything would be fine in Lindsay's hands and that the consultant would find out what was making her so tired.

Feeling even more under pressure Lindsay decided to bypass Erik and call Coralie's mobile. She had heard Erik say half a dozen times that it was switched off. Coralie answered immediately.

"Lindsay. How are you? It's been too long since we talked."

"Are you back home. How was the cruise ship?"

"Cruise ship?"

"Erik said you were working on a cruise liner. He thought coaching deck quoits."

"He's crazy. I've been a chalet girl in the Alps all winter."

"OK. Lots of hot wine and hot men I guess"

"Yes. Lots of the hot wine, but only one hot, well warm man"

"Is the job all year or are you fixed with something else for the summer?"

"Just had an interview for a job in The Algarve?" said Coralie.

"Not too much skiing over there."

"Would you believe 'in tennis'?"

"Heavens Coral. We need you here, not in bloody Portugal"

The phone went quiet

"Erik is still with Trocadero of course?"

"We are joint owners. Nothing changed."

"You had better open a branch somewhere else for me to be able to work for you again. Somewhere where Erik can't get a visa."

Another pause.

"When do you finish with the chalets, love?"

"Finished. All done. No more duvets. Yippee."

"Where on earth are you?"

"Not far from you. Still on the Algarve. Half waiting for the result of my interview and half holiday with my brother, David"

"Jump in Ethel and meet me somewhere tomorrow"

"Ethel is in England being very lazy. I could try to persuade David to drive over. It's his car."

"I'd come to you if I wasn't so busy in the next two days."

"Can you get away without Erik knowing?"

"He will have to hold the fort whilst I come out. I am sure I can invent a good reason. By the way, how is it that he hasn't called you? I don't know about recently. He was trying your number every day"

"He has tried a few times this month, but I don't respond when I see it is him. He knows I am not ready to pick up otherwise he would have used someone else's phone. He is respecting my privacy. He knows."

"Call me when you have asked David. I have missed you such a lot my dear friend." Lindsay rang off.

Coralie called back an hour later, having finally found David in the jacuzzi beside the indoor swimming pool in the nearby complex. She said that they could get to Marbella by midday. Where could they meet? Lindsay had been to see Clarence and hatched a plot. With Erik trapped at the Trocadero as Supervisor, Clarence had agreed to keep the secret and host the meeting.

As she came closer to the town Coralie became nervous and went quiet in the car. After almost a thousand miles together in his car David had heard from Coralie all about her relationship with Erik and where she felt the two of them were today. He reassured her that he would be with her all the time they were in the vicinity of the Trocadero Academy. Just before lunchtime he parked his VW Golf outside the Bar Lulu and was greeted in the doorway by Clarence wearing shorts and his red braces again.

"You must be David and I suppose you have brought back that cheeky young sister of yours to annoy me. Well you had better come in."

When Coralie appeared Clarence changed his tone and hugged her for fully a minute with a tear in his eye.

"Come and sit in your usual place, you lovely girl. I have often looked across the bar and wished you were there instead of some holidaymaker with no sense of humour."

Lindsay arrived a few minutes later and there was another tearful greeting until Coralie introduced David.

"I meant to be here first" Lindsay said "to greet you back to your old haunt."

"I did that, you ungrateful Kiwi" called Clarence from the Bar.

"Why don't you move into the alcove by the side window away from the other punters, where I can hear you but I don't have to look at you."

"He hasn't altered has he? Just as rude as always." said Coralie

"Not a bit. Rex says he probably shouted something rude as he emerged from his Mother's womb". Lindsay replied.

After the early drive along the coast from Portugal David sat back and took long draughts from his cool lager and listened to the two women catching up with each other's news.

"And what about you, David? No more ski instructing for a few months. What will you do?" asked Lindsay.

Before he could answer a voice joined in from the Bar

"Mmm. Ski instructor are you? I thought you looked rather fit and strong."

Clarence came over to the alcove. "I expect your partner is pleased you have all that exercise and the same lovely tan from the snow glare that your lippy sister has."

"He's still single" Coralie chipped in.

"Oohh. Then if you can't find a job instructing your skiing round here I can always find something to keep you occupied."

"What about Rex?" asked Lindsay.

"Variety is the spice, dear. You should know. If what that Charlie told me is true about your tennis tournament conquests in the nineties and the noughties"

"Charlie Mills is in serious trouble next time he comes to Spain" she replied.

Lindsay looked back to Coralie.

"Cards on the table. We are in the shit. We need another coach urgently to cope with the approaching summer season of events and the amount of 'one to one' that every student needs now. They have all improved so much. We also have a problem in that the 'string quartet' are revolting."

"They seemed quite nice, clean girls when you brought them to Lollo's Reception" added Clarence helpfully.

"Piss off, Clarence."

"Oh. It's like that is it? I can tell when my valuable advice is received ungraciously". He walked back to the Bar in short, quick steps, his heeled shoes making clicking noises on the wooden floor.

"They are all unhappy about not having you as their main coach and Lucy is talking to her Mum about she and Saskia leaving and trying to join where you are coaching now. They think you must be coaching tennis still. Scott, who replaced you temporarily, is great and a doubles specialist. We have just offered him a full time post, but I have now to advertise for another to care for the singles work. Is there any way we can persuade you to forget Faro and come back to us?"

David got up to order more drinks while Coralie thought deeply how to reply. He returned with the lunch menu and they each decided on a light lunch.

"I never make a bean out of this lot on food. They are all on some healthy eating plan. I suppose you need to watch your figure too" Clarence said to David as he placed the order.

"Not for a while. I'm going for the Steak and Ale pie"

"Good boy. You can definitely come here again. I'll bring the drinks over"

261

David went back to the table to hear Coralie say

"I had assumed you would get along just as well without me and I am very flattered. There must be dozens of good coaches out there, who would love to join your great outfit"

Clarence brought the four drinks on a tray

"Look, Ducky. You are all beating about the bush. There is an Elephant in the room. Look him straight in the eye."

"What do you mean, Clarence?"

"Oh. Come on. The decision depends on you and Erik and where you both are and where you both would like to be" he replied "David, cover your ears. Sweetheart, you won the lottery when you hooked him. Now you have to decide whether you want to win the 'rollover', as the actress said to the director and several of the cameramen"

"Clarence, he fell out of love with me."

Clarence and Lindsay looked at each other and started speaking together.

"No way" Lindsay went on "He had a funny five minutes and regretted it. He has tried and tried to find you to explain, but you covered your tracks too well."

Coralie looked surprised.

"I think I have finally got him out of my system. I was ready to move back into tennis, but move on at the same time."

"Could you work for us with him still around. He spends quite a lot of time away with his commentaries on the Slams. We could make sure that you accompanied our players to different events, never together."

David, having heard all this, butted in

"Lindsay. It wouldn't work. Especially, as you tell us that Erik still is anxious to start up their relationship again, if he can."

Lindsay nodded, realising that David was right. However, they could both see that Coralie was wavering. Maybe there was a small fire for Erik still burning.

"Let me go and talk to Erik. I will be careful and not say you are here. You are both on holiday, maybe you could stay the night nearby if I can't get back tonight."

Coralie hesitated, then looked at David, who nodded.

"OK. We'll stay. But don't tell him I am here." she said.

TWENTY-TWO

"You can stay here, you know. We have a guest room upstairs in our flat" offered Clarence. "I only let best friends stay there."

"Thanks Clarence. That is very kind. But we only came for the day and I am going to need a change of clothes." Coralie looked at her Brother.

"We only have two more days in the apartment on the Algarve. We may as well go back and pack our bags. Next stop is England and past here is one route home. The Golf Club will call her mobile anyway, so it doesn't matter where we are." David said.

"All right then. Bugger off then, but be sure to come back tomorrow."

"I'll call Lindsay and ask her not to come back until tomorrow" said Coralie as she kissed Clarence goodbye.

Lindsay was mighty relieved to receive the call. She was in a quandary. As she pulled into the car park and was walking towards the main building at the Academy a taxi drew up beside her. She leant in through the window to find Sally as the passenger. Lindsay had completely forgotten that it was Padmini's visit to the consultant in two days time and, of course Sally would want to be with her.

264

"Oh Sally. We should have met you at the Airport. Did Erik know you were coming?"

"No. I thought you would be too busy. I only told Padmini."

"God. He is a bloke. It wouldn't have occurred to him that you would want to be here for her."

She took Sally's suitcase and they went indoors.

"Scott. This is Sally Shaunessy. Padmini's Mum. Where's Erik?"

"Taking a shower. We have just played a set with Dan and Torgny. Listen"

They listened. From the floor above came the singing:-

'The Sun has got his hat on, hip,hip,hip, hooray

The Sun has got his hat on, and he's coming out to play.

*Everybody's happy, hip,hip,hip,.........*ow, ow! Bloody doorstop!!"

"He stubbed his toe again." laughed Scott.

"Does he always sing in the bathroom?" asked Sally

"Every time, and along the corridor, and in the loo, if there is no newspaper in there." said Scott

Scott left to take the next pair of players on court.

The two women went over Padmini's diagnosis and her recent tiredness, and decided that nothing could be done until after the hospital appointment. They talked about the successes and problems encountered by the Academy in general terms.

"Tell me." asked Sally "How are Erik and Coralie getting on?"

She had noticed Coralie's reaction when she last visited and intuitively knew there was a closeness between her and Erik.

"They aren't. Coralie left soon after you were here last time."

"Padmini confirmed they were close and had fallen out, but she hoped Coralie would be back by now."

"Can I be straight and totally honest, Sally?"

"Yes. Go ahead"

"I know, and so does she, that you are Erik's special love. I think your visit last time brought your whole relationship up to the surface with Erik. He changed and became distant, and it all became too much for Coralie, who thought that all that was in Erik's distant past and that she was the one for him now,"

"It was…..I mean it is all in the past. Memories, but nothing more" said Sally

"I am not sure either Coralie or, for that matter Erik would agree"

"Whilst I am here I will remind him, if it is not too late. I suppose it's too late for Coralie. Is she a long way away?"

Before Lindsay could answer, in walked Erik wearing an open necked white shirt and back in jeans, his curly blond hair still damp.

"Sally. I didn't know……" he said

"No-one did. I knew you would all be busy. I came to take Padmini for her hospital appointment."

Lindsay watched them as they looked at and over each other. Was she being fair to assume that such a strong love and memory could fade? Was it fair to them or to Coralie to stir the flames? She wondered if it was possible to love two people at the same time – one a lovely memory and the other hot and alive.

Lindsay left them and went to discuss catering with Carmen and Juanita because Sally would be staying for at least two days. On the way to the kitchen Coralie phoned to say she was returning to Portugal and would be back in the late morning with the car loaded for the trip North to the UK.

It was the last thing that Lindsay needed in her efforts to persuade Coralie to return to the Trocadero for Sally to appear and muddy the already cloudy waters. She no longer held out much hope of success. How could she approach Erik on the subject, and reveal that Coralie was so close by, when Sally's aura would be overwhelming his emotions?"

Scott came in and threw his racquet bag into the corner.

"I'm knackered. Going for a swim in the sea this time with some of the boys"

He left after this announcement and Erik jumped up.

"See you at dinner Sal. Cameron will show you to your room. He is on house duty today. I have the floodlight session this evening with Felipe."

The new floodlights over the clays courts were proving a bonus, giving them access to evening tennis and a more widespread programme.

Lindsay returned to join Sally in their sitting room.

Sally said "Can you give me Coralie's mobile number? I think I need to talk to her"

"OK. It can't do any harm and I guess it could help." Lindsay wrote down the number and Sally assumed, because it was a British mobile number, that Coralie would be in England.

Sally went to spend some time with Padmini and then went out to sit in the warm evening air to call Coralie. She sat on Lollo's bench, a little way from the court on which Erik was hitting balls to Felipe.

Coralie answered "Who is this?"

"It's Sally. Padmini's mother"

Coralie sat down on her bed in the apartment on the Algarve.

"What do you want? I don't work at the Academy any more"

"I know. I wanted to talk to you about Erik. Well Erik and me actually."

"This will cost you a lot of money, phoning from Oman. If you have Skype we could text or talk with video."

"I am not in Oman. I am actually at the Academy. I came to take Padmini to hospital the day after tomorrow."

"Did Lindsay give you my number?"

"Yes."

"She must think it is worthwhile us talking. Look I am in Portugal, not too far away, and I am passing near you tomorrow on the way to the UK. Maybe we could meet."

"Much better than on the phone. I have something tell you and it's better done face to face." said Sally

"I am meeting Lindsay at Bar Lulu at 1pm, but please don't tell Erik"

"Can you get there an hour earlier so the two of us can meet on our own?"

"Yes. I can get there by 12 noon. Do you know where it is?"

"No, but the taxi driver will know. I'll just have to find an excuse to leave here on my own."

Coralie went out of her room to find David. He was on the verandah reading a book.

"Erik's Special Love called. She wants to meet me tomorrow. Can we go an hour earlier to arrive by 12?" David nodded. "No problem."

"She wants to tell me something face to face. I'm sure she wants to warn me off because Lindsay has told her they all want me back. She wants to warn me off Erik, so they can preserve their memories without anyone trying to rival them."

"Maybe. But it doesn't matter if he is out of your system. Or is he?"

"Hallo. I'm Sally. You're Clarence aren't you?"

"How did you guess?"

"It may have been the braces, or the purple shoes with the bows."

"Coralie called me. Come upstairs to my flat where I have prepared a secret hideaway for your tete a tete"

"Will I be safe going upstairs with a stranger?"

"You will with me, Ducky. That's a promise. Now let's have a good look at you. You are rather lovely. No wonder that Viking Raider flipped his lid for you."

"You know too much, Clarence. But I hope you are discreet."

"What would you like to drink? Coralie was only 40 minutes away when she last called"

Clarence led Coralie up the stairs to meet Sally, carrying her drink and Sally's cup of tea.

"Don't you worry about young David. I have ways of caring for strong, muscular sportsman you would never imagine. Coralie meet Sally. Now, you two. If I leave you alone you won't scratch each other's eyes out will you? I hate the sight of blood. Come down when you feel hungry."

"Is he always like this? He sounds great fun" asked Sally.

"Oh Yes. Worse usually. Rude, and the exotic clothes. Heart of gold though. Like today, thinking about our privacy."

They sipped their drinks simultaneously.

"I think I can guess what you want to tell me" said Coralie.

"Maybe you can, but I still wanted to say it in a way you will always remember if there is ever any doubt"

"You want me to stay away from Erik and stay away from the Academy because it belongs to him and he will always be a temptation if I go back."

Coralie didn't really know why, but she was fighting tears.

"No. No. It is almost the opposite." Sally responded.

They took another mouthful of their drinks.

Coralie looked at her, wide eyed, not expecting a variation. Sally went on

"I came to tell you something in confidence. Erik and

I had a wonderful affair. Yes, that is what it was, because I was married with a teenage son. We loved each other to distraction from a distance, and then together for around two magical weeks. It was very special. Amazing for me and it seems, amazing for him."

Coralie listened, imagining fully how this could have been, as hers was a similar experience.

"I also loved my husband very much and had done so for 16 or 17 years. It was me who broke off our affair and went back to continue my life with Chris, my wonderful, brave man. I shall never forget my time with Erik and hope he will always be my friend, but that is all it is. That is also all it should be with him too. A memory contained in a bubble. I have heard from several people how much you and he were in love. My appearance should not have changed that one digit, and I plan to tell him so in a few hours time. I just wanted to see you and tell you first. You should both be together, enjoying a great relationship."

Coralie was speechless for what seemed like ten minutes.

"Sally. Thank you for telling me. You are so thoughtful. I don't think he is over you though. He carries your painting in the top of his bag everywhere and, after you visited, he had it on his bedside table. That was the last part of my agony before I left"

"I didn't know he still was doing this. He told me he had the painting on the wall in his house in Monaco and that he sometimes took it around with him, but that was years ago. Silly man. He is seeing in his memory of me everything that he has in you in reality. Don't go on with your journey yet. Give me a little time to try to make him see sense"

They descended the stairs and joined David and Lindsay, who had arrived. Lindsay was openmouthed upon seeing the two appearing together.

"Sally. You were going shopping in Marbella."

"Yes, I was. I met a new friend instead" she replied with a big smile.

"As you have not killed each other in my flat I suppose you are going back to the Academy after lunch to kill Erik" said Clarence nonchalantly.

"Nearly correct, Mr Braces. However, I shall probably do it alone." said Sally.

Sally and Lindsay left together and headed for the Academy. Sally explained that she had decided to clear Coralie's mind of the idea that there was still a romantic connection between Erik and her. She had hoped that this would be enough to bring them back, at least, to a friendship that would enable Coralie to take up her old post. The only problem now was something she had to clear with Erik.

They arrived to find the afternoon tennis coaching in full swing with Scott and Erik on court, each with a group of students. Lindsay had postponed her session with the 'string quartet' until the evening on the floodlit court in order to leave herself free to meet Coralie. They did not seem to be still in the complex. Lindsay thought they had gone to the beach to take Padmini's mind off the hospital visit tomorrow. Sally went to her room, telling Lindsay that she had gone for a rest. The journey from Oman yesterday was a long one.

Five minutes later Sally emerged from her room, now with bare feet. She made her way down the corridor to Erik's room and tried the door. Erik would never lock a door in his own house. A door closed downstairs. She walked halfway back and pretended to look out of the window. Quiet again, she went back to Erik's bedroom door, opened it, went inside and closed the door behind her. She had seen Erik through the window, still on court. Seventeen years ago, she thought, she would have draped herself across his bed in an irresistible pose and waited for him to return. No, she must not dream dreams at this time. Sally was doing this for someone else. She looked around, on surfaces, under the bed, in the wardrobe. No sign of it. She looked in his sports style suitcase, a floppy one with wheels. There it was, Sally

Shaunessy staring at Sally Shaunessy, red dress and flower and all. It was hidden away in the top of the bag as he once had told her it was.

Without waiting any longer in the room, in case Erik returned more quickly than she expected, Sally took the painting and tiptoed to the door as would any other burglar. She listened at the door for any noise. Just the occasional shout and the frequent plunk of ball on racket, all in the distance. She opened the door quietly, slipped out, closed it again and walked briskly along the corridor to her room. Once there she put the painting into a large sized 'duty free' plastic bag and laid it at the bottom of her own suitcase, quickly covering it with her spare clothes. She sat on the only chair in her bedroom, feeling rather tacky. The only other thing Sally could ever remember stealing was a Crunchie bar from Spar as a dare when she was nine.

'If he doesn't notice whilst I am here' she thought 'I'll take it back home, frame it and send it by courier to Jean-Marc in Monaco to hang back in the house.'

"Pssst. Clarence. Is she here?"

Clarence found himself looking over the Bar Lulu balcony at four pretty, but very young, faces?

"Is who here? Wait a minute. I know you lot. You were giggling in the back pew at Lollo's wedding. Come up on the balcony."

The String Quartet ran up the steps to the restaurant level.

"Right. Sit down"

"We can't" said Lucy "we're too excited."

"What have you heard?"

"Cameron was cycling by and he is certain he saw Coralie coming in here this morning. Is she still here? asked Gabby

"Look. There may be someone here. But it's more than my life's worth to let out the. ………….."

"It is Coralie isn't it? She's inside isn't she?" shouted Saskia

All four pushed past Clarence and ran into the bar/restaurant to the surprise of two holidaymakers enjoying a pot of English tea.

"Where? Where is she? Not in here!" They ran back to Clarence who was now standing smiling in the doorway. Gabby and Lucy threw their arms around him, jumping up and down.

"Dear Clarence, tell us, tell us"

In the commotion no-one had seen David and Coralie come down the stairs, having taken their bags up to Clarence's spare room. Padmini was the first to spot Coralie. She squealed and ran between the tables to hurl herself into Coralie's arms. Lucy, Gabby and Saskia joined her, all trying to hug a piece of their favourite person, who was grinning and only just managing to stay on her feet. To the amusement of the guests and David they began to chant

"You're back, you're back, you're back, you're back"

The scrum broke up and they all sat down, picking up the scattered chairs at the same time.

"Clarence. Champagne please" said Gabby

"You must be joking" came the reply, and everyone laughed.

All four started talking at the same time, throwing questions at Coralie so quickly that she could hardly answer any of them properly. David lapped up the popularity that poured over his sister like a proud father and went to stand next to Clarence. Clarence said.

"I'll produce a jug of something fruity in a minute. If anything decides her to take the risk of returning, it will be this. Did you know she was this popular?"

"Not really. She hadn't said much about her work at the Academy."

They listened to Coralie explaining to the girls that her

return to Trocadero depended on what happened in the next two days.

They looked a little bewildered. Saskia turned to look at David and asked Coralie.

"Is this your new lover?"

She shook her head, laughing, but before she could reply Gabby went to him and said

"You'll let her come back to us, won't you?"

"We'll go on strike if you don't" said Lucy.

"David is my Big Brother" Coralie eventually managed to say.

She went on to tell them that she would love to come back to work at the Academy, but there was one large obstacle that she couldn't really discuss that stood in the way. She was going to stay with Clarence for two days because there was a chance the obstacle may clear. In which case she would ask Lindsay and Erik if she could return.

"You will make sure she stays here, won't you David?" asked Padmini.

"And so will I" added Clarence, carrying a jug and four glasses.

Lindsay left Sally and Erik to eat dinner alone, excusing herself to catch up on office work. Erik carried their coffees out on to the verandah and they sat in the dim lights from the town and in the warmth of a spring evening.

"You and I are fully over aren't we?" asked Sally.

"Why do you ask?"

"Someone told me that Coralie left because you were still obscured by the memory of me and our affair all those years ago."

"The someone was probably right."

"The person said you were obsessed by the painting you had of me in the red dress."

"It's a reminder that I look at to recall that wonderful, unique love we had"

She turned to look at him.

"We had the most incredible love and it was unique to us. Life moves on and we have to move with it or we finish up like the bride in Great Expectations, out of touch with reality and frozen in thought. When new love appears we have to embrace it as a new jewel, not comparing and holding it up against other jewels we owned in the past. We need to put it in a bottle and float it downstream with gratitude for having held it as a gift. My love would not be so strong for Chris if I carried the bottle around with me."

Erik looked back at the distant twinkling lights in the direction of the beach.

Sally went on

"You found new, vibrant love with a special girl. Another special love, if you like. To keep it as a constantly blooming flower you must put the other flower in the bottle and leave it on the ledge, not carry it around or even gaze too hard at it in the presence of your new special person."

"I thought I had done that with Coralie, but your presence pushed me into a time warp and I withdrew my feelings for her and slipped into a dream world. She left and I slowly realised how selfish I had become. The realisation made me go to the UK twice to look for her and now I have to live with the penalty of losing her. Now I compensate by reviving my memories of us, aided by that painting I kept of you"

"That painting should be hanging on a wall. And, when you fall in love again, it should be on a wall in one of your other houses"

With that Sally stood up and kissed him on his cheek. They stepped back into the brighter light of the sitting room.

"Coralie"

"Hi Sally"

"He doesn't know you are nearby. If you call him in the morning I am fairly sure he will be ready to see you. I shall be off early to take Padmini to Granada. Lindsay is going to come with us. Good luck."

Erik waved to Lindsay's car as it moved away, heading for Granada Hospital. He was on the phone to Phil Mercer in Seaton to ask him to keep The Umpire's Chair free for him during the second week of July, after Wimbledon.

"You've forgotten, mate. You asked me last year to keep it open. We could have sold it three times over. As usual July, August and September are fully booked up."

He pressed the red button to disconnect and it immediately rang again.

"Erik?"

"It says 'Coralie' on the screen, but is it really you or a 'soundalike' robot?

"It's me"

"You are supposed to be avoiding talking to me."

"That is on hold if you want to talk this morning."

"Sure, go ahead"

"How about you come to meet me?"

"Are you in a port for a stopover?"

"No. I am with Clarence for a stopover"

"Bar Lulu? I'll be with you in ten minutes"

Clarence was waiting at the top of the steps on the balcony.

"Hallo stranger."

"Are all my chickens coming home to roost, Clarence?"

"Maybe they are coming to roast, dear. Don't ask me, I am only the zookeeper. She's inside, by the way."

Erik went inside the bar and saw Coralie sitting in one

of the alcoves. He thought she looked fantastic, better than the image he carried in his mind. He sat down beside her. She moved a few inches away and looked at him. For six months he had known exactly what he wanted to say and now, at the crucial moment, it escaped him.

"When do you have to be back on board?" he managed to say.

"I don't know where you think I have been but I am not there any more" she replied, managing to control a tremor that had crept into her voice.

"Shall we leave Clarence in peace and go for a walk?" he asked

"I'd love to walk again on the beach"

They stood up to leave. Clarence called to Erik from the bar.

"As the Wicked Witch said to Snow White, I hope you're not still feeling grumpy."

"No, my friend. Now I'm feeling happy. We're just going for a walk"

"Bar Lulu and Agony Uncle Clarence not good enough then?"

Coralie blew him a kiss.

Erik drove them to the beach car park. Coralie took off her shoes and they walked out on to the sand. It was only mid morning and the West end of the beach had only a handful of visitors scattered along it. They headed in that direction walking slowly. Coralie rejected the offer to hold Erik's hand.

"Do you want to know where I have been, what I have been doing?"

"Not really. I just want you back with Trocadero, back with me"

"Haven't you gone completely into your historical recollection of your 'special love'? Doesn't her continual reappearance fuel that love? I don't know why you don't just whisk her away from her husband and keep her with you all the time." said Coralie angrily.

"It isn't like that. That was over seventeen years ago. I made a mistake when she first came here with Padmini. It somehow brought the emotions I had had since our affair to the surface. I was selfish and didn't think of you or of us. After you left it brought me to my senses and it hit me between the eyes what we had. We were so good together. I was prepared to give up Spain and go wherever you wanted. But you concealed yourself so well I couldn't find you to apologise. There was no way I could even write to you as you had briefed your parents to man the defences."

"I was hurting so badly" she said. "We had everything. The most wonderful rapport and love. There was no obvious history that either of us carried. I couldn't get through to you. Then I found that bloody painting, on your bedside table, right beside where you would be sleeping and dreaming."

"I always carried it with me in my bag. When Sally came with Padmini and then left, I guess I must have taken it out. It was one of the things we did together. She was my subject and I painted her."

"You could have painted me too, if you had asked"

"I haven't painted anything since then, although recently I have been wondering if I should begin again."

They walked in silence, neither knowing what to say next.

"Tradition says the man has to take charge of this sort of situation but I don't want to bully you." said Erik, as they turned at the end of the beach.

"What would you have said? I mean, if you were going to bully me."

"Are you in love with anyone else?"

"No……..not much."

"Is that with this David fellow?"

"No, not David. He is my Brother. A little bit with a nice guy from Switzerland"

"A little bit?"

"For God's sake, Erik. You closed me out six months ago. I had to move on, find a job, meet other people."

"I'm jealous, that's all" said Erik. "I've been trying to catch up with you, to prostrate myself before you and crave your understanding and tell you, well to tell you I still ………to tell you I still really…er…love you."

She took hold of his hand and turned to face him.

"Why do men find it so difficult to say 'I love you'?"

They looked at each other. There was a longing in both their eyes.

Setting off along the sand again, this time holding hands, Coralie said

"I don't love Thomas in the way I loved you, you big ape."

"I only seem like a big ape because you haven't any shoes on and are lower down, and I have been blundering through my words this morning. "Will you come back to the Academy and work with us all? I promise to keep my hands off you and fit a new lock on your bedroom door"

"What about your feelings for Sally every time she turns up?"

"This is the first time she has been to us since you saw her. She has been sending Padmini with their 'switched on' housemaid each time."

"So you haven't been drooling over her memory all the time then"

"No I have not. Ask anyone. I have been driving and flying and phoning trying to find you, my Coralie."

She stretched upwards and kissed him properly. He responded eagerly, bending down a little to reach her.

"I shall have to spend hours now, phoning and explaining to everyone. Poor Thomas, The Algarve Golf Club, Mum and Dad, even Elena. David is just shell shocked and will believe anything. After the onslaught by the 'String Quartet' he will never be the same again. And Clarence, he has been a darling.

279

"The four girls came to see you. How did they know you were there and I did not?"

"Cameron saw me going into Bar Lulu and told them. Now that was definitely bullying. They swamped me with love and pressure to come back."

"Will you have to go back to collect your belongings from the ship?"

"Erik, my lovely man, I have not been anywhere near a cruise ship. All my clothes from the Les Carroz ski centre, yes ski centre, are in David's car."

"So, you could come back now, right now. No. Stop. Wait a minute. Can you spend tonight with Clarence and come over tomorrow?"

Coralie looked puzzled.

"Sorry. But, well, actually Sally is in your room!"

"You………" She chased him down the beach and hopped halfway into the car park as she tried to put her shoes back on.

David looked up from the Marbella English paper as they came in to the bar, holding hands. He called to the back of the restaurant.

"All sorted Clarence."

"Thank the Lord for that. I've lost nearly a stone in the last two days with worry."

"Clarence" said Erik "You don't qualify to thank the Lord for anything if you don't do Christmas or Easter."

"I don't do Christmas, ducky, because I see no point in sitting around in front of a dead tree or eating chocolates out of somebody else's oversized socks."

"Why not Easter then?" Coralie grinned at him.

"I do Easter all year round. I make a point of eating hot cross buns every weekend. And I suppose I am going to have to put up with your cheek again now you've kissed and made up"

"Have you kissed and made up?" asked David quizzically.

"Not enough yet" replied Erik. Coralie's tummy fluttered involuntarily.

"Lindsay phoned to check you had been here. She is on her way back from Granada. They are dropping Padmini off at the Academy and will be here quite soon."

"Thanks Clarence. Can I go upstairs and use the bathroom?"

"You may as well. You and Mr Superslalom here have taken over the entire building already. I couldn't find a clean blouse this morning"

Erik updated David and Clarence with his understanding of where Coralie was now, and told them that his plan was for her to begin work at the Trocadero very soon, come back with him to Wimbledon and to see Ted and Jackie afterwards for a few days. Before he could explain further Lindsay and Sally arrived with questions written all over their faces.

"The saga's over girls. I can put you out of your misery. Sweden and England have restored diplomatic relations, and whatever other kinds of relations are being left to speculation." said Clarence.

"Erik, I am so pleased." said Sally immediately. She gave him a hug, followed by Lindsay. Coralie came down and the hugs began all over again, with Clarence somehow involved and David a bemused bystander.

"How is Padmini?" Coralie asked anxiously.

"She is fine. Results in a week. They say it is unlikely that it will turn out to be leukaemia, but they need to eliminate it. Far more likely is that it's just anaemia that has been untreated." Sally answered as cheerfully as she could.

Lindsay asked whether they had been in the bar all morning, and was told that the beach was the stage for the reconciliation.

"I'll bet you were dying for a swim, Coralie, after a winter in the Alps. Did you go in?"

Erik replied. "We just talked a lot. I had no swimming shorts and I didn't want to add to the number of people who have seen me naked."

Lindsay, Sally and Coralie looked at each other and 'high fived' all round chorusing

"Been there, done that!"

Clarence returned to the bar in hysterics.

Sally had arranged to visit a friend in Menorca whilst she was waiting for Padmini's results. Erik took her to Malaga Airport and returned to join Lindsay for a staff and pupils meeting at Trocadero. They told the assembled contingent that Coralie was coming back to take up her coaching post again and would arrive tomorrow. There was so much joy amongst the students and some of the staff that it was a few minutes before they stopped talking and Lindsay could continue with the practical details.

"I'm Scott. They've pulled out all the stops to get you back. You must be bloody good. The kids have set up a kidnap unit in case you change your mind."

"Some of them were with me before the Academy started. I don't think I am anything special." replied Coralie. "Let me settle in and then tell me all about you"

She quickly put some of her essentials around her room, changed into tennis gear and went outside to join Erik beside the courts.

"You wore the same light blue colour when you took your first training session. You look even better now."

"I hope it won't show that I have not hit a ball in six months" whispered Coralie.

Agnieska and Soo-Jin joined them, both smiling.

"You come in best time for summer tournaments" said Aga.

The afternoon sessions finished and Erik waited for her. "How was it?"

"Good. They have all come on so much. I am sweating badly and need to get used to this warmer climate again."

Up on the landing of the first floor Erik pulled Coralie close and kissed her. She broke away and pulled him into her bedroom kicking the door closed and let him kiss her again.

"This is where the hero and the heroine frantically tear off each other's clothes and make passionate love" he said.

"This heroine is going to take a shower. The hero and the film cameras can go away." She pulled away again and headed for the bathroom.

Erik left the room and hurried down to his own bathroom. He quickly showered and dried himself and wrapped a dry towel around his waist, while Coralie let the warm water flow and make her feel fresh. Making sure no-one else was on the landing he went quickly back to Coralie's room and waited. She emerged covered with a large pink towel, the end tucked into the top and walked towards Erik.

"Are you a nice clean person too?"

He didn't answer but put an arm around her and tugged her close. She put her left arm around his neck as they kissed each other fiercely. Their other arms were up to no good and, almost in the same instant, both towels landed side by side on the floor.

"Ooops" she said, winding the other arm around his neck. "I've come undone."

As he kissed her again, he backed her steadily towards the bed.

"Mum" said Cameron in the corridor of the school area. "We need to talk".

"Is it urgent, because I have a crazy day ahead redoing the tennis rosters?"

"Yes, Mum. Serious and quite urgent"

"OK. I can spare five minutes now"

"Can we sit outside because I don't want the Staff to be scared by your screaming?"

"Move up and make room for me. Right. What have you done?"

"Made Sofia pregnant" He looked down at his feet.

"Jesus Cameron. How the hell have you managed to do that? I mean, I know how you did it, but why, where, and who on Gods Earth is Sofia?"

He explained skeleton details about the boat and their friendship and that she couldn't get the pill, because this is Spain. One day he ran out of condoms and it was the 'conceiving' time of the month for her.

"There is a 'day after pill' now, you know"

"Yes, Mum, but they haven't invented a 'two months after pill' yet"

Lindsay broke off to see Lavinia before school began, her mind whirling about Cameron's situation and what to do. She returned to find him still sitting on the bench.

"This is going to be an expensive mistake whatever you two decide to do"

"Yes. And the cost of the funeral." Added Cameron

"What funeral!?"

"Mine. After her Dad finds out where I live."

"Tell me about this poor girl. How long have you known Sofia?"

Lindsay wandered aimlessly around the complex all morning, feeling better if she was on the move. She had told Cameron to get on with his allocated chores and they would talk again in the afternoon when the tennis was in full flow. At lunchtime she decided to go to see Clarence, as Erik was wholly preoccupied with Coralie.

"Is the Agony Uncle still in business?" she asked him as he was writing the last of the lunch menu on the blackboard.

He noted that she was in a somber mood.

"Yes. But the fees are high. Come and sit over here. There are no customers yet. Coffee is finished and lunch not yet started."

"Clarence. I need wise advice from a good friend"

"You've come to the best place. I was once described as being the Suppository of all Wisdom. I don't know what it means, but it sounds impressive."

Lindsay smiled awkwardly, and then told him her dilemma.

"I don't know how to advise him. I would never abort a foetus so that piece of advice would be without conviction for a start."

She told him all she knew about the girl and their relationship with each other, their ages and likely futures without this surprise complication.

Clarence listened very intently, obviously thinking all the time.

"Let me serve this couple and call Rex from the kitchen. He can take over"

"This is Uncle's advice" he began, when he sat down again "A baby is a most precious gift and not to be given up lightly. Some people try for years without being able to conceive. These two are actually incredibly lucky to have a choice. Babies do have a habit of arriving at most inconvenient times though. It is probable that Cameron may not have a say in what happens, especially if Sofia's parents have strong opinions and are influenced by the Church or the neighbours.

I suggest you and he, as soon as possible, go and meet them in their home. Let Sofia's Mum and Dad rant and rave at Cameron to begin with. When they have calmed down, and are thinking clearly, find out what Sofia wants to do. They may love each other deeply even though they are kids and want to continue their association in some way.

That is the first step. Depending on all those things you will be able to determine the best outcome. Most important is to go there soon before everyone knows and the family become influenced by Auntie or the Priest's ideas of what should happen. And come back and tell me how it goes."

"Thank you, dear Uncle Clarence." Lindsay went back to her car.

Lindsay was more apprehensive than Cameron as they drove up to Sofia's home towards the back of the town. Senora Marquez answered the door. She looked at Lindsay and then at Cameron, uncomprehending who they were. Lindsay was unsure how to approach the subject.

"I am Sofia's friend." chipped in Cameron

"A mixture of relief and anger and concern showed in the mother's face."

She beckoned them inside and went out to the kitchen. They sat side by side in the living room. Mother returned carrying two glasses of fresh orange juice, which she gave to them. Sofia appeared in the doorway and hesitated.

Lindsay realised that the conversation would have to be in Spanish and worried that she may not be up to it. Cameron asked them to speak slowly to help his mother. She translated everything into English in her mind before being able to understand. Cameron moved over to sit beside Sofia on a wooden bench-seat and whispered a question. She nodded.

"Senora Marquez. I am the person responsible for Sofia's condition. She has just told me that you know. I wanted to tell you myself that it's all my fault for taking advantage of her"

"No. No. It was both of us" shouted Sofia.

"I am very sad." said her Mother. "My husband is very angry"

At that moment they heard the sound of someone entering the house. Sofia's Father walked into the room. He quickly calculated who the visitors were and stood in the middle of the room grimacing and opening and closing his hands. He said nothing, then sat in a chair with tears streaming down his face, gazing down at the floor.

Lindsay was stunned and began to cry. Sofia had cried so much in the last 48 hours that there was nothing left. Senora Marquez sat still with her hands clutched together in her lap. Sofia laid her head on Cameron's shoulder.

Lindsay thought 'These poor people. Probably their only daughter. Maybe doing well at school. And my bloody son has put her and them into an impossible situation.'

Sofia's Father then said to Cameron.

"I tried to stop you before and kept Sofia at home for weeks, months."

"Papa. It was me too. I wanted to be with him so badly."said Sofia

"Did you learn nothing from your Mother? Nothing from the problems created by Marisa getting pregnant before marriage? Who will care for your baby? We need the income from Mama's work."

"I will keep it and care for it, and be a good mother"

"You are just sixteen and taking Bachillerato at school. We are saving for you to go to university."

Lindsay had pulled herself together. She turned to Cameron and Sofia

"Do you love each other?"

They both nodded and Sofia added "I would go anywhere for him"

Cameron stared at her "I was going to say exactly the same in the same words."

"Senor, Senora, help me with this suggestion because it needs a lot of thinking through and planning." said Lindsay.

"They are very young, but they love each other. Let's see

if we can together make a plan that will give this baby, our grandchild, a secure life.

Senora Marquez responded

"Yes. Let's try. But how? I have been sleepless for two nights trying to think."

Lindsay continued

"If they were older I would suggest they marry, and maybe they will in due course. I am part owner of the Tennis Academy at Trocadero."

"I thought I knew your face. From the papers when they report your winning students" interrupted Sofia's Father.

"Part of the Academy's training is for the students to attend school in the mornings. The classes are small and the teachers are good. We have a few students who attend only the school. One of them is Cameron. My suggestion is that Sofia stays in her own school for the next two months until the end of the school year. The baby will not show until after then. Then, next school year she comes to the Trocadero. She can continue the Bachillerato. We have other students also taking it."

Sofia's parents were sitting up and giving Lindsay encouragement to go on.

"If Sofia stays with us until the baby is born your neighbours need not know until later. You can come every day, if you wish, to see her and when she has the baby. I need to confirm this is OK with my partner, because he is half owner of the Academy. Cameron and I will pay for her keep from as soon as she arrives with us, and we will pay for all her medical checks and hospital bills throughout. What do you think? Could the plan work?"

"It seems so good. A very good scheme" said Mother to her husband.

Senor Marquez looked at his daughter and sighed

"You, Sofia, are a very lucky girl."

Sofia and Cameron hugged each other and Lindsay shook hands with both parents.

"Can you come to the Academy tomorrow evening to talk some more about it? Come at 7pm and take some dinner with us."

TWENTY-FOUR

Erik checked that Lindsay was able to cope before he left for Paris. The previous evening she had taken him to one side and told him of hers and Cameron's challenge. He had agreed to Sofia becoming a student next year and told her to put the fees on hold to see whether they could manage without any contribution from her own funds.

"I'm fine with that and her staying here later. Now Coralie is back we will get by without any difficulty."

Erik was taking Scott this time as the emphasis would be on the doubles and he himself would be commentating for some of the time.

As the seniors had all gone to Paris the 'String Quartet' were given the afternoon off. They disappeared after lunch, only to return looking very furtive. Their search for Coralie found her in the gym on a running machine. She stopped and they surrounded her.

"Only three. I thought you four did everything together"

"Gabby will join us in a minute." said Lucy. "Coralie. We have decided that you may run away again now Erik has gone to Paris, so we have done something to ensure you have to always stay in Marbella"

Saskia and Padmini could hardly contain themselves and Coralie wondered what could be coming.

"Gabby" Lucy called

Gabby walked around the corner carrying a bundle of silky black hair. It was wriggling so much that she had to put it on the floor. It was a spanIel puppy!

"This is Pepsi" said Padmini "and he is all yours"

Coralie put her hand over her mouth

"My goodness" she said. Her mind trying to work out how she could look after a little dog as well as do her job well. She picked him up and he started licking her face. The girls all laughed.

"Do you like him?"

"He is absolutely adorable. I love him"

Gabby handed over a thin lead to attach to his tartan collar.

"We all wanted to keep him ourselves" said Saskia. "Now you have to stay here with us to care for Pepsi because he is only a puppy and can't leave the country."

"Why can't he leave the country?" asked Coralie.

"We've registered his chip and he can't cross the border without a document with Gabby's signature on it."

"You devious scheming bunch!"

She put Pepsi on the floor and he immediately peed a large puddle in the centre of the gym. This time they all laughed and the girls ran out.

"Hey you lot. Help me clean this up."

Lindsay took Coralie in the late evening to Bar Lulu. Soo-Jin had stayed behind to have physio on a damaged shoulder and was supervising the younger students. In between updating Clarence every time he could get away from the Bar, Lindsay listened to Coralie's week-by-week detail of the time she had been in the Alps. The last time Clarence came over before they went home he told them of a variation idea he had that may help out the young couple. It was that he and Rex could, if Sofia and Cameron wanted, care for the baby whilst it's parents studied in school. Lindsay thanked him for the idea, although she could imagine that it may not be acceptable to them or to Sofia's Mum and Dad for a variety of reasons.

In the car Lindsay's mood was swinging back to 'happy'. She asked Coralie whether the beds in the living area were strong enough.

"What do you mean?" Coralie suspected a double meaning.

"If you are going to use all the rooms in rotation, we will need to check the beds. You have already broken Erik's and it sounded as if yours was under some strain the day you arrived back" Lindsay laughed.

"Will you please stop listening. I will get all sorts of hang-ups if you don't"

"I'm just jealous, that's all" said Lindsay, still smiling.

Erik and Coralie reunited after the French Grand Slam and there was a fine four weeks with all the students before they took off for Wimbledon fortnight. Some of the Marbella Club members came along to see Felipe off and Maria Carmelita arrived with her chauffeur driven Mercedes to wish Nacho well, and see him join the minibus to Malaga Airport.

Coralie was sad to have to leave Pepsi behind with Cameron. She and each of the 'String Quartet' kissed Pepsi farewell and confused him so much that he ran over and peed against Maria Carmelita's leg. The following fiasco of Pepsi chasing Maria Carmelita and the Chauffeur chasing both of them with a box of tissues left everyone in the departing minibus rocking with laughter.

They all stayed in a rented house in New Malden, not far from Wimbledon. Entry qualification had been achieved by all the seniors and all the doubles combinations, including the two youngest pairs. Dan and Torgny reached the second week in the Men's Doubles and lost to the Bryan Brothers in four sets in the quarter-finals. Dan had a good draw and made the last 8 in the Boys Singles. Oksana lost in the final of the Girls Singles and Aga and Petra won the Doubles, having beaten Lucy and Gabby in the semi-final. All the others lost earlier in the tournament.

Erik was very pleased with them all and amazed that the two thirteen year olds had reached the semis. He praised Scott and mentioned him twice on Swedish TV. He saw them all off to Heathrow before collecting his Porsche and driving with Coralie in the July sunshine to Devon with the roof open.

They went straight to Coralie's parents in Ottery St Mary, where Jackie had prepared a cold meat salad lunch to be eaten in the back garden. Ted had made the garden look lovely with shrubs layered from front to rear of the side flower beds. Climbing roses dominated trellis work attached to a white wall with a different variety swirling over an archway.

In the late afternoon they collected the key to the water tower, 'The Umpires Chair', and Erik drove into the parking space underneath the unusual structure. He climbed up the stairs with Coralie close behind and opened the hatch with the folding staircase. Cathy, Phil Mercer's wife had left a cream tea with fresh scones on the little central table. As did every visitor, Coralie went straight to the picture window with the magnificent view across Lyme Bay and the East Devon coastline.

All his memories from the past remained in the depths of Erik's memory as he put his arms around his new love. He realised that he had put this overwhelming restriction into its rightful place, buried for distant recollection only.

They rose for a late, primitive breakfast, raiding the basic items that Cathy had put in the fridge and then went for a walk along the clifftop towards Lyme Regis. On the way back they met George inspecting his crop that was ripening in one of the fields next to the path.

"I heard you were coming down. Come and join us for a bite of lunch"

Callum was at home, having finished his 'A' levels. He and Erik talked about Viti Levu while Coralie updated Helen with Lucy's great achievement at Wimbledon. Helen was sad that the farming in Midsummer had meant they couldn't get away to watch the matches. George and Felix had gone back to the fields as soon as lunch was over and it had crept on to 3.30pm, when Luke arrived from Primary School, starving hungry

"Mum, can I have one of those bloody oranges?"

This was a good show stopper.

Helen, rather embarrassed, quickly replied

"Luke, please don't call them that. I told you they were blood oranges, but they are just like any others. They are given that name because it looks as though they are bleeding inside"

"OK. Can I have one of those bleeding oranges then?"

Helen just nodded in the resigned way that defeated mothers often do.

Erik hinted to Callum that he may be able to join the sail down to the Mediterranean if one of Callum's sixth form friends was unable to go. If he can get away for a few days he would love to go along, or maybe join them somewhere down the French coast. He, secretly, would feel better being alongside Mr.Edworthy, the teacher, when he navigated the shipping lanes near Gibraltar.

The next day, Coralie wanted to take her Mum shopping in Taunton, so Erik drove her over to collect Ethel, who had been nurtured by Ted for the last six months. He called in to the Burrows Sweet Shop in Seaton and told Saskia's parents how well she was progressing and maturing as a tennis player. Then he returned to see the young tenants, who now lived in Kirkhaven House, next to 'The Chair'. He had not met them before. All negotiations and rent collection had been done by the agents in Sidmouth. They seemed very pleasant and he sat in the garden with the husband, while his wife brought out tea and a black coffee, and the two little girls played hide and seek behind them in the bushes. Ralph was a wood turner and made ornaments for the holiday trade. He was using the Barn to work in, the same Barn that Erik had used for some of his painting years before.

"It's a bit of a mess, I'm afraid. Wood shavings everywhere. I wanted to ask you, if we ever met, about some things I found in one of the corners of the Barn soon after we arrived here. Come and have a look"

Erik followed him to the Barn, which seemed unchanged from his memory of it. There were piles of wood shavings and some partially finished shaped wooden bowls laying on a table and the floor. They went to one corner at the back where four bundles wrapped in corrugated cardboard lay. Erik knew instantly what he would see.

"Yes. Thanks. They are mine" He took them all and tucked them under his arm, bade the couple farewell and walked through the coppice across to 'The Chair'. Once inside he pulled up the hatchway, sat down and unwrapped the bundles one by one. The first was a painting of an old caravan. The second made his heart leap. It was his painting of Sally, lying naked beside the River Axe.

It was the only other painting he had ever made of a human being, of his Sally. He carefully dusted the canvas and lay it against the big window facing him as he sat on the sofa. Every memory of every moment they had been together now flooded back into his mind and his vision. A large tear escaped and ran down his cheek. He sat facing the painting, toying with the desire to keep it to secretly produce whenever he was alone. After quite a long time the realisation dawned that he didn't need this prop any more. His emotions had completed their period of mourning. It really was time to move on with his 'new' special love. He took something from the kitchen work surface and went across to open the hatch.

Nearby was one of George's fields. He took the painting, still in its frame, down the stairs and climbed over the gate into the field. There was no-one around. It took only two strikes of the match to light the dry wooden frame.

Erik stood back and watched his work burn with a bright flame for a few minutes. The canvas curled and disintegrated. As the flames died and the wood turned into ash he saw, through the heat haze and the thin smoke, the welcome sight of Ethel being parked beside the road and his beautiful new love walking towards him.

EPILOGUE

As readers will know the Zanzibar has become one of the leading world chocolate bars. It has even reached the shelves of Kate Burrows' sweet shop in Seaton. The staff in the Cremona Plant are 80% African refugees, who have their own extension of the village higher up the valley helped by a major housing project from the Spanish Government. Cremona is respected internationally as an example of the best co-operation and harmony in towns between established local residents and a large influx of immigrants.

Felix and Sink have stayed with their new families, each having been granted asylum retrospectively by Spain and the United Kingdom in view of the horrors of their childhood and the fact that they are orphans.

The Spanish Border Police have now taken extra precautions to stem the flow of illegal immigrants entering the country via Isla del Perejil (Parsley Island) and the use of Alboran as a stepping stone from Africa. They are now as secure as other Spanish enclaves in Morocco i.e Ceuta and Melilla.

Sofia delivered a healthy daughter and is earmarked to take over from Carmen as Household Supervisor at the Trocadero Academy when Carmen retires. She plans to take her degree in a few years time.

Cameron passed Spanish as one of his Bachillerato

subjects and is a mainstay at the Trocadero. They are helped during busy periods by Clarence and Rex as babysitters, who are getting much pleasure from sharing the baby that they would love to have been able to call their own.

The Academy is well established as one of the foremost junior tennis training centres in Europe. The first students have moved on to their chosen careers, most remaining in the 'tennis world':-

Oksana is one of the top 10 singles players and earns even more as a model.

Soo-Jin aggravated her shoulder injury and had to retire from competitions. She has followed Lindsay into PE teaching in New Zealand.

Felipe continued to win on clay courts and with the continuing assistance of the Marbella Club Members now runs a sports college for disabled students in Córdoba.

Dan makes a good living from his singles performances. However his doubles world ranking with Torgny gives him entry into every men's tournament and an annual income that already exceeds the lifetime earnings of most professionals.

Torgny shares Dan's strong finances and sponsorship, though his winnings come principally from their doubles. He has relaxed his personal aggression now that he is reconciled with his Father, who reappeared after two years. His aggressive, positive tennis continues and he and Dan are the Swedish Davis Cup doubles pairing, just as Erik had hoped.

Thomas suffered badly with 'tennis elbow' and had to retire from playing regularly. He now works for a chain of sports shops in Geneva.

Petra is married to Kurt. They hold the record for the longest unbeaten run in Mixed Doubles, which continued into the Senior Events. She also won several singles events, which has enabled her to buy a house and grounds by a Lake in Switzerland. Now Petra is concentrating on being a good mother.

Kurt is a good tennis coach, discovering that this skill Erik had spotted in him makes for a good long-term career in the sport. He hopes one day to work back at the Trocadero Academy.

Kas has returned to Poland to work with his Father.

Nicholas learnt a lot in Marbella and is a well-loved PE teacher in a secondary school in Belgium. He still plays practical jokes on fellow staff and pupils.

Agnieska (Aga) still splits her time between horses and tennis. The Polish Councils for each sport periodically try to wrench her away from each other, but she loves them both. She has won many equestrian events and tennis tournament singles and, until Petra became pregnant with her first child, reached finals in doubles as well.

Padmini and Ignacio (Nacho) became closer as time went on. They are the successors to Kurt and Petra in Mixed Doubles and rarely lose. They are both still at the Academy, where they both coach as well as enter Senior Tournaments to supplement their income. They live happily together but haven't troubled their families by getting married, thereby saving Maria Carmelita social heartache.

The 'String Quartet', or now the 'String Trio' without Padmini, are all living in the UK. Lucy and Gabby are both married and expecting their first babies. Together with their husbands they have started their own tennis academy in England in association with the Trocadero and with advice from Lindsay and Erik. They want to specialise in taking pupils from Britain and Italy. Saskia has been accepted at Sussex University to study Geography and is an asset to the University tennis team. She is still waiting for Judy Murray to call her into the British Ladies Tennis Squad.

END

This was the second book in 'The "Erik" Trilogy.'

Read the introductory novella 'The Tennis Racket' and the first in the series 'Second String to a Tennis Racket'

The final book of the trilogy 'The Court Jester' will be available later in 2018

All the above may be obtained as paperbacks or as Kindle reads from Amazon.

The proceeds from all these books will be donated to Stuart's two charities:-

Star Action (Reg. Charity No. 1111137)
www.staraction.org

The Quiet Mind Centre (Reg. Charity No. 1029636)
www.quiet-mind.org

About the Author

Stuart Neil lives in East Devon. He played tennis at Junior Wimbledon and was a Scotland Hockey International. For many years he has led Emergency Medical Teams for European Charities working in crisis zones in Asia and Africa.

He has finally given in to the temptation to write and the novella *'The Tennis Racket'* leads into his 'Erik Trilogy':-

'Second String to a Tennis Racket.'
'The Marbella String Quartet.'
'The Court Jester'

Three romantic ventures into the world of Tennis and Ladies Golf.

Each of these books or the 'Erik Box Set' may be purchased through the Amazon website.